The Knoll

Ginger Cucolo

Allen House Publishing
2013

Cover Image taken by Mackie Cucolo
Designed by Abbie Cucolo

Inside sketches by
Ginger Cucolo
Tony-Allen Cucolo

Published by

Allen House Publishing
2013

www.allenhouseprinting.com

ISBN 978-0-9833057-3-6
Library of Congress Control Number: 2013900312
Copyright © Ginger Cucolo 2013

Printed in the United States of America

For my husband and children…
telling a story is so much more fun when you play along

Table of Contents

Chapter 1
A Blessing and a Curse

Knock, Ireland, 1845

It is bitter cold. I am awake and wet wishing I were somewhere else. Ma always places me next to an earthen wall, hoping the dirt will keep me warm and protected. It is usually a good spot, but the constant rain has proven Mother Nature is stronger than this shanty we call home.

A flogging of water gushed down the lower part of my back. Whoever in the sky, aiming at me, picked a perfect spot. There were only two parts of my body open to the air, and it did not seem as though my leg was their first choice. I scoot over slightly to get away from another possible drenching and lie there with my cheek next to the earth, staring into a dark space, my upper body soaking wet. I want to be dry and fall asleep again.

My thoughts wander to Moira, and I allow myself to daydream. I began to recall a time when I was on the floor and could see the shadows of those dancing around me on the ceiling as flames flickered brightly from the candles that were lit. My eyes wander in the darkness, and I am only able to see the shadows from the moon's light.

Time passes and I grow drowsy, imagining the flickering of the flames. My eyes get heavy and without understanding how, the moment transforms and I am there, the same place but a different time. Everyone is laughing and singing. Ma seems to be the most joyful tonight, and her laughing pleases everyone. I lie there catching my breath a moment longer before jumping up and dancing again.

Da is sitting in a chair at the end of our table watching all of us, while Ma goes back and forth playing with our neighbors, dancing and singing and trying to get Da up to dance with her. He does not think he is any good at dancing, but this worry about ability to dance does not seem to be in the minds of anyone else as they frolic about looking as though a medieval creature is amongst us and has just bitten them.

Da enjoys watching the shenanigans and has the best laugh. A deep, contagious laugh that lets you know he is honestly enjoying the moment and happy his family is so merry. And we are, stomping and singing as loud as we can.

"Come on, Da!" Moira yells. "Dance with us!"

Moira and I run over to pull at his arms.

"Whoa! If you pull any harder, you'll be dancin' with just me arms!" He flails his arms as if they were free from his body, but it doesn't stop us from pulling.

"Get in the middle, Da!" We scream as we try pushing him to the center of the room. "Do that jig you always do!"

Moira slaps me on my back and my body jerks. It wasn't Moira at all but another gush of water from above. Those memories were just a dream. I take a deep breath in and let it out with utter disgust. As I lie there, I try not to move hoping I will slip back into that dream, but my being wet and cold keeps me from those memories and the escape I desperately want.

Our home leans up against a hillside and the roof is made of straw mixed with mud. The rain comes down through the spot where our roof meets the soil. This shelter works well enough, but time has worn it down and it now gives way under the pressure of the rain.

As I stare into the darkness, I remember my dream and the festive gathering. It had Ma and Da, my older sister, Moira, my younger brother Quinlan, and two other families. I don't think it was any particular celebration, just a gathering. How I wish I could get back to that dream. It was such a wonderful time, but it is only a memory.

While we still gather, it is no longer as lively as I remember, and it is rare. The sounds have changed. Sounds have always been peculiarly intense to me. I do not think of the intensity as a bad thing, but as a gift. One where the sounds heard are instant memories for me to picture in my head. There are new sounds now, and ones I would rather forget, but right now, they are part of my life, and I do not know if I will ever be able to forget them.

Memories can be both a blessing and a curse. I am glad I have them. I see them as a blessing knowing those that were with us, even for a short amount of time, loved us. My sister, Moira, is gone. She died this past year from a fever and terrible headache. I think they called it typhus. I miss her desperately, and so, you see, I have her memory. Memories of her laughing. Memories of her singing, even memories of her scolding me.

She was only 15, but Moira always seemed to be so good. She helped Ma and Da, and had quite a bit of responsibility on her as the eldest. With our grandmother's spindle, Ma taught Moira to spin yarn and sell it to a neighbor who would make cloth from it. I remember the rhythm in which she turned the spindle, and the clicking of it at regular intervals.

I have new memories, now, and they include a different group of people. There is not too much to celebrate, but Ma and Da do their best to bring cheerfulness into our home. Even if it is just the four of us.

I don't hear much about Moira anymore. I don't think Ma allows herself to think about her. She spends too much time working and taking care of Quinlan and me. Quinlan was born unable to speak. Oh, he can make noises, but not really speak like the rest of us.

Ma has always said, "Quinlan is a gift from God; A gift that sees and does things different. He may not be able to talk, Allie, so you must always watch o'er him and take care of him. If we teach him the correct things to do, he'll do fine."

The rest of us have strong Irish accents, with Da having the strongest of all. Ma and his friends call him "Mac". I don't even know if any of his friends know him by any other name than Mac.

"How did you get that name, Da?"

"I'm glad they call me Mac. It's a fittin' name for me, don't you think?"

"I guess so, but Da fits you, too."

"Of course you silly girl, but I am your Da, so that's a fittin' name for me to you! But Mac is our word for son. Our ancestors were the sons o' Crearys, and we kept the name. If your name had an "o" in front of it, you were the son o' the father's first name. Guess I should be plenty grateful they call me Mac and not O!"

"And would I be an O'Allie?"

"O'Allie? Heavens no! It's not my first nor my last. Your Ma always liked the name Allena, and we ended up shortening it to Allie. I think it tis fittin' for you, too."

"I like it. I like Allie McCreary, or should I say Allie Mac?"

"No you shouldn't, you should just stay with Allie McCreary. If you shorten all your names you'll end up being called Aaaaaaaa, and what would people think of us!" he pulled me over on his lap and called out to Ma.

"Katherine Kelly McCreary, your twelve year old daughter is callin' herself Aaaaa! What do you think of that?"

"I think the two of you are sillier than Martin O'Murray at the pub. At least he has the excuse of drinkin' too much"

"Now, Kate, don't knock poor Martin. You know in heaven there is no beer, so that is why he must drink it here."

"Yes, but to think he is spendin' all of his family's money on drinkin' is a selfish thing to do. Especially with everythin' that is happenin' now. At least your foolishness is natural and not spurred on by the likes of additional spirits. You are able to work in the fields rather than work the bloats partakin' the ale alongside of you. What might the Farradays think of that?"

The Farradays were the landlords of the property my parents lived and worked on. They were school educated and only had the slightest Irish accent. They spoke a more proper English and knew other languages like French and Italian. They were the landlords of the property until the English came through and claimed all Catholic property for Protestant ownership. The Farradays are Catholic, like us, and while their station in life was above us, they are now to be tenants on what used to be their own property. How could this be? It didn't make any sense to me.

"It is the same God, isn't it? You said God chooses forgiveness and acceptance? If people are judged and separated down here, why would God take the time to separate up there?"

"Try not to let it bother you Allie, there is nothin' any of us can do about it. If you want to make a difference, love all, and treat people as kindly as you can. That's it. The Farradays are a wonderful family who are doin' the best they can under the circumstances and our questionin' it will only remind them of their condition more."

The Farradays were always kind and helpful to my family. Ma worked in their household and Da in their fields. Ma often brought home special treats from their table, or hand me downs of clothing they no longer wore. She was always very appreciative of this and thus wanted to help them in any way she could.

Even as last year brought about the beginnings of change, the Farradays allowed Da to pay what he could for his piece of land. I don't know what was owed, but their loyalty to the Farradays must have meant the Farradays were generous in the overlooking of payment not paid in full.

"Kate, I want to do what we can for Mr. Farraday. He's never treated us like the Kinneys or the Tremains. Why, the Kinneys put out the Radcliffs just the other day. Out on the road, he did. Not a place for them to go or farm. Mr. Farraday could do the same if he had wanted to. In time, they will be like us, and on their own property!"

"What?" I shouted.

"You've heard us talk about this, Allie. The Brumleys have taken their land, and will be here any day now," Da said. "The Farradays have lost almost everythin' in a matter of weeks, and have to go from being waited on, to growin' and farmin' their own land and payin' for it."

I was confused by the whole situation. The Farradays had two boys. Before now, we only saw the family when they went by in their carriage or when we stole a peek at their playing in the yard or riding their horses, or listening to their mother read them a story under the mulberry tree on the knoll. I saw the boys as rather arrogant, but Ma said they were strong and determined, and typical of boys of their importance. They were actually nice, young men. No, just arrogant to me. They never gave me, my brother, or sister any time of day.

Now they must put their "strength and determination," as Ma put it, to good use. This would be helpful in the tilling of the land, but there was nothing for the parents to pass on to the boys for inheritance.

Before the stealing of their property as I call it, Brody, their youngest, had secretly been bringing books to our home. Da and he dug a hole for hiding the books, and during that time period Brody would sneak out four to five books at a time from their home to hide in the hole. The hole was in a corner of our home, and Ma would put the spindle on top of it to cover the tousled earth.

"Why are they hidin' their books? What are we supposed to do with them?"

"It's not for us. We offered our home to them so they can bring things over here and save for the future. They have no other place now. They can't get to England."

"Out of the entire house, he only brings books? They have so many beautiful things, and Brody is only hidin' their books?"

"For now. His parents told him to bring a few other things of value like silver, pewter, jewelry, and the like, but all of their paintings, china, even clothes are to be left for the new landlords."

"Da, does this make any sense to you? Wouldn't you bring something more fun, or more treasured? I'd bring the horses."

"The horses? And how would you hide the horses? Are we to bury them and hope they will be all right in a year or two?"

"No, but what will they do with their horses? They can't just leave them there."

"They are goin' to have to. I know it does not make any sense, but the larger items, and the ones anyone could tell were missin' can't be hidden. If we or the Farradays were caught with any of those things, we might all be charged with stealin'. We have to pick and choose what the best and easiest things are to hide."

The oldest Farraday boy, Patrick, would soon be on his own. But for now, the entire family tried to adjust. Of course, with Brody being fourteen and Patrick seventeen, they weren't really boys anymore.

Their whole life up until now was geared towards their being raised as gentry, and the change in their status was a huge shock. They could stay in their home until the new landlords arrived, it just wasn't theirs anymore. They began moving out and trying to face the realization of their new home.

Moira and I always thought Patrick was the best looking of the two boys. His face looked like his mothers, and his hair is the color of ginger, thick and at times curly when there was moisture in the air. He had a long and lean body that looked so nice in his clothes.

He looked the part of a gentleman and Moira once told me, "There are many girls in town that like him. It's silly, though," she said, "because he doesn't give any of them the time of day. He's rather lawdy daw. His voice and body posture are like his father's, but he definitely isn't like him in his actions."

Brody looked more like his father, in a smaller body. He was slender and dark haired and tried to act like his older brother and father, but his interests were more like his mother, more reserved and quiet. Funny, they both shared characteristics and traits from both parents, and yet they were different from each other. Brody enjoyed being with his mother and wasn't interested in everything the two other Farraday men seemed to be interested in.

We never called Mr. And Mrs. Farraday by their first names, but they called each other Thorne and Maureen. The names fit each of them. Thorne, not like something prickly on a rose bush, but as something strong and majestic. Maureen being kind and cultured. As they talked to one another, they spoke in calm tones and with ease. They didn't have the strong Irish emotion in their speech as I was used to hearing from everyone else. I guess their dealings in Britain and the times they lived there helped shape their language and behavior.

We loved to watch and listen, and Brody was the most entertaining during this time. His voice did the most blarney things. It would change in the middle of a sentence, or seem to crack as he pronounced certain words. Quinlan and I would laugh our cacks off. We tried not to in front of him, but sometimes we couldn't help it. It was so amusing.

Of course, Brody didn't think so and would often get very agitated with us, "Away with you! Go bother someone else!"

But as soon as he tried saying it, it would break in the middle, and Quinlan and I giggled harder. He tried to speak with such a formal tone around us at first. I think this is what Moira must have meant by calling Patrick lawdy daw. That's the way Brody seemed to us. He did not want to spend any time with us, and our laughing at him did not help. We hadn't been around either of the Farraday boys very much, but with Brody bringing items to our house to hide things, we would overhear him speaking to Da.

"Stop being so coddin' you two! You have no business eavesdroppin'. Go play outside or be quiet, and respectful."

"Aw don't let 'em cod you Kate, they have nothin' better to do, and it doesn't bother Brody or me."

I knew that wasn't true for Brody, he had already told us to get away.

With the Farradays out of their home, Ma would no longer be working for them. They had to put every bit of money they now earned from being tenants, and farming, back to the British landlords, so that meant some of their former tenants would have to move.

"Kate, did Mrs. Farraday tell you about their havin' to ask the others to leave? It's an awful thing," Da said to Ma.

"Yes, and she is quite upset about it. Four families were asked to leave. I'm feeling rather guilty myself. I don't think the Lambs or the Van Ingens will understand. You know how they think we are already the favorite ones of the Farradays. What do you think?"

"I don't know. I talked with the O'Branigans, and while they aren't very happy about it, they knew it was probably coming. They're headin' East to be with family over there. He tells me it is not as bad over there."

"And the Yorks? Have you heard anythin' from them?"

"No, but that doesn't mean anythin'. You know how they keep to themselves most of the time. I was thinkin' we should go over and see if we could help any of them."

"Let's do. At least we can offer."

We helped move the few items they had out of each of their hovels. The Yorks and the Lambs chose to immigrate to Canada, and the O'Branigans chose to move to Eastern Ireland where they heard the situation wasn't as bad. The fourth family, the Van Ingens refused to move and it was both a humiliating situation for the Farradays and the Van Ingens. The Farradays didn't want to force them off, but they had no choice.

"Mr. Van Ingen, this is not something we relish doing, but we must. If you do not leave, the Brumleys will have you evicted just as soon as they get here. I am trying to keep you from going to a workhouse or jail. Don't do this to your family. Don't you have somewhere to go?" Mr. Farraday pleaded with Mr. Van Ingen.

"This is our home. You have allowed us to raise our family and farm this land. It should be ours to keep. I've earned the right to stay and live here," Mr. Van Ingen told him.

"You have, but the English courts have ruled, and you are not the only ones having to make adjustments. We all have family and friends being forced out. Some, like you, have no place to go, so they go to the road and just stand there. Surely you do not want that for your family? You can go to Canada, America, England, or to another place better off here in Ireland. You do have choices. Don't let the government make those choices for you. "

"I don't see you leavin' the land. You are stayin' and allowin' the McCrearys to stay, too. I refuse to leave until I am forced from this land."

So, on the day after they were scheduled to leave, Mr. Farraday called the local Priest to help the family. He could have called the Constable and had them evicted, but the Priest was much better.

"This is not easy for Mr. Farraday," Ma told us, "he doesn't want the Van Ingens to be removed, but they have to go. If he waits on the Brumleys to remove them, he couldn't be sure what would happen to their family. This way the Church has more say and can be more considerate. Asking all of these families to move is weighing heavily on Mr. Farraday's conscience. And the adjustment for his family must be shaming. Everyone looks at them differently now, and treats them unkindly. They either see them as the mean Landlords that kicked out their tenants, or as people who finally received their come-uppance."

"What does that mean, come-uppance?"

"It means people who do not know them think they have lived off the sweat and toil of tenants without thought of their difficulty, and then enjoyed the fruits of other people's labor. These people want them to suffer since they are sufferin', too."

"But they weren't mean to their tenants."

"I know," said Ma, "but many times people don't take the time to find out the truth about people. They want someone to blame, and the Farradays are taking the brunt of that anger and blame."

Within time, Mr. Farraday became involved with the community again. The other three were slow in coming around. Mrs. Farraday didn't know what to do. She had no skills and working for one's self did not seem like a Lady-like thing to do. Ma treated her as if she was still working for her, so both seemed uncomfortable trying to figure out this new situation.

My parents worried about them, and often talked about the Farraday boys.

"Patrick seems like such a different person," Ma said.

"This is hard for him," said Da, "I know he's trying, but he doesn't fit in. He is defiant."

"But this is his land, too," I said, "and he has a right to work alongside any of us."

"It was their land, but he never had to work on it before. Anyway, I don't think his problem is actually having to work the land, but being told he *has* to work the land," said Da.

Patrick enjoyed us, but seemed irritated. We could hear them talking when the wind was blowing just right, and his frustrations were a big reason they had disagreements.

"You have to try and make the best of it," Mr. Farraday told him.

"But I want to stand up against the English and make them give back what they have taken from us," Patrick said.

I understood his point, but what could he do? He and Brody ended up fighting often. Sometimes they fought over who did what as they worked, or who was able to sit down, or eat first. It seemed out of character. They quarreled in the field or going to and from their home. We knew we bickered, but to hear the Farradays' quarrel was a bit unexpected. We thought they lived a perfect life with no disagreements. We were wrong.

Whenever there wasn't much for my brother and I to do, we would go over to the Farraday home and listen in on what was happening in their place.

Ma caught us once and told us, "You must stop doin' this. We must all ignore the discussions comin' from their house and respect their situation."

"Japers, Ma! Have you heard how they get all worked up? It's a fairly good row on most any topic. It's entertaining for Quinlan and me."

"And at their expense!" she said.

I knew she was right, even Moira would have scolded me mercilessly for eavesdropping. However, the eavesdropping turned into an opportune experience. Listening to them as I sat against their wall or laid outside on the grass, I could imagine a scenario as they played out the lines. Of course, it was real to them, but my imagination turned it into a play and they were my actors. Fortunately, we were never caught again, and we continued to listen even though I knew it was improper. By being in their world, I could totally forget what was happening in ours.

The awkwardness that once felt so strong between us began to ease. Mrs. Farraday learned things from Ma. Things that seemed so simple and ordinary like cleaning clothes, baking, cooking, taking care of her family members, and herself. Mr. Farraday and their sons were also learning. They spent many days with Da learning how to grow potatoes and work with the few animals we had on the property. Potatoes were the only crop everyone grew. Even though farming was totally new to the Farraday men, they picked it up quickly. Mr. Farraday treated Da with respect.

When together, it always seemed as though they came to our house, not theirs. Fine with me. I heard more when they were with us, but I did ask Da about it.

"The Farradays come to our home so we don't feel too uneasy. If we went to their home, they might feel as though we would be reminded of their previous status."

"But their place is no better than ours," I said.

"You're right, Allie, but wouldn't you agree that their comin' here makes us feel more at home? If you were in their home, I bet you would not talk as much as you do here. Maybe we should go to their place more often!" Da said as he tried to grab me and tickle me. He loved to tease me.

In our home, they would have long discussions on everything from politics to culture, and travel to economics. I had no idea what they talked about most of the time, but Da allowed me to sit by them and listen. Well, as long as I was quiet. And that was very hard for me to do because I had so many questions of my own. Still, just being able to sit with them and listen to Mr. Farraday was a delight. He knew about so many things.

Mr. Farraday was such a gentleman. Before, he was always well dressed, clean and crisp looking, and handsome, too. Now, his clothes might not always be as clean, but his hair was always neat and combed, and he must shave daily because I have never seen him with a beard. However, he was not as strong looking as Da. He is slender and fit, in the most gentlemanly of ways. He seems kind and polite. He would rise from a chair when my Ma would come or go from a table, or help her into a chair when she chose to sit down.

Ma wasn't used to this. Not that Da didn't love Ma or respect her, he did. It was just a different way of life. I think Ma was self-conscious at times of his actions. I think she saw herself as being below the Farradays. She spent a lot of her adult life working for them, and now things had changed, it was to be a slow process.

When they were together, I found myself being embarrassed of Ma's inability to see herself as anything more than a common worker.

"Why can't you accept Mr. Farraday's kindness?" I asked her.

"It just makes me uncomfortable," she said, "I don't have the same upbringin' or education as Mrs. Farraday."

"Is it only about *that* for you?" I asked, "They do not treat you any different because you do not have the same upbringin'."

"One day you will see the difference, Allie," she said, "I appreciate the gesture, really I do, but have a difficult time with it."

"Well, you are just as good as anyone else." I said.

"Maybe you've been listening to Patrick."

"Would that be so bad?"

"No, but remember there are consequences with any action you take." She stroked my head, then went back to her work.

Mrs. Farraday did not do as well as Ma with the everyday chores. She was much frailer than the women who were reared to work the land and raise a family on their own. Whether it was too much pride or her delicate nature in truth, she was incapable of working like Ma. She was slender and small boned with a waist that must not be more than six broomsticks put together. Her hair was always neatly brushed and fixed with waves lying against her head outlining her face beautifully.

She was petite, but not unwilling to try and help her family. Mr. Farraday did not force the issue. I think he felt he owed her a much better life than they were living, and he was not going to let her feel humiliated more than she was. What she could do and we couldn't, was read and speak English well, and her ability to do both made her feel as though she was worthy of something.

Ma told Quinlan and me, "Mrs. Farraday has been kind enough to offer to teach you two how to improve your readin' and writin'. We want you to be attentive and considerate of her time."

"Why don't you and Da do it?" I asked them, "You could learn how to read and write, too? Don't you want to know how to?"

"We don't have the time," she said. "Maybe one day, but for now, we want you to learn.

"I will," I exclaimed. "It will be wonderful. I will love learnin' to read."

"And to write," Ma said. I smirked, but knew what she meant.

We started with the basics, and learning to write our name. It all seemed very boring. I wanted to read and learn the things the men talked about, not the alphabet, grammar, and rules.

Ma told us to be appreciative enough to listen and do what she says. Therefore, we did, or at least I tried. Ma wanted us to have more of an education than she and Da. My family all had thick Irish accents and Mrs. Farraday knew proper English. Her other languages might be helpful in the future, but English was a good start.

Ma had a brother, Brennan, who traveled to America almost four years ago. He had written to us many times, telling us, "People don't understand my accent very well and it is difficult finding work. Even social situations are hard, but, it is still a huge country with many opportunities and the Irish that have already come to America have formed a tight knit group. I will send money whenever I can."

Da was excited about this, "If we could save enough money we could all travel to America. With the money Brennan sends us, it's possible. I think America is our best chance. We must work hard to get there. That's why it is important Mrs. Farraday helps Quinlan and you learn how to read and write. It is a stroke of luck for us."

I did not agree with him about leaving Ireland. I did not want to leave, even if things were bad right now. However, learning how to read was fine with me. I had always found it much more enjoyable to sneak into the Farraday's world and listen to them.

My favorite memory was of Mrs. Farraday reading to her family. She would take the family under a mulberry tree up on the knoll, and read to them. The tree itself had a strange trunk. It was large and leaned over as if someone had pulled it down but the branches stretched far enough up and out to give shade to a large area beneath it.

This tree had berries on it every Spring, and we always grabbed some when they were ripe, and eat them. You had to be careful when the berries were spread on the ground, because sitting on them or rubbing them on your skin or clothes could stain whatever they touched. Ma always knew if we had been up on the knoll during that time because we would come back with stains on our elbows and backsides.

The entire Farraday family could read, but Mrs. Farraday had a wonderful way of making stories come to life. She would sit against the tree, in the shade, as the men lay on a quilt in the moist, green grass on the hillside. She leaned against the split in the tree. The boys often used the root that stuck out of the ground as a head rest.

Quinlan and I would lie on the far side of the hill straining to hear her every word. The knoll sat up beyond a stream that trickled loudly at times. There was never a shortage of sounds. It didn't even matter on the days the weather was cloudy and misty, or even cold. What was happening as we listened to her reading was much more important to us than any displeasure the weather brought upon us.

One day Quinlan and I overheard Mrs. Farraday reading the book, Last of the Mohicans, by James Fenimore Cooper. We lied there as she read from the book, sharing words from a character of Coopers:

"His head was large; his shoulders narrow; his arms long and gangling; while his hands were small if not delicate. His legs and thighs were thin, nearly to emaciation, but of extraordinary length; and his knees would have been considered tremendous, had they not been outdone by the broader foundations on which this false superstructure of blended human orders was so profanely reared."

The story was full of so many adventures it lent itself to my own imagination of what was happening.

The Irish are wonderful story tellers, and while I always enjoy the almost musical way in which the Irishman can tell a story, this book opened up a whole new world to me. The interesting part is the language and the way another tells their story through the written word. It was English, not Gaelic, and my understanding of the English way of speaking was now encouraged by the words Mrs. Farraday read. I remember the thought of one character, Hawkeye, who told Cora,

"I have listened to all the sounds of the woods for thirty years, as a man will listen whose life and death depend on the quickness of his ears."

It took her about two weeks to read the book in its entirety. My little brother listened, too, and wanted to act out the characters. He longed to play with Patrick or Brody. He really didn't have any boys to play with so he spent many hours playing by himself and acting as if he was an Indian or an American fighting the French.

While my imagination was stirred, too, no one had any idea how learning to read would become so important to me. I already knew the power sound and smells had, but reading was going to change my life. It would ignite a whole new thought process for my imagination.

My imagination was always of great help to me. In the worst of times I could let my imagination go and think about the Irish stories I had heard in the past. Now, I could think of Cora and Hawkeye. I had heard this was the second book in a series. And the next book? Could it be as good? It would have to wait because there were other matters concerning the families that were tenants. Something was happening to our potatoes.

Chapter 2
The Mulberry Tree

Ireland is magical. I can't imagine living anywhere else. The green hills appeal to the senses; truly a feast for the eyes. Grandma always told us about the great and proud Irish people and the folklore they have passed on for generations. She said it is their lives and the farming of this beautiful land that is much of the Irish story.

Potatoes seem to have been all the Irish people farmed, or at least in our area. That is all I remember. This beautiful land had field after field of potatoes, and whole families helped in the harvesting of it. It was not only their main staple to eat throughout the year, but what they sold to pay for use of the land and for other things the family needed.

Da said it is an easy vegetable to grow, and all the Irish people need. "This plant starts with a little flower and grows into an underground miracle full of goodness, hardy enough to be stored for a long time. We can use it for so many different things, and it keeps throughout the winter. We can do no better."

Or so he thought. I watched this year as what were hearty plants only a few days ago turned brown, and withered. Da and his friends were bewildered. It started last year. One day plants were alive and healthy, the next, they were withered and sickly, turning blacker as the days went on making them bad, even for the animals. No one knew what was causing this, or how to stop it.

Most of the Irish people we knew were optimistic, and after last year's dreadful crop, most believed this year would be different. And, everyone thought that way as the new crops began to grow and look like they were supposed to, until…until it happened, again.

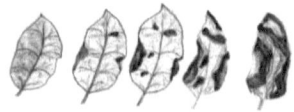

The plants turned black and were ruined. People tried to harvest any part of the potato plant that seemed acceptable, but even these parts rotted within days. Not even the animals would eat it. Our pig, our goat and our two dogs rummaged for grass or leftover crumbs we might have. We had to save the crumbs for ourselves. We watched the animals wither away, and what we had to use them for was worse. We had to eat them.

I remember Quinlan crying something terrible because of what we were doing and what we were eating. I couldn't stomach it, so Ma wouldn't tell us if one of our beloved pets were part of the meal. You cry and are upset, but you do it anyway. What kind of creatures are we that we go ahead and eat what we once loved?

Losing their homes was disheartening, but the worst was the starvation of people. People tried to think of every option for feeding their families, and fishing became one of those options. Mr. Farraday, Patrick, Brody, Da and Quinlan traveled miles to fish. Fishing took an entire day, and most times only two to three fish were caught. They would throw the tiddlers back because they were so small.

Whatever fish were caught, we split and used it in a variety of ways. Eating one fish from a whole day of fishing was wasteful. Ma was quite creative with fish. She used it for rubbing on bread, or dripping it on potatoes. When Ma hung the fish above our table, she could put the potatoes under it and let the aroma and flavor of the fish drip down and be absorbed by the potato. One fish could not feed the entire family. But if she did it this way, it would last for a few meals, not just one. You could use the dripping method with any kind of meat, so those lucky enough to have a ham or bacon could drip it for days, and then we could have "potatoes and point."

Ma taught Mrs. Farraday how to do this. It was difficult for the Farradays to think of this as tasty. They were used to eating much better and their taste for food was much more particular. I guess fish drippings on potatoes are very different from pastries, meats, and fruits.

They had to get used to our way of eating. The drippings were an improvement for us. How strange, this was a good meal for us, but an unpleasant meal for them. They ate it though, because, once again, when you get hungry, even this type of meal is welcomed.

We saw so many changes in our neighbors and friends. People began begging and stealing and getting into trouble for things. Ma and Da told us many of these people would never even think of doing these things if they had money and food for their families, and we should remember that when we spoke of them. Not one of us could get out of a status lower than poverty. How can that be? Our present circumstances seemed to have no end in sight.

This situation only spurred the outrage of the people. You could hear people talking everywhere about their dissatisfaction with the conditions and that the British were not doing enough for them.

Patrick was talking to his father and mine, and said, "The British view us as ungrateful and say we are not willing to work for a living, that we only want handouts. Is this how you want to be thought of? Can you honestly stand by and have them treat us this way?"

"If they were here, they would see the people had nothing to farm; that they no longer had animals to eat; that they no longer had a shelter over their heads," said Mr. Farraday. "We must find a way to show them we want to work and don't want to take handouts."

"We must face this somehow," said Patrick. "We must discuss the poorhouses and the workhouses."

"All right, what about the Society of Friends? They are a group of people who use the money they have left and try to distribute soup, bread, rice, oatmeal, and sometimes meat and vegetables. They are trying to help those that need it."

We needed it, and Ma and Da were grateful. They also used the church for handouts, but the church would often be limited as to what they had, and we tried to go without so others could have something. We had shelter, and the many that didn't have a place to live needed the food so much more.

"We need the British. If there is more starvation, fightin' will break out between our own people," said Da.

That disturbed me. Was it possible we should be afraid of our own people?

"You never miss the water 'till the well has run dry," Da reminded us, and "Half a loaf of bread is better than no bread at all."

I love the way people use these sayings. I don't know what they all mean, but it's almost a contest to see who can come up with the cleverest ones, and most adults nod their heads and agree or laugh and that makes it worth the comment. Sometimes I smile, acting as if I understand their meaning, but am saying "what does that mean?" in my head!

"We all know work is limited. People move rocks from roads, break rocks for walls, then use those rocks to build homes and walls. We can see the walls slowly going up around towns or lining roads," said Mr. Farraday.

"Yes, but the rocks are also used for work in the workhouses," Patrick added.

"They are trying, though. They are searching for any labor they can find," Mr. Farraday told him.

"However, by doin' this, they are unable to work on the land. I realize there is nothin' to work on the land and it makes for a terrible situation. I believe some people want to be arrested and put in workhouses so they'll get a regular meal, get clothin' and have it better than the just waitin' and starvin'."

"You're right, Mac, but once they are thrown in the workhouses we rarely hear from them again, and all we can do is hope they will be all right. Is this acceptable?"

"Patrick," Mr. Farraday said, "The Society of Friends brings in seeds for farmers with the hope people will try growing other crops."

"And many try, but does it make any sense? They are so weak and sick and the land itself is so barren it is difficult to get people to plant the seeds and wait for plants to grow. This seems pointless. It brings us back to the original point. Our inaction fuels the belief by the British that the Irish are unwilling to improve their own situation."

At another meeting Patrick went on and on about the latest situation he heard from some friends he had in Dublin. He told the fathers, "The crops grown by our own people who are starving are being harvested for the English who then sell these crops to other countries or use them in England."

"That can't be," said Da, "Why?"

"Because of greed and disgust for the Irish people," Patrick said, "and we need it right here. Do we not?"

"Of course we do," said Mr. Farraday, "but violence will only make the British more hateful of our position, and thus support their reasoning on our inability to make things better."

"Well, doing nothing only allows them to continue to keep us in this horrid state. I can't accept that." said Patrick, "I have to do something about it."

"And if you do," Mr. Farraday said, "what good will it do you if you are in a workhouse, or poorhouse wasting away. Or worse, dying?"

It didn't make any sense to me. I didn't actually see any other crop being farmed in our area, but if they were going to send it somewhere, couldn't they have sent some to us?

Patrick thought about it for a moment, and then asked his father, "Have you not heard about Catholic Priests who are so frustrated with the situation they are turning away the poor and starving because they can do no more for them. What are they to do? Many of these people do not even have a home. Why, they are living in their scalpeens just like an animal that burrows in to have shelter. Sometimes their whole family is huddled together for warmth and shelter. Others are sleeping in ditches on the side of the road. These types of situations make people irritated and disturbed. Many are fed up with it."

"It's not that I do not agree with you, Patrick," said his father, "we do not agree about how we should go about making the changes for our people."

Patrick continued to be the most irritated amongst us. He spoke out the most and gathered others who felt the same way to discuss it as often as possible. Patrick was a natural leader and people listened to and flocked to hear him raise their spirits in the hopes something could be done.

Mr. Farraday and Da wanted to help with changing the circumstances, but did not feel getting everyone worked up was the correct way to do it. They were disgusted, too, by the deaths occurring daily and the despair of the people, and our own situation, but they felt going against the government was not the best way to handle it.

Mr. Faraday felt this way just as Mrs. Farraday became ill. She had not eaten well in months and with her frail nature, was sick quicker than the rest of us. This past month had been disheartening for them.

The Brumley's arrival from England and taking possession of their home forced the Farradays to complete the recognition of their losses. The Farradays were living in the house next to us now all of the time, and Mrs. Farraday's health declined rapidly. Ma and Brody took care of her the most, with Mr. Farraday doing what he could to take care of his family. Their house, not very far from ours, and all of the windows open, privacy was just not possible.

"This is another challenge God has given us to test our faith," Ma said.

"That doesn't make any sense to me, Ma. How can you remain faithful to a God that has taken so much from so many people?"

"Because it is what I believe," she said. "That's why they call it faith. You have to have faith. Hopefully I can help the Farraday's durin' this time."

"And what if they don't feel the same way?" I asked.

"Then I will just be there for them," she said, "and continue to believe in God. You know what you're grandmother used to say,

"For the fullness of days spent together,
The friends that we pray with will be with us forever,
The feelings we've shared, the food & good fun with faith that God's
blessings have only begun."

I knew Patrick wasn't very open to religion. He didn't believe there was someone out there who would watch over us and take care of us. He didn't feel as though anyone was looking out for anyone. He was bitter and sometimes Brody felt the same way. As their mother's health worsened, both boys grew angrier.

There was nothing anyone could do for poor Mrs. Farraday. She quit eating; hoping the food she didn't eat would be given to her boys. I think deep down she knew she was dying and didn't want to take food away from them.

Mrs. Farraday continued with Quinlan, our studies, and me as long as she could. I think it made Brody jealous sometimes because we spent so much time with her. My favorite time was when she read to us. Her favorite stories were those by Jane Austen and poets like John Clare, and Lord Byron. She loved their works. She was a romantic at heart and believed in what she read even though she no longer lived the life she was accustomed to.

She always seemed to get lost in the words. She became entranced by them. I loved watching and listening to her read, but as she became weaker, the joy in her words changed. She was sorrowful, and the words came out as if they were her last ones. As if she was sad at the thought of never reading them again.

Every day she would end our lessons with,

"With the first light of sun…Bless you
When the day is done….Bless you
In your smile and in your tears…..Bless you
Through each day of all your years…Bless you"

One day she read to us a statement by Morgan the Poet. She explained this was something he said after a series of defeats to the Viking invaders,

"Do not weep, not all suffering is forever. Not all darkness can persist before the light of day. One day, we will return, and be all the stronger for weight and hardship. Our people do not pass into darkness without complaint, but shout into the din of the abyss with great triumph and defiance."

Sometimes she drifted off into another world and Quinlan and I would just sit there and be with her. Once Brody came in and saw what was happening and pushed us outside. I think he was embarrassed because we saw her this way. Even when she drifted off on some wild story, she was interesting. She was a kind person so we knew better than to mock her.

Ma was worried about her and one day came in when she was asleep. "You must leave Mrs. Farraday alone. Come now, you can see her tomorrow."

Mrs. Farraday opened her eyes and said weakly, "They're not bothering me, Kate. I enjoy their company, truly."

I think she enjoyed someone sitting with her so she was not alone. She would smile sweetly at Quinlan and tell him, "You remind me of my boys when they were your age. They also found it difficult to sit still, and they would make pictures in the dirt on the ground or twirl a piece of grass between their fingers, just like you."

"He likes to use his imagination and use grass spears as soldiers and enact scenes of Vikin's in boats, or foot soldiers from some story he's heard about from Da," I told her.

"And he should continue to use his imagination like that. You will, won't you, Quinlan?" He nodded, and we both sat there until she fell asleep again, then we headed home.

One day we quit early because she was very, very tired. On this day her mind didn't wander, she just lay there, staring. I was worried about her, so I left to get Ma. I found Brody before Ma and asked him to come to their house.

Quinlan stood up to leave, but something kept us at the door. We watched as Brody sat on the ground next to his mother and held her hand. He stroked it softly, and then laid his head next to her side and held her arm under his head. A few minutes later, we could hear him weeping softly. I went over to him but he yelled at me to get out. Startled, Quinlan and I turned to run from their shack.

Quinlan ran home, but I stayed outside their doorway wanting desperately to stay. I stood there with my back against their outside wall, by the door. Frozen to it as though I was being pushed against it by a mighty wind.

Should I go and find Ma or Da, or Mr. Farraday? Should I stay and help Brody? Should I get something for Mrs. Farraday? She would hate Brody being so upset. I was moved by the tenderness he had for her and I knew how much he cherished her. His heart must be breaking.

Quinlan found Ma behind our house and she ran to see what was wrong. She ran inside, and then slowly walked back out. She stepped outside the door about two steps and just stood there.

"Ma?"

She turned and looked at me, and I knew something horrible must have happened.

"Mrs. Farraday is gone," she said. "I need to find Mr. Farraday, do you know where he is? Have you seen him?"

I shook my head from side to side, and remained stuck to their outside wall. Not able to move. Ma didn't pay any attention to my circumstance, but told me to go home and stay there.

Go home? I was stunned. So many people had died around us, but Mrs. Farraday, too? I knew she wasn't well, but this was the second person close to me who had died and it brought back all of the memories of Moira dying and what a loss that had been.

Now the Farradays were going to have to live through it and I couldn't stand it for any of them. What would my going home do? I obeyed Ma, reluctantly, and as I did I could hear Brody talking to his mother. I could not imagine being without Ma. As I walked through our doorway, I peered back to see Mr. Farraday running into his home. The only thing I could imagine was Brody, still weeping. I no longer saw anyone, just the image of Brody with her, beside her.

Where was Patrick? Did he not know what had just happened? Their house looked empty. I knew Brody and his father were in there with Mrs. Farraday, but the house seemed empty. There was coolness in the air as always and a heavy mist, and under the current setting it was an eerie scene, fitting for my memories of this moment.

I thought of the knoll and of a story Mrs. Farraday told me before she was ill. It was about the Mulberry Tree and how it was part of a very old folktale. People called it a symbol of unhappy love but she told me to look at it another way. Look at the tree for its beauty, its significance, and the fruit it bears for all.

The story, she went on, was of a young boy and girl in Babylonian times who grew up together. When they were grown they fell in love. Their parents told them they could not be together. Whenever they could, they would sneak off and tell each other of their love for one another.

One night they agreed to meet underneath a Mulberry tree. The girl arrived early and saw a lion that had just killed on ox. In her haste to leave, she dropped her scarf and the lion dirtied it and tore it apart leaving the blood from the ox on the scarf.

When the young man arrived, he found her scarf and believed she was dead. He took out his knife and killed himself. When she returned looking for him, she found him dying under the Mulberry tree. She then took his knife, and stabbed herself. Their spilt blood was absorbed by the Mulberry Tree, thus giving it its dark red fruit. I could see the deepness of that red fruit in my mind as I thought of the story.

I looked back towards the Faraday shack. Ma came to me and turned towards their house. She put her arm around me and we just stared in their direction. I thought of Mrs. Farraday and the home she had lived in for so long. Their beautiful mansion, full of the things she loved. Now she was gone, having died in a shack. It was ugly, damp, and bare. I hoped her mind had slipped to better times her last few moments, and the memories she had of earlier years had come back. Maybe she died thinking she was still in that world, not this one where she watched her own children struggling to eat and live.

That's what I wanted for her, and her family; the sounds and memories of their other life. The poems and stories she loved to read.

Grandma always said, "You've got to do your own growin', no matter how tall your grandfather was."

Now this saying I understood. Well, once it was explained to me, I did. No matter who they were before, the Farradays were going to have to "grow" through this situation themselves.

The Farraday men, my father and Quinlan helped dig a grave for Mrs. Farraday. They chose to bury her in their family plot which the family had had for generations. I guess the Catholic Church had not turned everything over to the English government, or the English government had not bothered to meddle into the business of gravesites, too. She was there with her parents and a brother.

There were spots available for Mr. Farraday and their boys, but for now, we looked at the site where Mrs. Farraday would remain. New earth spread across her body, wrapped in a quilt passed down to her by her grandmother.

They continued tossing dirt until the spot was level with the earth around it. No headstone was placed by her gravesite, because there was none to be had, and even if there were any, it would cost too much for any family. They placed a wooden cross at her head and vowed to come back one day to honor her with a headstone.

Ma was stoic, as always. I never saw her cry for Mrs. Farraday, but her sadness was there when she spoke of her. She knew what a blow it was to the Farraday men, and she realized her focus must now be on two families.

Because of this, she agreed to work for the Brumleys. It was difficult, because she partly blamed them for Mrs. Farraday's declining health. The Brumleys didn't seem to be disturbed by her passing, and that disturbed Ma. Da could not get himself to work for them, and while Mr. Farraday considered it, he, too, could not get himself to ask for work from them.

"I understand why Mr. Farraday cannot work for the Brumleys," Ma explained to me. "Even a small thorn causes festerin' and the Farradays losing their home and status was no small festerin'."

"I'm bitter, too," Da said.

I always wondered if their bitterness to the Brumleys was because of just that, or everyone's situation as a whole. Of course, I didn't really know the Brumleys, but I thought rather lowly of them myself that they did not seem to have much sympathy for the Farradays, or the local people. They rarely ventured out amongst the rest of us, so they were almost a mystery to everyone. It was probably better they didn't go out much. Everyone hated them and what they stood for.

"Don't speak poorly of them. You never know when the tables might turn and someone might speak poorly of you," Ma told us.

So, we did not do it in front of her, but we did speak about it to Brody and Da, and we always listened to others who spoke about them. I think it was kind of healing to listen to others, but Ma reminded us repeatedly about the "thorn and festering thing." I guess she was right. I watched others get worked up more and more as they spoke not only about the Brumleys, but the whole situation.

I overheard some of the men talk about "Mere words do not feed the friars."

"That statement means actions are better than words, and just talking about it was doing nothing to change the situation. However, I'm getting worried actions will only get us all into more trouble," Ma begged Da and the Farradays. "Be dog wide. Please keep your heads!"

"Keep their heads?" I said, Da smiled, and I continued. "What else would they do with their heads?"

I hadn't known it, but Da and the Farraday men had been part of a group that supported a man by the name of Daniel O'Connell. He was well-known by the name of "The Liberator". They would meet and discuss how to change the Irishman's situation. Up until now it had been just talk, and the organizer of the group tried to go about making the British aware of these awful situations, but many of the younger men didn't think talking was improving anyone's situation.

Many of the younger people in this group believed, like Patrick, it would take violent tactics rather than peaceful tactics to bring about change. The younger group split off and called themselves the "Young Ireland" movement.

We found out about their connection to this group when Da and Mr. Farraday were arrested at a peaceable protest. They were arrested amid others who were trying to demonstrate against the government. The awful thing is some of the "Young Ireland" supporters acted out of hand and caused the lawmen to arrest as many as they could, including Da and Mr. Farraday. It was a horrible day for all of us.

Ma was shocked. She went down to the place where they were holding both of them to talk to Da.

"How could you let this happen?"

"I'm sorry, Kate," he said. "Action is sweet to drink, but bitter to pay for."

"I know, Mac, but we all will have to pay for what you've done. I'm so thwarted. I don't want to fight through this without you."

He lowered his head, and then Mr. Farraday spoke up, "Will you watch over Patrick and Brody, Kate?"

"You know I will treat them as if they were mine." He placed his hand on her shoulder and squeezed it.

The Sheriff called for all prisoners to follow him. Da looked at Ma and told her he was sorry, again. She put her fingers up to her mouth and touched her lips.

Mr. Farraday told her, "I'll do what I can to get us out of here. Tell Brody."

And then they were gone.

Ma came home and found me digging in the hole that held the Farraday's books and other items. Even the money they had been saving for our travel to America.

As soon as she walked in, I held some of it up and said, "You can use this to get them out."

"They wouldn't hear of it," she said, "and neither do I."

"What? You want to leave them there? Why?"

"Givin' them the money might not guarantee their release. Then we would not have any money and lose our chance of leavin' Ireland."

"But you must try! We can't leave them there!"

She didn't want me to go see him, but I slipped off anyway and ran down to where they were keeping him. Da was in a crowd of men, all tied to one another, and being watched over like a herd of cattle. Some of the men were speaking loudly and yelling at the guards.

I did get a glance from Da and he smiled in an almost remorseful way, if that is possible. I stared at him wanting to run up to him, but afraid of what might happen if I did. We didn't get to speak, and I was afraid it might be the last time I would see him.

I don't know where he went, except that he was taken to a workhouse. We didn't even know where.

These workhouses had more people in them than they were supposed to and the overcrowding led to the spread of disease. We heard of the dying and the dead being huddled together. Lack of space and food and the ever-spreading diseases were not limited to only the poor. Sickness attacked the officers, priests, and caregivers of the workhouses as often as the inmates themselves.

We could only hope Da was not in one of the more dreadful workhouses. We never received word of how long he would be there or what the exact charges were. Since he did not know how to write, it would be by word of mouth if we were ever to hear from him.

We did know he and Mr. Farraday were sent to different workhouses, and it just happened Mr. Farraday was close enough for us to be able to see him at times.

He was sent to a workhouse near us called, Claremorris. It was a day's journey to see him, but by seeing him, Quinlan and I could imagine what Da's situation might be like.

Mr. Farraday had lost weight and looked weary, but he was alive and doing as well as could be expected.

Chapter 3
Uncle Brennan In America

Ma did her best to bring Brody into our home. We hadn't heard from Patrick, so Ma went about her days working for the Brumleys, and then coming home to work for us. Quinlan and I tried to help. We gathered any food that could be found. Sometimes that meant grass spears or bark from a tree, or handouts from the local church. It might just be soup or scraps, but we would take anything.

Brody was lost in thought most of the time now. He would show up for bedtime and a meal every now or then, but that was about it. Ma was worried about him, but she was too busy herself to do more than she was already doing.

Quinlan and I spent some of our days looking at the books Mrs. Farraday had given us. I often tried to get Quinlan to act out the stories we read since he always loved doing that so much before. It kept us busy, but one day I noticed Quinlan wasn't playing like he normally did.

When Ma arrived home that night, she found Quinlan with a fever. He was already weak from so little food, and the fever took him quickly. Ma said he was doing poorly, and he moaned because his gums hurt and he was weak.

I felt badly for him. I tried to help Ma take care of him while she was at work, but I didn't know what to do except sit with him and stroke his hand like I had seen Brody do to his mother. Sometimes my touching his skin really bothered him and he hit at me to help him. I hated him at times. Not really him, but the situation and how I couldn't seem to do anything right.

I finally remembered how soothing reading seemed to be to Mrs. Farraday, and I tried my best to read to Quinlan. Sometimes it was more of me just telling the story as I remembered it because I had not practiced my reading as much as I should have. How hard could that be? What was wrong with me? Why could I have not taken more time to practice my reading?

Brody was only there a few times. He seemed so distant, and while Quinlan wanted Brody to spend time with him, Brody didn't want to. I hated Brody for not spending more time with my brother. He was so selfish. It takes nothing to sit and be with him. Ma had done so much for his family, and he just didn't seem to care.

Quinlan suffered for weeks, and as the weather turned colder, the dankness made the situation worse. It seemed as though nothing was going to help Quinlan. One day I went out to get some scraps from the local Parish and when I returned, Quinlan looked gray.

I said his name as I walked back into the house, but he said nothing. I slowly walked over to him realizing what might have happened, but not wanting it to be so. I kept saying his name hoping to awaken him, but he didn't move.

I bent over him and shook him hoping that would help. I grasped his jaw with my hand to move his head and I realized he was cold. I took his hand and realized the same thing. I dropped his hand, frightened at the thought of what it meant. My little brother was gone and I wasn't there for him when he had taken his last breath.

I left him at a time when he needed me the most. He died without anyone there to be with him. I would never forgive myself. How could I tell Ma I was not there for him? I was too ashamed to admit to anyone I had left him alone.

Where was Brody? Now, I was mad at him.

He finally returned home before Ma, and my being ashamed of not being with Quinlan was unleashed on him.

"Where have you been? If only you had been around, one of us could have stayed with Quinlan while the other went to get the food!"

"What are you talking about?" He asked, having no idea what I was railing him about. He walked toward Quinlan but turned and left after looking at him motionless on the ground.

Furious, I yelled at him, "What? Where are you goin' now?"

I sat there next to Quinlan crying for hours it seemed until Ma returned home. She and I spent the night right next to him, crying. She could not hold it in this time. She was exhausted, and we were both so sad. It was bad enough losing him, but I didn't know if I could live with myself for not being there with him. I had hinted to Brody, but I couldn't get myself to tell Ma. I hated myself.

We did not have a place to bury him like Brody's mother, so we dug a shallow grave for him next to the place we had buried Moira. It was on the Farraday's property, or I guess the Brumley's property, but they never knew it. I don't even think they knew about Quinlan or his passing away.

Ma tried to go on with her work as if nothing had happened. I couldn't stand it. Sometimes I would go out to his gravesite and lay next to him. Even when it was raining and cold, at least I was next to him. Maybe I was making up for not being there when he needed me. Whatever the reason, I found myself lying next to him daily.

Often I would notice Brody off in the distance, but he never came down with me. I don't even think he ever said anything to Ma or me about Quinlan dying. I didn't care. I hated him now, anyway. He was not the same boy Ma spoke so highly of this past year. See? It's amazing how many changes can occur in less than a year. I don't even know what he does with his days and Ma is too busy to be concerned about him all of the time.

Da used to say, "You must live with a person to know a person. If you want to know me come and live with me," so I guess we never really knew Brody like we thought we did. I didn't like this Brody.

How could he be this way when he had had such a beautiful and wonderful mother? If it's true what they say, "As the big hound is, so will the pup be," then why is Brody so different from his parents. And I guess, Patrick, too, wherever he may be.

As time went by, Brody came around more and teased me constantly about the flitters I wore. They were actually rags and were my sister Moira's, and were a much better fit, if you can call it that, than wearing Ma's or his mother's clothes.

Anyway, he didn't look much better in his scraggly old clothes. They might have had a finer weave, but they had been worn through in places, and were dirty beyond what he used to wear in the years before. And, he had a few more to choose from since his father and Patrick were gone.

He didn't tease me in front of Ma, so she never really believed what I said about him or that it was as bad as I said it was. I tried to get back at him with smart remarks, but I was never very good at it. I could have picked on him about his tousled, grown out hair, or the few scraggly whiskers on his chin, or even his silly voice that cracked and broke at times, but I wasn't quick enough. Oh, I could think of something to say later on, but by then it was too late, and my accent was so thick even if I had come back with something clever, it didn't go over as well as his comments in his proper, silly voice.

I used to hear my grandfather say, "If you want to be criticized, marry," so I decided to change it slightly and say," If you want to be teased, get a brother." Yes, that was my own thought in regard to Brody.

Maybe it wasn't true for all brothers, because Quinlan had never teased me like Brody. As much time as Brody and I began spending together, we might as well have been brother and sister. His brooding was annoying and I had no qualms about telling him the things he did that annoyed me. He may not have really been my brother, but that did not keep us from bickering like siblings.

The wintertime didn't help with the shortage of food or clothes. We wrapped anything we had around us, and burned anything we could find for warmth. We even ended up tearing down pieces of the shack the Farraday's used to live in to use for wood. We also used pieces of it to fix parts of our place which needed reinforcement. Brody did help with this, but continued to brood.

Ma started to worry Brody was on the doss, laying about or being useless. She thought he might be joining the same group that the fathers had been involved with.

He was keeping something from her, she knew that. She tried to find out what was wrong with him, but had no luck getting it out of him. She often wondered if he knew where Patrick had gone, or what Patrick was doing.

He wouldn't talk about Patrick, but he did speak of his father. I knew Brody visited his father at times, and he saw him on the road when they were doing work. I didn't really know if he was ever able to talk to him, but I did know he ventured to the workhouse a few times.

Ma also visited Mr. Farraday at the workhouse and didn't tell him about her worries of Brody because there wasn't anything he could do to change the situation and she didn't want him to worry. She said they did discuss the whereabouts of Patrick.

"Have you heard anything from him? What do you think has happened to him? Was he in a workhouse? Had he been killed? Had he traveled to another country?" Mr. Farraday would ask of her.

"You know I would tell you if I heard anything. I'm still waiting on word about Mac, but I promise if I hear about either, I will tell you right away. How are you doing in here? Can we do something for you?" Ma asked.

"No, thank you. I am getting along fine. I think the most important thing is to stay busy and try to remain strong. I eat what they give me, when it's edible, and work when it's available. Getting out of here is on my mind the most. I know I can trust you with Brody, and forgive me. I know you would tell me if you knew something, but not hearing anything drives me senseless."

"I do understand. I can't imagine being stuck in here not knowing about your children or what will happen to you."

"I do not care about me, except, if I were out of here, I might be able to do more for all of us."

"We do what we can. We'll be all right, and your boys will be all right. You focus on yourself and what you need to do to stay alive."

"Thank you, Kate. I do not know what I would do without your's and Brody's visits. I really do appreciate your coming when you do."

"I think we both have our children in our best interests and if we can make life better for them, then we shall make it."

I didn't know it at the time, but Ma and Mr. Farraday also discussed me. He made suggestions to her that shocked me when I found out what the suggestions were the following month.

One particular time, Ma came home and seemed so different. She pulled out the letters Uncle Brennan had written to us over the years. She looked at them, lost in thought. She could not read the letters, so I thought maybe she missed her brother and was thinking about his being so far away. He was the only family she had left from her birth family.

Sometimes Brody would read the letters to her. She did not ask me to read them to her. She asked Brody to look through the letters, especially the most recent ones, and see if Uncle Brennan said anything about where he was in America. Brody didn't find anything specific. It seemed as though Uncle Brennan was traveling wherever there was work. He moved around a lot and would sometimes be in New York, or Pennsylvania, or out in the west working on railroads. Ma seemed frantic trying to find out where he was.

After another trip to the workhouse and having seen Mr. Farraday, Ma took Brody aside. "Your father and I have been discussing something, and need you to do something for us. We know it is not something you want to do, but we need you to go see a friend of your fathers in Galway. He says he has always been a loyal and trusted associate through business."

"Why?" Brody asked. "Can't we ask someone else? I bet there are others who would jump at the chance of leaving. It's been years since I have been to that town. What could be that important?"

"I understand your questionin' it," Ma said, "but your father can explain it to you much better than me. Please go talk to him, and then you can decide if you will go or not."

Brody went to see his father at the workhouse, and when he came home, he had agreed to do this for Ma. I didn't know what was happening and Ma wouldn't tell me. I was hurt that she, Brody, and Mr. Farraday had a secret and I was left out. I was her daughter.

"Why don't I get to know what is going on?" I asked her.

"Because this is business for Mr. Farraday, and we have decided not to get you involved. The less you know the better."

"Then can I travel with Brody?"

"No! I won't hear of it. If I am to go, I will go alone," he said.

"Allie, he's right. For this trip, he needs to make it on his own. Anyway, you would only get in each other's hair. You know how you two cannot stand to be together for more than a couple of minutes without bickerin'."

I crossed my arms and stomped out the door. I had to pass Brody on my way out, and he smiled as I passed. I kicked some dirt up towards him and continued walking out the door.

The next few days, Ma gathered as many scraps as she could from the Brumleys without their knowing it. If she had been caught, they probably would have had her arrested. I did not want her to know I was worried, but the prospect of losing her, too, was unnerving. And for what?

Brody was to travel with only the clothes on his back, and a tied piece of fabric full of the scraps Ma had gathered. He also carried a scribbled note from his father. I had no idea what it said. It was all so secret.

I remember Ma telling Da before he was arrested she was worried about the organization he was involved with because the British might find out and not like what they were saying.

They had said, "It is not a secret if it is known by three people."

Well, Ma, Mr. Farraday and Brody knew what was happening right now, and it was still a secret. So much for that saying!

I stomped around the house and let it be known I was not happy with being left out. Ma let me be unhappy which was so unlike her. She was always the strongest of us, and she always tried to make sure everyone was happy, whatever the circumstances. She went to work and came home seemingly unmindful of my feelings.

Brody left early one morning, and all I knew was he was heading toward the seacoast. Ma doted over him before he left and they spent a long time whispering to one another. I couldn't hear. I played as though I was still asleep against the wall, but I strained to hear anything I could to figure out what was happening. Without hearing enough to put any pieces together, and without my telling him goodbye, he left.

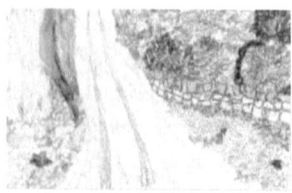

Ma prepared for work, kissed my forehead, and headed out the door. I rolled over to watch her leave. I didn't know whether I should be mad or worried. I still felt left out.

For the next couple of days I slipped away to the spot that was always comforting to me. The spot Mrs. Farraday would read to her boys. That tree on the knoll with so many fond memories. The Brumleys didn't gather as the Farraday's did, so even though I was close to their home, they would have no idea I was there.

I snatched a book from the Farraday's pile. A book by Jane Harvey, "The Castle of Tynemouth. A Tale." It was about a girl who narrowly escaped being burnt for witchcraft. It was set in the 15th century.

I have never traveled far, so thinking about a castle named Tynemouth, and its area and people were so intriguing. As I read, I did not always understand the words, or even how to pronounce them, but I skipped those I didn't know and tried to imagine the story as I read what I could.

The days went by quickly as I read this book. I read as long as there was sunlight, underneath my special tree. I became the character of Rosetta as I read the story. Sometimes I would close my eyes and try to envision her and the places discussed. Some of the story was cruel, but in its entirety, it kept me captivated.

Around the fifth day, Ma came home ever so anxious. "I wish we would hear something from Brody. We haven't heard a thing in over five days, and I am worried about him."

"Why?" I asked. "Is he doing something he might get into trouble for?"

"No, but being out there alone has its own dangers. I'm sure he's fine, but I will feel better when he gets home."

On the sixth day, she just happened to get a letter from Uncle Brennan. She took the letter to Mr. Farraday and had him read it to her.

She came home and told me all about it. Uncle Brennan had written from a place called Boston. He said he did not know how long he was going to be at his boarding house, for there were rumors of work available in the west.

He had been out west before, but this time there was work for logging and mining, too. Many of the jobs on the East coast were being done by what he called, "Free Blacks." We didn't know what that was but he said the competition for jobs was very high and many of the Irish were being discriminated against along with the "Free Blacks", and there weren't many jobs for everyone.

This letter made Ma more nervous about Brody's whereabouts. She paced the floor, talking aloud to herself about different areas of America and trying to guess what Uncle Brennan's plans might be. She needed to write a letter to Uncle Brennan, but she needed Brody to help her write it.

"Where is Brody?" she repeatedly asked herself.

Day six went by, then day seven, then day eight.

During this time, I was able to finish my book. At the end, I realized it was one part of a two-part story. I don't believe the Farradays had the other part, or maybe they had not saved it as part of the items they had hidden.

I couldn't be angry with them, but I yearned to read the second half of this one, and the other ones to the *Last of the Mohicans*. One day I would find the other books and read them. If I ever became a writer, I would not do that to a reader. A book should be written in its entirety so the reader could know the whole story. Humph! I would have to wait.

Finally, on day nine, Brody came in right after Ma had gone to work. I ran over to the Brumleys, hiding beside the kitchen window listening for Ma to come into the kitchen so I could get her attention. It seemed like hours, but finally I heard her come in to get something for Mrs. Brumley. I tossed a twig through the open window in the kitchen, but she did not hear it or see the twig on the floor.

"Ma!" I whispered, but there was no reaction. How could she not hear me? Why would a twig fall into a window without a purpose? I then picked up a pebble and threw it in the window. It must have hit a dish, cup, or saucer because it made a loud noise. I was afraid someone else might have heard it. Ma came to the window to peak out and I swatted at her to get her attention.

She was stunned, "Go home, Allie! You know I'm workin' I can't talk to you right now."

While she was finishing her last sentence, Mrs. Brumley came to the kitchen to see if Ma had dropped one of her precious china pieces. I dropped down on the ground beneath the window sill. Ma played it off as if she were shaking crumbs from her hands and turned around to face Mrs. Brumley.

"What have you broken, Kate?"

Ma motioned around her to show that there was nothing broken, "Everythin' is fine, Mrs. Brumley. I accidentally slipped while placin' the teacup on the saucer. The cookie on the saucer was underneath it, so I was brushin' the cookie crumbs from my hands as you walked in."

Ma held up the cup and saucer to show her that it was fine.

"Well, go ahead and bring me my tea in the drawing room, and place an unbroken cookie on another plate. Watch what you are doing from now on or I will take the price of the broken piece from your payment next time. Do you understand?"

Ma nodded, "Yes, ma'am. I'll bring it right in."

Mrs. Brumley turned and walked out without saying a word.

Ma waited a moment, then looked out over the window sill and down towards me, "Allie, now go home. We can't afford to lose any money. I have to get back to work."

"But Ma…"

"No, 'but Ma,' you go on home! Now!"

"But Ma, Brody has come home."

"Oh!" she said, "Oh! I will think of somethin' to tell her and get home as soon as possible. Is he all right? Has he said anythin'? Did he bring anythin' with him?"

"No, no, and no!" I said.

"Run along and I will hurry home as soon as I can."

I didn't quite obey her, but waited for her beyond the nearest ridge beyond the road. It didn't take her long, and I grabbed her as she hurried by on her way home.

"Oh, Allie, you startled me. I thought I told you to go home and wait?"

"You did, but I wanted to wait for you and walk you home."

"You wanted to hear what I might tell you about Brody's trip. Isn't that true?"

"Well, maybe. Will you tell me?"

"Absolutely not! We will hear what Brody has to say, and then I will tell you what I can."

"How did you get away from Mrs. Brumley? What did you tell her?"

"I told her I must be comin' down with somethin' and felt quite faint. She then told me she did not want me breakin' any of her dishes or makin' her family sick so she told me to go home for the day. We were lucky this time."

"I don't like her, Ma. She's not nice to you."

"But she pays my wages and we need anythin' we can get. Most people do not get anythin', so I will put up with her oddities and demands to continue gettin' paid."

I scrunched my mouth in a way to show her my disgust of Mrs. Brumley, but Ma didn't pay any attention to it, she was mindful of the fact we had to get home.

We held hands as we ran towards our house. I didn't know what the hurry was, but I knew Ma had been anxious for days, and maybe now I would find out what all those secrets were they were keeping from me.

We ran into the house and Ma broke her hand free from mine as she ran to Brody and grabbed his shoulders. He stood there without much of a response. He did look exhausted. He was dusty and more scraggly than normal. Even if he had wanted to tell her things, she didn't let him get a word in.

She spouted a stream of questions to Brody as she poured him some water and he drank it thirstily and slumped down to the ground.

"What happened on your journey? Did anything bad happen? Did you see Mr. Leeds? Is he going to help us? What did he say? Did you have enough money? Is it going to work? What did he say? Can he help? What did he say?"

"Ma!" I yelled. "Stop and let him speak!"

She looked at me, and then at Brody anxiously. She knelt down next to him, and said, "Are you all right?"

"I'm about to fade. My legs are so tired," He scooted back to a wall and leaned to rest. "I am just so exhausted. He is going to help her, but can I take a rest? I promise I will tell you everything? There's still time."

"Time for what?" I asked impertinently.

"You go ahead and sleep Brody. When you are rested, we will hear your story. I am just pleased you are home safely," she then pulled me outside.

"Who is her?" I asked. "Who are you all talking about? Come on, Ma, can't you at least tell me what is going on, now?"

"You will find out everything when he wakes up. I won't keep any more from you, but we have to let him rest."

I couldn't stand it, and it didn't seem as though Ma could either. He stayed asleep the rest of the day and most of the night. Ma and I tried to sleep, but both of us were restless for different reasons, and yet the same ones…What was he going to tell us?

Chapter 4
Brody Tells of Galway

When he finally awoke, I found out who *she* was - *she* was *me*.

"And ya couldn't have told me this before?" I asked, "Why not?"

"I didn't want ya to get your hopes up or get involved in something that might not happen. Now, let's be quiet and let Brody tell his story."

"Yes, you're not going to learn a thing unless you let me tell my story." He said.

He gave me a disgruntled look, and then returned to Ma and began telling his story of the past nine days.

"The trip took longer than expected. On the way there, I wasn't quite sure where I was going. I didn't sleep well at nights because there were always suspicious people around, and I was fearful because of all the money I was carrying with me, and the note from Father. Father told me not to let anyone but Mr. Leeds get his note because someone else might use it without Mr. Leeds knowing that the person bringing it to him wasn't actually me. You already know that Father has never met Mr. Leeds in person, but he said they were business acquaintances through another friend, and so Mr. Leeds had no way of knowing what father or his children might look like.

"Along the way a very nice family, the Goddards, let me stay one night and helped me find the right path to Galway. They also told me how to find Mr. Leeds. They didn't know Mr. Leeds, but they knew where I should go and who to talk to about finding him. They gave me what little food they could and told me I could stop there on my way back.

"I was so grateful for them because I was much more tired than I thought I would be and I really didn't know if I was going the right way or not. They warned me of the mass of people that would be in Galway and around the city. Most had traveled from far away to take ships that left from port cities. Galway was one of the cities they found refuge in.

"I followed their directions and finally made it to Galway. They were right about the large number of people, everywhere. There *were* people everywhere, of all sorts. The streets were crowded, the pubs were crowded, the alleys, everywhere! I couldn't believe my eyes! I didn't know how I was going to find Mr. Leeds in all of that mess, but I remembered what the Goddards said and who to talk to about finding him. They had given me a piece of paper and I followed their directions to the town library.

"I found myself fighting and pushing my way through crowds of people. There were so many people here. I was startled and wondered, what did they think they were going to do? I pressed on. I saw everything from wealthy looking people to beggars; babies to the elderly, and families to those looking all alone. It was a horrible sight. Many looked sickly and starving, and there was no place for anyone to go. There was no shelter available and no food for anyone. It was kind of like home, but there were so many more.

"I finally made it to the library, but I was met at the door by a guard. One that told me I couldn't come in unless I had business there. I guess I did look rather pitiful. My clothes were even more ragged now. I must have looked like anyone else out and about on the street. I told the guard I was given this address as a place to find a Mr. Leeds who I had business with, and the he let me in.

"The library had magnificent wood that outlined the walls, the ceilings, and the tables. A deep, dark wood that had a wonderful aroma of what I remember libraries smelling like." He stopped for a moment.

I scrunched my mouth and shifted my eyes from side to side wondering why he would think this was significant enough to tell us about it. I had no idea what he meant, but he seemed to love to talk about it, so I closed my eyes and tried to imagine the library and the smell of the wood as it surrounded all the tables and books.

He went on, saying, "I was caught up in the majesty of it all and almost forgot why I was there, but a woman came over and interrupted my gazing. I was startled for a moment, and then collected myself to ask about Mr. Leeds. She told me she didn't know of him personally, but she could find someone who did. After about 20 minutes, she did just that, and another woman came up to me and said she would take me to Mr. Leeds's right away. She introduced herself as Finola Abernathy and that her mother was a friend of Mr. Leeds's.

"Miss Abernathy was an attractive young lady. She told me she volunteered in the library after school and in the summer months. She had black hair that went down her back beyond her waistband. She had the front pulled back and folded under, letting the loose part lay down against her back. It swayed as she walked flowing from side to side, brushing against her fitted jacket. She was smartly dressed with her jacket and skirt that hung down to her boots that were polished nicely as though she did not walk on the open dirt very much."

I leaned back with my face returning to the scrunched expression. I had never heard him speak with such detail. Especially about a girl! He just kept going and going on about her. Ma was gripped with every word he said, not even glancing my way for acknowledgment of my reaction to his story.

I pushed her arm to get her to look at me, but all she could do was say, "Stop it, Allie, let him finish."

Not a peep my way!

"We went out a back way and slithered through the crowds of people. She told me to keep my head down and move with a purpose, staying as near to her as possible the entire way. I did as told, and when we reached our destination, I looked up to see a handsome townhouse. I didn't know if it was Mr. Leeds's home or office, but I was grateful to finally be so close to the man I had traveled so far to see.

"Miss Abernathy rang the doorbell. A servant opened the door and must have recognized the young lady who brought me there, because she let us in right away. She told the woman, Betsy, about me and that I needed to see Mr. Leeds. Betsy explained that Mr. Leeds was in with another client and we would have to wait.

"Miss Abernathy waited with me so she could introduce us, but hours seemed to go by and she had to get home before it was dark. She told me to never go out by myself, especially at night. It was just too dangerous. She said if I needed anything else, I could come by the library to find her. She then said goodbye, and I was left there all alone.

"As I sat in the parlor, waiting on Mr. Leeds, I must have fallen asleep because I didn't hear Mr. Leeds come in."

I did hear him when he belted out to Betsy, 'Where are these people you said are waiting for me?"

Ma and I breathed loudly, and Brody smiled and continued, "I jumped up quickly from the settee where I had been lying and stood at attention. Scraggly looking and tired, but trying to be presentable. Mr. Leeds had a look of amazement on his face when he realized I had been in the room all along. Betsy stepped in to show Mr. Leeds where I was, but by now, he knew.

"I shuffled through my clothing and rags trying to find the one letter I had kept so close to me. When I finally came across it, I gave the crumpled letter to Mr. Leeds, and stepped back waiting for him to read it. He took it over to the light, put on his spectacles, and read through the letter. When finished, he slowly turned around and eyed me up and down. I felt like a chicken hanging on a hook at market waiting to be chosen for the evening meal."

This time Ma and I laughed, and I said, "There isn't enough meat on ya for anyone to want ya for dinner!"

Ignoring me, he went on with his story, "Mr. Leeds came over to me, twirled me around and eyed me some more. When he finally spoke, it was with a loud and familiar tone as if we were long lost relatives. He started talking about Father and how, even though they had never personally met, they had years of a business relationship and he had wondered what had happened to him when the correspondence had stopped so abruptly. He had heard rumors, but it was wonderful to now get the truth from his son.

"I tried to remind him of the letter and my purpose for being there, but Mr. Leeds kept talking over me and asking me question after question. Maybe he's kin to you two the way you kept on asking questions when I arrived home!" Brody said. "Mr. Leeds told me we would have plenty of time to look over the letter and its contents, but let's eat dinner, first. I was worried about the letter and what I needed to do, but felt that Mr. Leeds was controlling the entire evening.

"However, I was starving and the aroma coming from the kitchen overrode my desire to discuss the letter at the moment. I was glad to get some dinner, and be in a home like that.

"And," Brody said, "dinner was delicious. They had pork cutlets and corn and baked apple, with wine no less."

Ma and I were stunned. "Where did he get the food?" I asked.

"In the port towns, some people could get food before it is shipped out to other countries."

"What do you mean, shipped out to other countries? Where was the food a goin'?" I asked.

"Mr. Leeds said it was a horrible situation and England was doing Ireland a disservice by exporting so much when the country and its people needed it."

"All of Ireland seems to be starvin'," I said, "and yet, food is being shipped out?"

"That's what Patrick talked about months ago," said Ma.

"But how did this Mr. Leeds get the food?" I asked.

"I didn't ask specifically because I thought it would be impolite to ask when I was his guest," Brody said.

"Well, maybe if you had asked, we could get some of that food for our own family, or for our friends." I said haughtily.

Brody acted snooty right back at me, "I can do nothing about it!" he said, and then went on with his story.

"Mr. Leeds asked about Father, Mother and Patrick. He had heard rumors about our losing our estate, so I told him the whole story and about the terrible year we had all had. I told him about our current situation and that is why Father had asked me to come and make a special request of him in the hopes of his getting his help.

"Mr. Leeds sat there looking stunned and shaking his head. I didn't know if that meant he didn't believe me, or he was commiserating. After a few moments, he stood up and told me he would help me anyway he could, but that first I was to bathe, and have a good night's sleep. Then tomorrow we would start a fresh day and decide what to do."

I laughed. How funny that Mr. Leeds told Brody he needed a bath! No one else seemed to think it was funny, so I just shrugged it off, twisting my mouth, yet once again.

"His house lady, Betsy, took me to a guest room where she lit a fire and prepared it ready for me. She even put out bed clothes for me to sleep in." This time as he spoke, he almost seemed melancholy.

"I felt so guilty about being in his home, knowing Father was in a workhouse and you two were sleeping on the ground that very same night. It just wasn't right." He took Ma's hands and leaned forward.

"Oh, Brody," said Ma, "please tell me ya did not turn down their kindness?"

"No," he answered, once again sounding melancholy, "I took advantage of it and lied at first by the fire, and then I crawled into bed and the sheets, under the comforter. I remembered sleeping this way in our old home, but had forgotten about it over this past year.

"I remembered the smell of clean sheets and those of a fire by your bedside where the aroma of petals in it made it ever so sweeter. I slept the night through and dreamt of Ma. I didn't want to wake up, but I did.

"I thought of Betsy and her station in life, and how she was similar to you, Kate. I had a special feeling for her and her situation. She was a slender lady with a husband and son, but spent the majority of her time with Mr. Leeds. She was kind and considerate and seemed genuinely interested in my well-being. She did not have much education, but she did her job well and worked hard for Mr. Leeds.

"The next morning, I sat up in bed and tried to rationalize my good sleep with what I knew the rest of you were having to live with, and knew I had to go through with my obligation of the letter and the request.

"As I looked around, I saw a set of clothes lying on the settee in the corner of my bedroom. Betsy must have snuck in at some time while I slumbered and laid them out for me. I couldn't get myself to put them on. I knew Mr. Leeds meant well, but how could I wear them knowing how all of you were struggling here? The clothes were clean and starched and hole free, and probably fit me, but my own guilt weighed heavier than the liking of a new set of clothes, so I dressed in the clothes I had worn, and went downstairs.

"Mr. Leeds was sitting in the drawing room having his breakfast. Scones and jam sat around a plate with one spot vacant. He must have eaten that one, but there were more sitting there, and when he saw me come in, he offered the plate to me. I took one and remembered the smell of fresh baked bread and scones in the morning, and the fruit that had such a fragrant aroma in the jams and jellies I used to have at home. That must have been what woke me up, the smell of the items baking.

"Mr. Leeds realized my distraction for he brought my attention back to him and told me it was all right to eat his scones and fill my belly as long as he was there. He also said the clothes in my room were for me and I was welcome to wear them home. He said Father had brought him a lot of business throughout the years, and the least he could do was take care of me when I was under his roof.

"I told him how much I appreciated his consideration, but did not want to take advantage of his hospitality. He laughed and slapped me on my knee."

"On your bony knee!" I said and cackled. Once again, no one else did, and Brody looked at Ma after he rolled his eyes and continued his story.

"I must have eaten four scones! I could not remember having eaten so many before, but as I looked down on the plate, there were now five spaces open and Mr. Leeds had not had another bite. I tried to pull myself together so as not to look so taken with it all, but I really was. It seemed so long since I had eaten two wonderful meals in a row.

"Inside his home it was a different world, because if I strained ever so slightly I could hear the noise of a crowd outside. The hustle, the bustle, not like Christmastime in the city, more like noises at a rally for the Liberators before it all gets going and people are talking loudly. I was warm and safe and my stomach was full.

"I was thinking about all of this when Mr. Leeds spoke of the request for the first time. He said the request was quite achievable, but there were certain things he had to go over with me to make sure we did everything correctly. We must discuss the costs, the current situation in Ireland and America, the Uncle, the boats that were available, and much more."

"What?" I stared at Ma, "Please tell me what he is talkin' about! Why America? Why boats? Why discuss the costs? Da is not here so how can we even think about travelin' to America without him? Who were ya talkin' about? What was Brody doin'?"

Ma turned towards me and took my head in her hands, "We are plannin' a trip to America for ya. We want ya to get out of Ireland and make a place for yourself in America. Ya will be so much better off, and Da and I have saved for exactly this situation. We all want to go, but I can't leave and I couldn't live without tryin' to get ya there and to a better life. 'There is hope from the sea, but none from the grave.' And, I couldn't stand to bury another child."

I was stunned. I heard the words coming out of her mouth, and her lips moving, but I couldn't believe them. They didn't register. It was too much to take in. Blimey! What is she thinking? I had so many questions running through my mind, I just sat there, stunned. I looked back at Brody who continued with his story without allowing me the time to process this information and ask questions.

"Mr. Leeds spent the day with me. We went out to the ships in the harbor and met a few of the Captains. As we were talking, I couldn't help but notice that so many people were waiting to get on the ships. It seemed as though there were more people than the size of the ships could hold. People were everywhere, and Mr. Leeds said there were waiting lists of people who were trying to get to Canada, Australia, England, and of course, America. We picked up the paperwork that was needed to book passage for Allie. And then we asked around for what might be needed in America.

"After spending time at the harbor, we went to a bank and opened an account. We placed the money Father had allotted me in an account in mine and Mr. Leeds's names."

I truly didn't understand. I was still stunned, but the story went on.

"Mr. Leeds brought me back to his house and he took some time writing down everything he could think of that would help us get prepared for the journey. I was so thankful because I would never have remembered all of it if he hadn't taken the time to write it down.

"Towards the end of the day, Betsy called us in to dinner and we sat down to roast duck, dressing, and plum pudding. With wine, again." Brody said smiling.

I rolled my eyes and laid my head down in my open hands that lay on my knees. Not to cry, but to rest and take in more of this surprising story that involved what was going to happen to me, without me even knowing about it!

"As we finished dinner, I told Mr. Leeds I would have to be heading back home the next day. He offered for me to stay another day or two to rest, but I told him I must get back to tell you and Father about my trip and the plans we needed to make.

"Mr. Leeds said he understood, and asked Betsy if my room was ready. He said he was going to spend a little time reading and if I liked, I could look through his books and pick out something to take upstairs and read. I did just that, and chose, Gulliver's Travels by Jonathan Swift. I took it upstairs, and fell asleep by the light of the fireplace.

"Mr. Leeds must have come in to check on me, because someone had come in and jostled me to get up and on the bed. Whoever it was, they smelled of pipe smoke and leather bound books. I was aware, but not awake. I spent another night curled up on this soft and warm bed with dreams that took me away.

"The next morning I awoke to the smell of scones baking again, and I turned over to check the fire and realized I had to step back into reality and head home. As I slipped out of bed, I saw the clothes Mr. Leeds had purchased for me. I decided they were a gift, and Mr. Leeds had been so nice, how could I not accept them and wear them on my trip back home?"

Brody looked down as he continued his story.

"I picked up each piece and looked at it before putting it on. The shirt made of silk, soft and sleek with a tie in the front. The trousers, warm and long, stitched nicely. Much better suited for a cold day than the knickers I had been wearing. This outfit had a vest and a coat jacket, socks and shoes. They fit so well and I felt so handsome and smart."

I cackled at loud at the ridiculous notion of his thinking he looked handsome and smart. Ma stopped my mocking of him, and motioned for me to continue listening to his story. He moved on from his egotistical description and continued with his story. It took him back downstairs and to another breakfast of scones and jam.

"Mr. Leeds spoke of how good I looked and he was glad I had decided to wear the clothes he had bought me. These would do much better than the clothes I had worn on my way here, and I could discard the old clothes if I wanted to. I told him I wanted to keep them, but appreciated everything he had done.

"We finished breakfast and I excused myself to go and get the rest of my things. I wrapped up all the information Mr. Leeds had gathered for me, and prepared to leave. Betsy brought me some scones for my trip, and some tidbits of food which I could carry with me. She hugged me as if she were my mother and was worried about my journey. I though it so strange since I had made it there without any consequences, and I no longer had the money or the request letter Father was worried about.

"I went downstairs and bade Mr. Leeds farewell. I thanked him for everything, but he stopped me and said we would be seeing each other again and no thanks were needed. What was needed was a safe journey home and back to our house where I could make sure Father's request was fulfilled. Until then, he said.

"As I headed out the door, Betsy reminded me of what evil there is out there and I should be ever so cautious. She told me, 'Youth does not mind where it sets its foot,' and, 'Why should you never iron a 4-leaf clover? You don't want to press your luck.' I smiled as if I understood, and turned from their doorway and out onto the street. I remembered what Miss Abernathy had told me about walking with my head down and with a purpose, and I did just that as I found myself leaving the town of Galway, and heading back home.

"I strolled on the same road the Goddards told me about. I was looking forward to stopping by their home again and telling them about the city and the harbor and everything I had seen and heard.

"My mind was focused on that when something terrible happened. I was only about one thousand paces outside the city when I passed a grouping of trees, and out jumped three men who grabbed me.

"They went on and on about my clothes and how they had found them 'a good un, a rich un, looky here.' I tried telling them over and over again I wasn't rich and had just been given these clothes, but they didn't believe me. They pulled at my wrappings and items and tore them apart.

"I tried fighting them but two of them held me while the third went through my things looking for money or food. They weren't interested in any of the papers, but were glad to find the food Betsy had packaged for me not more than three hours ago. And what was it she had said? Something about ironing a four leaf clover?"

I guess he had pressed his luck, and I had a rush of guilty feelings about my previous ridiculing of his self-description in his new clothes. How humiliating for him, and scary to be out there alone. He didn't sound very scared, but he must have been.

Ma was horrified. She grabbed him by his shoulders, "Brody, I'm so sorry. I never wanted to put ya in such a position."

He made nothing of it. "I'm fine now, so you shouldn't worry."

"I don't know if this is worth it. I'm afraid to hear anymore."

"They didn't hurt me," he reassured her, "They did steal the clothes given to me by Mr. Leeds. They may have left me there unclothed, next to the trees, but they had not taken the paperwork and instruction given to me by Mr. Leeds. And, it was good they did not get me on my way into town since I had the money and the request from Father."

Ma began pacing the floor, realizing what danger she had put him in. He stood up and stopped her from pacing.

"Kate, I am all right, and I'm home now." She hugged him, then sat down and motioned for him to finish his story.

"After I collected myself from the attack, I found my old clothes and put them back on. I was glad I had not let Mr. Leeds take them away from me since that is all I had for clothes. I felt a little silly thinking about Betsy and how she was worried and I had thought her silly. Who was silly, now? I lost those handsome clothes given to me by Mr. Leeds, and set off looking like a poor beggar, again.

"The strangest thing came to mind after putting my clothes back on; I felt more at home in them than in the nice clothes. Don't get me wrong, the other ones were wonderful, but I no longer live that way, and I should have known better than to not have changed out of them."

Ma reached for his hand and said, "I'm glad ya are all right, Brody, but we must seriously consider whether we should go through with our original plans. I'm just not sure it's was worth it. What if something happens on the journey back? What if ya don't make it?"

It was an eventful story, and it must have taken hours for him to tell us because by the time he was finished it was morning and Ma had to go to work. She was tired, but she had taken off early the day before and she didn't want Mrs. Brumley to be upset with her. She knew in the months ahead, she might have to take more time away from work, so she needed to do as much as she could for the Brumleys, now.

I walked a way with her, not saying anything. I was still in shock. She didn't say anything to me, either. She hugged me and kissed my forehead before she turned towards the house.

After Ma and I parted I went to the knoll. I lied there and looked up at the fog in the tree. It was a musty smell, damp and cool. I closed my eyes wanting to think about everything that had been brought to my attention over the night, and I guess I fell asleep.

I dreamt about the library Brody talked about and the bedroom he slept in. He wasn't there in my dream, and I don't think I was there either. It was a tour of sorts from above the rooms, and I was absorbed. I tried to smell the aromas Brody talked about, but I couldn't. It was as if they had no smell, images only.

I must have been asleep all day because Brody came up to me and sat down next to me. I awoke to his speaking to me in a tone I hadn't heard in months.

"I have such good memories of this spot. We always knew Quinlan and you were up here and hiding over the hill. Mother would not let us say a thing to you. She was afraid you might not come back. She was always glad when you all were there, listening."

I didn't say anything, but looked at him as if to say *What?* I then spoke, hearing myself denying it and saying, "We didn't. Ma would never let us bother your family like that."

He bumped his shoulder against mine, acknowledging my comment, without agreeing. I was self-conscious about it and kept quiet after that.

So what if they did know? It was part of my memories, too, and only good ones. We could both share something that was good. I had my brother, and he had his whole family together as part of that memory. Yes, it was a happy one for both of us.

I remembered Mrs. Farraday's story about the Mulberry tree. Her words were comforting even now. I didn't look up at its branches, but I could hear them swaying in the wind. It was alive and part of both of us. The berries were growing and getting ready to ripen. Soon they would be their dark red color.

As I slowly came out of that uncomfortable feeling, I remembered Brody and that huge secret he had kept from me. I became furious with him, again. I stood up and stormed around the knoll as if I was lecturing him, hands on my hips, throwing my hair from one side to the other. "How could ya?"

He stayed seated and told me, "It wasn't up to me, Allie. Your mother and my father made the decision for me to go to Galway and see if I could find passage for you to America. They didn't know if it was going to happen or not. They didn't want you to be involved because you might question everything and get worked up."

"What?" I said. Well, yah, I did get worked up at times, but wasn't it about me? "Shouldn't I have a say?"

He didn't really acknowledge my comments. He sat there patiently and waited for me to finish.

Then, he stood up and said, "We need to get home. Your Mother will be home soon. If we're not there she might get worried. She might also want to start discussing what plans need to be made."

I went through periods of anger, then sadness, and then excitement. Ma and Brody organized what they could, and discussed with Mr. Farraday the consequences and plans of my trip. That meant over the next month, I wasn't really a part of this plan – again! Oh, I was allowed to hear it, but the actual planning and coordination of it all was out of my hands.

Their minds were set and June was to be the magical month I was to set sail for America. They all figured this would be the best month to travel before winter set back in and sailing would be too cold. Otherwise, we might have to wait a year more, and Ma didn't want that to be the case. She didn't want to take the chance.

It was the last few days of May, and we were working on our plans and what we were to travel with. Mr. Farraday told Ma he wanted to give me whatever he could to make sure I would have something in America to sell if need be.

He was still so kind, and here he was in a workhouse, not knowing when or if he was to ever be free again. Ma felt guilty at taking anything, but she knew he was right. If I didn't have these extras, I might be put in an orphanage or not given the best possible chances as a passenger.

As the day grew closer, I wondered why Brody was not going with me. I understood about Ma. She couldn't leave without knowing about Da, or helping Mr. Farraday anyway she could, but Brody? Why weren't they making him go? I asked Ma.

"Brody was given the option and he refuses to leave his father."

"Why don't I have the right of refusal?"

"He can still help me and his father by stayin' here, while you will have a better chance in America with your Uncle Brennan."

I didn't truly understand it, but I had no choice, they were sending me whether I liked it or not.

When the day arrived, my mind was racing. I was excited and yet scared, happy and yet sad. How in the world would I ever get my stomach to relax? And my mind, would it ever stop racing as fast as my heart was pounding. Ma was determined. She wanted me to go, but she seemed downhearted. She did want me to go, didn't she? Shouldn't she be just as excited as me?

We were finishing the small bit of packing we had to do when out of nowhere came the sound of a man, loud and obnoxious. His voice moved closer and closer until Ma realized he must be coming into our home. She grabbed me and stood in front of me. Brody darted to the opening of our doorway. He greeted the man and then brought him back to our doorway with his arm reaching up around him.

The light was behind them so it took us a second for our eyes to adjust. When they did we realized who it was. It was Patrick!

He was going on and on about something, and Brody was talking at the same time, so we just stood there and stared, mouths gaping open. When Ma regained her composure, she went up to Patrick and gave him a hug, welcoming him home.

She looked back at me. Her face revealed a message. It was a look of remorse. I had always heard, "As you slide down the banister of life, may the splinters never point in the wrong direction!" I guess Patrick was a splinter going the wrong way. Without really knowing, I knew deep down this would change things. I wouldn't be leaving in the morning, and my trip to America would have to wait.

Chapter 5
Patrick Returns

Patrick kept Brody and Ma up that night. I couldn't follow what he was saying and went to sleep not really knowing whether I should feel disappointed or happy.

The next day, Ma told me, "Patrick was numbs last night. He had been drinkin' too much because he is in trouble. We can't tell anyone, Allie, that he's here. All right? He is very active in the Young Ireland Movement and part of this movement has done some things the British consider illegal. I'm going to go see his father this afternoon and see what we should do."

Patrick and Brody were still asleep when Ma went off to work. She told me to let them sleep it off and she would be back as soon as she could. I grabbed a book and went to the knoll. I was extra hungry today but I was used to it. I knew any of the extra food we had packed was in the satchel Brody and I were going to take on our trip to Galway. No one had touched it even though I knew the next boat scheduled for America was not until October.

It was warm now, but October would be different. It would be cooler, then. I tried to forget about the journey, so I opened the book and began reading.

Today I grabbed Persuasion, by Jane Austen, and became lost in its tales of the seaside and ships and love.

It must have been mid-afternoon and I found myself eating grass spears as I read. There were still some dried berries left from Spring, but they were out of my reach. I looked up and Brody was sitting against the tree. I hadn't even heard him come up and sit down.

"How long have ya been here?" I asked.

"For a while, now."

"What's the matter?"

"I'm mad at Patrick for coming back and putting all of us in jeopardy. No, that's not right, I'm glad to see him. I don't know what I feel about the whole situation, right now."

I'd never seen Brody like this. He stood up and walked around.

"I know he didn't know we were leaving today," said Brody, "but he never seems to put much thought in his actions."

"But his life seems so exciting! He's traveled so many places, and he's fighting the British to make it better for us. You should be proud of him. You seem jealous, Brody, of his adventures and standing up for his beliefs. Is that what it is?"

"Jealous? Do you not understand what he is doing? It may seem fanciful and fun, but his being here puts us all at risk. I am the one that stays here and remains responsible. Taking care of you and making sure you get to America is what I get stuck with!"

That made me mad because I didn't need him to watch over me, and I really didn't think we spent that much time together. "Listen Brody, as soon as I am on that boat, ya can do whatever ya want!"

He stood up firmly and took off. I lied there a little longer, then stood up and headed back to the house.

The sun had moved to the other side of the sky and as I returned home, Ma was heading off to see Mr. Farraday. Patrick was up now and wanted to go see his father, but he knew he couldn't because he needed to stay hidden. We both sat there, but he couldn't sit still.

"Patrick, you're makin' me nervous. What's wrong?"

"Nothing, Allie. Tell me about everyone's plans to head to America."

"I am the only one going. Your Da, my ma, and Brody cooked up this scheme without even talkin' to me about it. Ma doesn't want me to stay here anymore. She's worried somethin' might happen to one of us, and she says my best chances are in America. What do ya think?"

"Think, I think Brody ought to be going, too. Your ma is right. You shouldn't stay here if you don't have to. The situation is not going to get any better for quite some time. In fact, it might get worse.

"Worse? How could it get any worse?" I asked.

"Someone else could die," he said. "That's why Brody needs to leave, too."

Just then, Brody came in and shouted, "I can't leave. Someone has to stay here and make sure Father is remembered. And Mother, what about her? Where were you Patrick when Mother died?"

"Brody, I'm trying to change things. For our Country"

His comments didn't seem to help Brody and he seemed mad at all of us. Patrick tried to calm him, but Brody was in a foul mood.

Mad at Patrick, mad at the situation, and mad at Ma for not waiting on him to go see his father. I told him he should have been there when she returned home, but that didn't help him either. He was in a mood.

Patrick changed the subject and started telling me about some of the places he had been and seen.

"Have ya ever been to Galway, like Brody?" I asked.

"I have, but it was too crowded and we didn't get a very good response from people about our cause."

"Brody said there were people everywhere, waitin' to get on boats."

"That did seem to be our problem. The people there were more interested in getting out of Ireland, than helping those that were staying here. We have been luckier in getting support in areas where people have been struggling the most."

Brody listened in and Patrick went on. "It's going to take a lot more people feeling the same way as us to bring about change."

"Why do ya feel violence is better than peaceful ways? Your da thinks more people will be respected if they make changes through peaceful demonstration."

"Peaceful demonstration? And what good has that done for your father or mine? Are any of us any better off with the way they went about it? Daniel O'Connell tried his peaceful ways and it did not help him. Ireland doesn't have time to wait. It is the British who are making this worse. They deserved to be shocked into our reality."

He was passionate, and he had the stories to go along with his passion. Later that evening some of his friends came over. I didn't know any of them, and while I don't think Brody did either, he stayed with them. It was too loud and gruff for me, but I had no place to go to get away. Ma wasn't home, yet, and it was too dark and foggy outside to go to the tree.

Tonight, the fog was a blessing. This way Patrick and his buddies could hide in the fog without worrying about being caught. When the fog was as thick as it was outside tonight, no one could get through. That meant Ma, too. She would probably be staying somewhere else tonight.

I always worried about Ma on nights like this. She was alone and after hearing about Brody's attack, I worried something like that could happen to her, too. Patrick took a moment from his friends to check on me. He must have realized that I was worried and came over to check on me.

"Your Mother will be fine, Allie. She's used to our weather and will know what to do. She'll be home tomorrow. We'll be here tonight. You're all right. Go to sleep." He covered me with his coat and said, "Would you feel better if we left? We could go over to our shack if you want us to so you can go to sleep?"

I knew Brody would hate that. They would be over there talking and having a good time, and he would only be reminded of his Mother.

"No" I said, "I'd rather you stay here. I don't really want to be alone."

I knew that soon enough I would be all alone, and listening to their banter, even if it was gruff and loud was better than none at all. At least for tonight.

The night went quickly and Patrick and his friends were still there when I woke up. Not as loud, but 3 of the seven of them were still deep in conversation, and on the same subject. Japers! They could go on and on. Had they been talking about this all night? Those Farraday's were talkers. I laughed to myself.

All Irish people seemed to be talkers. What was I thinking? Talking and story-telling should not surprise me at all. Ma told me a long time ago, "He who comes with a story to you brings two away from you." She was right. This night was a part of my memories. I have the stories they told, and mine about theirs.

I didn't see Ma that morning so I went over to the Brumley's to see if Ma had gone to work. It wasn't quite as foggy this morning, so

I was hoping she made it to their home. I didn't see her in the kitchen, and I waited quite a bit for her to come in and get something for the family.

I decided to go over and wait down on the road between the town and their home, hoping I would eventually see her on the road. I didn't and I was worried sick. I ran home later that day, furious with Patrick. Maybe Brody was right. He had brought bad luck to our home and now Ma might be in trouble. I ran up to him and beat on his chest and wailed out loud. I was so mad.

He let me finish my raving and beating on him, before he spoke. He grabbed my arms and tried to calm me down.

"Allie! You have every right to be upset with me. And if it makes you feel better, you can stay mad at me all day. Brody went to the workhouse to check on her and see if he could see our father."

I was calmer, now, but remained silent, not even looking at him. I finally couldn't take it anymore and stepped outside the door to wait outside. As I did, Brody came over the hill and headed our way.

"You mother is fine. She sent word to Mrs. Brumley and has been in town taking care of things. She stayed at the church last night to be safe. She'll be home later tonight." he said.

I was still mad at Patrick, even if what Brody said was true. Ma was all I had and if his selfishness had brought trouble upon her...grrr.

It seemed like forever, but Ma finally came home. It would be another late night of stories and planning. We all ate some of the scraps we had and settled in for whatever stories they had for Patrick.

Ma started her story by looking at Patrick, "I saw your father yesterday, and he has given me some suggestions for ya. Brody wasn't able to see him, but he helped me in town today."

She then looked at me and said, "I'm sorry I didn't get back last night, Allie, the fog was just too awful. It was good I stayed because I listened for any rumors about Patrick. And there were some so I waited to see if I could talk to certain people Mr. Farraday had suggested I talk with. One of the people we saw was Father Donovan."

"That's where I found your mother this morning," said Brody. "Father Donovan was acting guarded about helping us with Patrick's situation, but he told us he would be silent, and do what he could to help us."

"He can't help us directly because too many people count on him. If he is arrested, they would be without direction and guidance. He knows the faithful will try to continue helpin' those in need, but many need God and his teachings." Ma said.

Father Donovan told her the great Scotsman, William Wallace, said, 'In order to find his equal, an Irishman is forced to talk to God.'

"And thus, there are many that want to talk to God in these trying times and if Father Donovan was arrested for helpin' one man he would be hurtin' all those that needed him more."

"Blarney! We're not just barreling, we have a purpose and it will help all Irishmen. Doesn't he understand that?" Shouted Patrick.

"It is better to exist unknown to the law. It is too late for ya, Patrick, but there is no reason Father Donovan should get into trouble when he is needed by so many more. Your father wanted me to remind ya of, 'When fire is applied to a stone it cracks.'

"I know that," Patrick said, "but it is too late. We have already gone beyond the point of turning back. Don't you understand that? Does Father? You either need to help me, or I need to leave now and keep moving to stay away from the law. The law will eventually know to check this home, so we don't have much time."

Brody spoke up, "Father has given Kate some suggestions for your moving about and staying away from the law. And, he said you should leave as soon as possible so as not to bring the law on her, Allie and me. He's worried about this, Patrick. He loves you, but his choice to defy the law was peaceful and put both he and Mac in workhouses. If their peaceful actions have had negative results, just think what your actions might bring about"

"Yes, but I really feel what I am doing is the best for the country, maybe not the few, but for all."

"Can ya see that it is kind of like the way Father Donovan explains his situation." Ma said.

"Not with the same outcome, but similar none the less." Patrick thought out loud.

"Patrick, let me finish tellin' ya what your father told me. He thinks ya need to get out of the limelight for a while and see what happens to the other followers. Possibly get out of the country, maybe go to America, and try to figure out what else can be done to rectify the situation in Ireland. Ya won't be any help to anyone if you are arrested or killed. And," said Ma "he wants ya to take a portion of your personal items we saved and use it as payment for getting out of Ireland. Ya can take it with you to America and make sure Allie makes it safely."

Patrick paced the floor listening to Ma. He nodded at times, and shook his head at other times, making noises as if he wanted to talk, but Ma and Brody held the conversation trying to get Mr. Farraday's point across.

When they stopped, Patrick turned to Ma, and asked her, "What do you really think, Kate?"

"Your father has done so much for me; I don't feel right givin' my own opinion in this matter. Patrick, ya are his son, and understand his position."

Patrick knelt in front of her and took her hands, "Please, Kate. Please give me your opinion on the matter since it involves both our families now. I want your opinion."

Ma hesitated, looking down at her lap, then back up at Patrick, "I do like the thought of you goin' to America with Allie on one hand, but on the other it frightens me."

"What do you mean?"

"I don't want to prevent ya from goin', but I am worried since ya are a wanted man, if ya are caught, somethin' might happen to Allie. Where would she go if they thought she was mixed up with ya? Otherwise, I agree with your father. I know he is trying to do what is best for both families."

"Let me think about all of this." said Patrick, "All of you go ahead and go to sleep. I'll sleep on it, too, and make a decision in the morning. I promise whatever my decision is, I will not stay any longer than I have to so as not to endanger you, Brody or Allie."

We were all rather gloomy knowing whatever his decision it would be meant a separation again of Patrick from us. Da and Mr. Farraday were on our minds, and to lose Patrick again was not anything any of us wanted, so we all went to sleep.

We must have slept very soundly for when Brody woke up first thing in the morning, Patrick was gone. He was frantic and ran outside looking for him. I scooted over to Ma to lie next to her and she hugged me as we lied on the ground.

"Patrick's done the right thing," she told me. "This proves he is a man now, and if he does not come back, he has made a decision that is a very unselfish one. I believe he's thinkin' about us more than himself. He knew deep down what might happen to us if he stayed. It might not be easy for Brody right now, but it will be the best thing until things turn around."

I thought it would be best for Brody. She hadn't heard him and how upset he was when Patrick came back. He might miss his brother, but Brody was probably glad he left.

Ma had to go to work so she stood up and fixed herself and hurried off to the Brumleys. Brody didn't come home and I figured he might be at the knoll, so I wandered up there myself.

He was there, and rather than annoy him this morning, I stayed behind the knoll just like I used to do when his mother read to them. I said nothing, and Brody didn't act like he knew I was there. We both stayed there, quietly, and the day slipped by.

At sunset, I started to walk home and heard footsteps behind me. I knew it was Brody, but I dared not turn. I wanted to respect his sense of loss at the moment. We both walked home without saying a word.

Ma came home that night and told us a Sheriff had come to the Brumleys looking for Patrick. They were mortified thinking Ma must have hidden him somewhere in their house since they would have absolutely nothing to do with him. Ma was worried they might fire her or remove them from their property.

"If anyone comes to see us," she said, "Brody or ya have to tell them Brody is Quinlan so they do not think I am harborin' people from outside our family. Ya should have seen the way the Brumley's reacted when Patrick's name was mentioned. It scared me to death and I don't want Brody to be sent off or get into trouble."

"I hope they melt off the earth like snow off the ditch." Brody said spitting mad.

She smiled, "You mustn't be so mad. We will make it through all of this and we must now focus on plannin' your next journey to Galway. I will deal with the Brumleys and hope they forget about the visit from the Sheriff and move on to some other frivolous worries that occupy their days."

Ma went off on a story about the Brumleys which she had never done before.

"They never seem very concerned about the people they live around, and they are quite harsh in their speakin' of anyone not British. Once I overheard them speakin' poorly of famous Irishmen like Theobald Wolfe Tone who they said was an idiot because he was a Protestant who tried to bring Catholics and Protestants together and challenge British rule. They even mocked Oliver Plunkett who was hanged for his martyrdom for the Catholic faith.

"I want to tell them ever so badly that Arthur Wellesley, the First Duke of Wellington who had defeated Napoleon, was an Irishman. Oh, how I want to tell them where Wellesley had been born, but I know it will only bring more wrath on myself or all of us!"

She hated how they talked about the Irishman. And most of all, she hated how they talked about the Farradays. She didn't tell Brody this, but sometimes she would tell me how they would make fun of their collections and destroy things as if they were trash. It took everything she had to keep her tongue.

I don't think I could have done it. Ma was always patient. She told me there was a time and place for choosing your battles, and with our station in life, there weren't too many battles that could be won. She wanted to remain out of trouble as much as possible with the hopes Da would be home one day.

She told me, "If ya do not sow in the spring you will not reap in the autumn."

How appropriate, because it will be autumn by the time Brody and I were to leave, so Ma was right. We must stay out of trouble now so that we can prepare for our journey in the fall.

Chapter 6
Searching The Workhouses

We spent the rest of the summer trying to get by, and watching so many more die. Disease, starvation, and the idleness of so many people were dreadful. Even the smell of our land that was once comforting to me makes me ill. I can't explain it. The fog and dampness is more of a mildew smell than fresh, and the land is more of a rotten smell than of green grass.

But the worst is the human smell. It is now foul. We have gone months with no way to clean ourselves. Our streams flow with dirt and waste. We can only clean ourselves in it or drink from it when there is a strong rain that flushes much of the waste downstream. The times we walk to town, you not only see the piles of dead bodies; you smell the dead. It turns our stomachs.

There is something for us to think about besides all of that, I am still planning on going to America, and Brody has found an interest in a young girl in town. Her name is Mary Knapp. We all like her very much, but he is actually very shy and she does not know he likes her.

He hasn't told us, but Ma says she can tell because he makes a point of going by her house and showing up at places he knows she might be. He has even taken to going to church more, and Ma thinks it is because she might be there. Ma is glad because she thinks whatever his reason is, Father Donovan can help Brody and be a positive role model for him. Father Donovan uses Brody to help hand out food and soup on the days it is available.

I want to tease him about it, but Ma has threatened me. She warned me if I was to upset him and he chose not to help me get to Galway, I wouldn't be going. So, I had to think of other ways to taunt him without doing it directly and have Ma catch me.

I found the easiest way to torment him was to use her name. It was a very common name, so I could easily find people in history whose names were the same, and play on that.

There was The Mary Rose, Henry the VIII's ship that sunk, and of course, Mary Queen of Scots who was beheaded! There was Mary Shelley who wrote Frankenstein, and of course, there was Mother

Mary and the Virgin Mary. Yes! Maybe in America I could go to Maryland. Hah! This was fun! He caught on and could barely stand my mischievousness. It probably made it worse since it was his mother who had taught me about these things. I think he saw it as me tormenting him, and that was all right by me.

One of the easiest things for me to play with was her last name, Knapp. Since food and the cold were such big issues for us, both could be easily brought up. Oh, but all I had to do was rhyme with it. Oh, I was so tired I needed a nap! Or, have you seen my cap! Yes, this was more fun than Quinlan and I had when Brody's voice began to change.

However, after a few days, Brody wouldn't stay around me because he knew I was going to cod him about her. He was spending more time at the church, and I don't think she was coming anymore. Maybe I was a bit too unkind, especially if she didn't like him.

There was another benefit to helping Father Donovan. Brody was able to go with Father Donovan to the workhouses, and sometimes that meant he could see his father. He couldn't talk to him for very long when they were there, but he could see him, and his father was happy to see him and see Brody helping others. Brody said his father was quite skinny and it amazed him how quickly his hair had started to turn gray.

Ma told me it was sad to see Mr. Farraday in the Workhouse with so many sick people. She knew the longer anyone stayed there, the quicker their health might decline, but she reminded us both that he was able to get food and a place to sleep, and he was close enough for us to see.

One time Brody and Father Donovan traveled to one of the workhouses in the southeastern part of County Mayo. They were gone for weeks, and when Brody came back he had so many more stories to tell.

"You just wouldn't believe," he said, "how much worse this workhouse was than the one Father is in. And there were many children in this one who had been abandoned by their families. There were children and adults without legs or arms, and their being sick meant much more than starvation and disease. There were many with mental illness and strange diseases that worried Father Donovan much more.

"In fact, he wouldn't let me go to the Workhouse on the second day. I stayed at the local church and listened to some of the townspeople discuss their issues and problems. I overheard them discussing a workhouse in the southeastern part of the country that was worse than this one and they said they had moved many people from this one to it not knowing it was worse. They were talking about it because many of their friends and family members had been moved and they were quite worried. They knew this workhouse had been assigned as an overflow workhouse from other areas in Mayo and it was too crowded and needed to be thinned out. They discussed the issue of seeing their friends and family, and what was to become of them."

Brody took a different tone and leaned forward. "This made me wonder about Mac and I begged Father Donovan to ask around at this Workhouse to see if there was any word on Mr. McCreary."

He said, "Father Donovan asked some of the prisoners, but no one knew anyone by the name of McCreary around the age of 40. There were younger men and one about the age of 65, but no one Mac's age. One prisoner told him to ask the clerical office because they kept records of some of the people that came through. Father Donovan remembered they had begun recording the names of those who worked with him at his father's workhouse, and on the third day he went to the office and asked if he could look through some of their records."

I wasn't sure where he was going with this, and I glanced at Ma to see if she looked as puzzled as I felt. She didn't, so I looked back at Brody and listened some more.

"The member of the church that had begun the records was not there on this day, but one of the other parishioners showed Father Donovan where the books were. He told him they had not started recording names until this most recent move to Dungarvan because so many of their family and friends begged for a record of loved ones. A mistake, Father Donovan said, they were sure to regret. Starting a list now didn't help those already gone, but hopefully they could make a difference for others.

"This man spent more time talking than giving him the books he needed to look through, so he asked the gentleman if he could bring me back and have me help. Father Donovan told him he needed to get back to his work with the prisoners at the workhouse, and I would gladly look through them if it is all right. The man said 'yes' and Father Donovan left me to do some research.

"I was glad to look through the books and I was hoping to find something to bring back to tell you," Brody said. "The man was a talker and while he surely had a lot of stories to tell, I wanted to focus on the names and not be rude. I figured out a way to look up, nod, smile, and then look back down at the names."

Ma and I tittered as Brody showed us his method of acknowledging this man. He kept repeating his gestures, telling us he never had to say a word. This man just kept talking without any real need for a two way conversation. Ma began laughing, then more and more until she was crying from his gesturing. I loved that – Ma enjoying Brody and his gesturing.

He went on, "The first afternoon I had the books, I looked over them quickly trying to find the last name first. They were listed that way, last names first, so I thought it would be an easy find if it was on the list. They weren't listed alphabetically, but looking for McCreary would surely be easy.

"I made it through the books the first afternoon, and had not found Mac's name. I had seen another name of a man that was arrested on the same day as he was, so I was encouraged by the fact someone had been at this workhouse and was transferred to Dungarvan. There was a Mr. McGraw on the list and while I did not know for sure if it was Mac, the age was close.

"That night I told Father Donovan about the name, and Father Donovan asked me if I was sure I had gone through the names carefully enough. I told him I thought I had. He reminded me we only had one more day before going home and he thought I should try one more time. He thought Mr. Addington, the man who was doing the recordings, would be there tomorrow and maybe he could help me find Mr. McCreary, or other names from Knock.

"That next morning I started early and waited at the door of the clergy's office in the hopes of rechecking the books and speaking to Mr. Addington about the names. The man who talked all the time showed up first and opened the door for me. He must have slept well, for he still had no shortage of breath or lack of stories to tell and it took me a good bit of time to get enough courage up to interrupt him and ask about Mr. Addington. He said Mr. Addington should be in sometime, but I was welcome to get back into the books and check again.

"I did so, and tried to force myself to read each last name clearly, and go more slowly. After some time, Mr. Addington showed up. He was slightly perturbed with me. Not necessarily for looking through the books, but for being impatient and somewhat demanding. I realized I might have come off as being rude, but I was worried about losing my chances at getting any information about our Mac.

"If he was there, Mr. Addington told me, he did not remember writing down such a name, but there was one more person that had done some of the writing and maybe they had written down the McCreary name. He told me to check any name that was close to McCreary: Creary, Creery, and McCrea, or even the reverse of the name. Sometimes the names transposed and McCreary might be listed as their first name. I hadn't even thought of that and was renewed with energy at the thought I now had a new angle to look up your name.

"I started over with the books, and this time the room was quiet because Mr. Addington had given the talking man a project which took him out of the office.

"Mr. Addington himself was not much of a talker, so the two of us sat there, doing our own business. He was doing some research and I didn't know what it was, but that was fine with me because I didn't want to lose any time in reading through the names, again."

Ma and I sat there listening intently, waiting to hear the words we needed to hear. First, we needed to know if Da was alive, and then, where was he?

"Finally," Brody said, "I came across the name of McCreary, a Johnathan, and listed as 48 years old from Claremorris which as you know is right by us."

"That couldn't be him," Ma said.

"Wait!" said Brody, "I read on beyond the one name. I first thought of quitting, thinking this was him, but Mr. Addington, told me to go on in case there was more than one. I turned back to the books and kept going. I knew I needed to cover all the names before Father Donovan returned, and I was glad I did."

Ma and I sat up and looked at one another. Had Brody found Da? "Did ya find him?" We asked.

Brody pressed on with his story without giving up any clues, but we couldn't stand it any longer.

Finally, Brody said, "He was listed, backwards, as McCreary John, 42 years of age, from Knock."

We were so excited. That meant he had found him. "What else did ya find out, Brody?" Ma said, "Are ya sure? Where is he? Did ya talk to anyone that knew him?"

"As soon as I finished going through the names, and knew I had found Mac, I thanked Mr. Addington and ran over to the workhouse to tell Father Donovan and ask him what we should do next. Father Donovan was pleased, too, and decided the best thing we could do was ask the head of the workhouse, Mr. Dowell, how we could get more information on Mr. McCreary.

We found Mr. Dowell and Father Donovan questioned him on Mac and the names listed as being sent to another workhouse. Mr. Dowell said while he was not in charge of the names written, he did know that this group of people were sent to the workhouse in Dungarvan. Mr. Dowell said those that had been sent to Dungarvan were well enough to be transported, so that meant Mr. McCreary was well enough to be able to make the transfer, and he must be all right."

Ma and I were elated. Da was all right.

"I asked Father Donovan if we could make the trip to Dungarvan, but Father Donovan told me it was too far and out of his jurisdiction. We needed to get back to his regular parishioners and that I should be grateful I at least knew where Mr. McCreary was, now."

Ma and I knew he was right. We were glad to know where Da was and that he was still alive. Ma said she would try and make the journey sometime in the future, and we could write to him right away and let him know they knew where he was.

Ma asked Brody to help her write the letter, and I told her I wanted to since I could write, now. It might not be as good as Brody's writing, but it would be from me and would mean more to Da. Ma agreed and we talked about everything we should tell him.

Brody was tired but said it had been a rewarding trip since he saw other names on the list, and he and Father Donovan could tell those families about their loved ones. He enjoyed being with Father Donovan and helping around the parish.

I don't know if he meant whether it was because of Mary Knapp, or not. He didn't ask about her when he returned home, or even hint. Maybe he was too embarrassed to inquire. Ma did talk about her family and Brody listened, but he fell asleep before she finished all of it, and Ma covered him and kissed his forehead. I think she actually loved Brody and was glad to think of him as part of our family.

It was a good thing Ma and Brody were so attached because the next few weeks were confusing for everyone. The local magistrate was trying to get rid of vagrants and trouble makers and was weeding out as many people as possible.

Ma reminded us we were to tell any strangers who asked that Brody was Quinlan so he would not be taken away. Brody reminded us, too, he saw many children and young people at the workhouses and lawmakers had no recourse but to put many of the destitute and abandoned children in workhouses.

The local sheriffs were caught in the middle. They knew many of us had no way out and were hanging on by a thread, trying to make ends meet any way they could. Moving them or separating families were putting the families in a worse condition.

However, as the law of the land, they had to follow through with what they were being told to do, or else it might be their own family taken away.

Ma couldn't be at the house at all times, so every day she went to work reminded of the current situation. She knew the Brumleys had no love for her, and while they liked her working at the house, any excuse to get Ma and us off their land would be fine with them.

The sheriff did come by with some thugs to check on our home. The Sheriff knew us, but the two thugs didn't and when we told them Brody was Quinlan, the Sheriff looked at us as if he might say something.

We did our best to act as brother and sister, but the thugs asked why we didn't look alike. Brody told them he looked more like the father, and I looked more like my ma, but we were definitely their children. It was clever, Brody didn't actually say it so it was my ma and da directly, and he played on the words.

Very clever, I told him later. He did look more like his own father, and I like my own ma. Hah! I wish I could think that cleverly on my feet. I think the Sheriff caught on, and knew of our situation so he let it go. Lucky. Because they had about eight people tied together outside waiting to be carted off to who knows where. It was a close call, and Brody had pulled it off.

Ma came home late that night, and had already heard about the incident. She said the Brumleys talked about it is though she was coming home to no one. Had they set her up? She wasn't sure anymore and knew our situation was getting more grim as the months went by.

She knew two of the people tied up together and felt awful she could not help them. I would have to go to America so Ma would know I would be all right. There might not be so understanding a sheriff the next time they stopped by, and we couldn't wait for them to come and take one of us.

The more people there were, the harder it was to feed us and get by day to day. I would have to be ready for an October sailing date, and this time nothing could stop us, Ma said.

Brody pulled out the information he had brought from Mr. Leeds and we went back over the instructions and information. It was so much information. I hoped Ma and Brody understood it all and inside I was grateful I was not going to Galway alone. I understood the basic picture: pack food for the trip, walk a long way, carry as little as possible, don't talk to strangers, follow directions on the ship, go through the proper procedure in America, find Uncle Brennan, live with him, wait for Ma and Da to travel to America.

What you don't know, you don't know until you live it and I would not completely understand any of this until I had lived through this new adventure. And even then, would I ever understand all of it? My brain was full, and I was tired. I went to sleep as Brody and Ma discussed the trip, again.

In the next couple of days, we heard the eastern ports were charging more for people trying to immigrate to America. It was cheaper going to Canada, or Australia. Even for England the prices had gone up. Seems the British did not want any more Irishmen to immigrate to England. We were worried the price might have gone up in Galway, so Mr. Farraday had Ma plan on Brody taking more items to sell in case we had to pay more for me.

It just didn't seem right. I was using a lot of their personal money and items for my being able to travel to America. Brennan hadn't sent enough for the cost of traveling, and Mr. Farraday was gracious enough to give up what he had. Ma told me she wasn't going to allow him to give all of it to us because she worried he might need something for himself or Brody in the future. She wanted me to get to

America safely, but knew what a sacrifice it was for him to give her so much.

We went through some of their items, and Brody found it most difficult going through some of his mother's personal items. Ma decided she wouldn't take any of Mrs. Farraday's personal things. She understood Brody's feelings and wanted him to be able to keep what he could, especially of her things.

There were other things we could take like silver pieces, pewter items, gold trinkets, and some of Mr. Farraday's items. We hadn't hidden many larger items, so the items we had were small enough to carry. They would have to, because we couldn't look like we were carrying much, and traveling far and carrying too many items would be difficult anyway. Brody needn't remind Ma about his being attacked for she knew we were going to have to be extra careful with what we had. She was worried most about that, and I could tell.

We organized the items so Brody carried the most. I was to carry a small handkerchief sized wrap, mostly of food. Brody carried the important items. I didn't bring a change of clothes, because I really didn't have any. Ma was going to give me some of hers, but they were too big and I thought having more only meant I had to carry more. I would rather carry more food since it would be a long trip to Galway, and who knows how long the boat trip would take.

Brody said Mr. Leeds said it could take anywhere from one to three months to get to America, and that most of the boats fed the people on their trip, so I should only have to carry enough for us to get to Galway. I had no idea what I was up against, but I thought I was ready. Well, ready or not, my time was near.

Chapter 7
The Allure of Miss Abernathy

I wasn't sure this day would ever come. I remembered the day I thought I was leaving, before, and Patrick showed up and changed everything. Would it happen again? I was filled with anticipation.

Ma let Brody and I travel to Claremorris to see Mr. Farraday. He was excited about my leaving and I thought it so strange. Here he was locked away in this awful place, and he was excited for me. He was supportive and thrilled about my trip and he never once made me feel guilty about his situation. I was glad we went and I saw him before we left. Brody was lucky to have him for a father, and I was lucky that he considered us friends.

Saying goodbye to him and making the trip made me face the reality of my situation. I couldn't sleep the night before, and I lied there staring at Ma. I wanted to remember everything about her. Her hair was disheveled most of the time, now, and her skin weathered and worn, but that's not what I saw. I saw a loving and giving woman who had gone through so much and didn't ask much for herself.

She was beautiful to me and I hoped I would grow up and look like her. She worked for people who didn't treat her well, and she deserved much better. I wanted her to go with me, but I knew she would never agree. I begged myself to please remember her; her smile, her laugh, her everything. Surely I wouldn't forget any of those things. The only thing I had of hers that was going with me was her handkerchief. This would have to do until I saw her again.

Ma was strong this morning. I knew she was worried, but she seemed at peace at the thought of my being able to live a better life. She said she would never say goodbye, because she would see me again someday.

She blessed me, "May God hold ya in the palm of his hand."

Brody hugged her as they went over some of the final instructions.

All of a sudden I panicked. No! No! I thought to myself...I can't leave! This is all I know!

Brody sensed my panic and turned from Ma, reaching for my arm.

I ran to Ma and hugged her. Holding on tightly! I felt a sense of doom and my heart was racing! I could hear it pounding

Ma took my face in her hands, "I love ya, Allie. This is an adventure of a lifetime and ya will be able to show me the wonderful land called America when Da and I come over ourselves. Won't that be exciting? We will have so much fun and be able to have such a wonderful life together! You go on with Brody. May your blessin's outnumber the shamrocks that grow, and may trouble avoid ya wherever ya go."

She gently turned me from her and nudged me forward. I obeyed her and turned to Brody and followed him out the door.

I felt a stubbornness rise up in me. I didn't know why, I should have cried, but I couldn't help myself. Something was wrong. It just didn't feel right, but I knew I had to go.

Everything was planned and set in motion, and Ma was counting on me to follow through. I couldn't let her down, but I could be sad without her seeing. So, as we walked away, I was defiant to cover my sadness. It made no sense, I thought. Brody didn't bother me, he walked ahead of me making sure I was following, but not saying anything.

We walked the entire day without saying a word. When we finally stopped, Brody found a spot between five trees.

"This will give us some cover and give us a place to hide."

I lied against a tree and I tried to hold off from crying, again. Brody left me alone, but sat up to watch and make sure we were safe.

"We'll have to take shifts and watch out for one another so no one can sneak up on us and steal from us." He said.

I nodded, and tried to stop sniffling. I finally fell asleep, and Brody let me sleep the entire night. He didn't wake me up for my shift. I had stopped whimpering, slept and was now determined to be better about the trip and try to be strong.

The next day started off as another quiet day, and Brody began talking about the people whose house we might be able to stay in tonight.

"They are so nice. I think you will enjoy their company. Make sure you let them know how much I've talked about them, and how they gave me food and I had a good night's rest. I want them to know how appreciative I was of their graciousness."

Towards the end of the day, he said he was tired, and was looking forward to sleeping at their house and seeing them again.

We followed the exact same path as he had taken before, but he said it looked slightly different. When we arrived at the spot where they should have been, it was no longer there. There was a dirt bed with broken boards and straw littered around. He was disappointed, and sat against the mud wall that had once been the side of their house.

He was exhausted and asked me if I would let him sleep awhile and then he would wake up and let me sleep. I agreed and sat next to him watching over our stuff.

Late in the night, a man came by and startled me. I must have slipped off to sleep because I didn't hear him come up. I jumped up and jumped away from the man. He grabbed Brody on his shoulder and shook him awake.

"What are you doin'?" the man asked

Brody looked at him, then me. He was stunned, wondering what I had been doing and how someone else could venture so close to him. I must have looked shocked myself because I did not know what was happening. All of our items were sitting there by themselves, and Brody glanced down at them realizing the situation.

"Aah, whatcha got there?" he said, "Did you steal this from someone else? Let me see whatcha have. Hand it over!" The man looked at our items, and bent down towards them.

Brody grabbed a board from the dismantled shack we were next to and whacked him on the head. The board broke in two. The man stumbled, yelling something at Brody, and then fell over. Brody then grabbed another board and hit the man in the head as he was trying to get up.

He must have knocked him out because the man stayed down this time. Brody grabbed all of our items, grabbed me, and drug me away from the scene. I was still in shock and looking back at the man.

Brody yelled at me to come on, continually pulling me. I finally snapped out of it and began running with him.

We ran as far as we could. It was pitch black outside and the fog had set in.

"Try and stay quiet" he barked at me.

He was furious with me, I could tell. He must have figured out I had not stayed awake and I had put us at risk. All of our items could have been stolen, and who knows what could have happened to us.

Brody found another grouping of trees to hide within, and we both sat against the same tree, wide awake. I was scared to death and the whole situation had disturbed me so much I was shaking.

We stayed up the entire night and at dawn were both in the same position. Brody had calmed down enough now to talk to me, but he gave me a talking to. I just sat there with my head down.

He was right, and I knew I had done wrong. I had scared myself enough for both of us, and had learned my lesson. I hoped to never be in that situation again. When Brody finished his lecturing, he grabbed his bag again, told me to get mine, and said it was time to keep walking. It was a foggy, cool day and Fall was definitely in the air.

It took us two more days to get to Galway. Brody gave me the same advice Miss Abernathy had given him about walking through the crowds, but I was awestruck at the sheer numbers of people everywhere.

They *were* everywhere and even though Brody had told Ma and me about it, I just couldn't believe it. Everywhere! There were people who looked worse off than us, and then there were those that looked as though they were the Brumleys and didn't have a care in the world.

Brody ended up pulling me along, again, repeatedly reminding me to look down and move along. I tried my best, but was dumbfounded. We finally made it to Mr. Leeds's, and the woman Brody had told us about, Betsy, answered the door.

"Brody!" she yelled and reached for him to hug him.

"Hello, Betsy, it's good to see you again!" He said looking back and down at me as I stared at his being hugged. "Betsy, this is Allie McCreary."

She turned to me and hugged me, too, even though she didn't know me.

"Brody, we've been so worried about ya. Especially since we hadn't heard a word, and we were expectin' ya both in June." She went on to tell us, "Mr. Leeds is goin' to be gone until tomorrow, but ya are both welcome to stay here tonight. He will be glad to see ya both, tomorrow."

She led us in and took us to separate rooms on the second floor.

We put our few things down and she said, "After that trip, I'm sure ya would like to take a bath before dinner. I'll draw one for ya."

I stood there with my mouth gaping open. Brody noticed me and whacked me on my arm. His eyes were looking at me piercingly and his eyebrows were scrunched down.

"I'm not taking a bath with ya!" I whispered at him.

He flicked me on the head and explained to me what she meant.

"We have separate rooms with separate baths. And, we even have our own hearths."

Why was I going to America? I wanted to stay right here. This was better than America could be, surely!

I stared at the bath for the longest time before finally sitting next to it, on the floor, and running my fingers through it. Feeling it's warmth and watching the little waves I made in it.

I had never had a bath before – never! This was beyond remarkable. I knew what I was supposed to do, but if I stepped in this tub, I would get the water dirty and it was such a beautiful vision as it is right now. Why would I want to make it filthy?

I must have stayed in the bath for an hour, because Brody knocked on my door and said, "Come on, Allie, dinner is ready."

"Dinner? Food? I'll be right down!" This was heaven and it would take a lot for me to leave this place. It would take a lot just to get me away from the bath. It had a wonderful smell, and it was warm. Well, it used to be warm. I quickly washed off just as I had with a bucket at home. I leaned my head over the side to wash my hair.

I suppose I should have stepped into the tub, for by the time I was finished washing the way I was used to, the water was as dirty as any I remember it being back home. The fragrant smell was gone, it was murky, and the towels that were left for me were no longer one color.

Hurry, Allie, hurry, was all I could think about. What was better, the aroma of the water beforehand or the food for dinner? Dinner! I jumped back into my dirty clothes and headed down.

It was just Brody and me at dinner, and it was wonderful. It was almost like a dream. There were candles, and a fire, and food. Food like I had only seen through windows.

"Allie, can't you act like a lady? Quit behaving like a heathen!"

"I don't know what ya mean. It is just the two of us, who cares?"

He rolled his eyes and told me to do what he did. He showed me the differences in the forks and the spoons. He showed me how to butter my bread by the bite, how to cut my meat, and how to hold my fork. The right way that is.

I was kind of liking it. I felt special. I felt like a princess. My clothes and hair were still ratty and ragged, but I was clean and this place was sheer delight. Oh, if only Ma could be a part of this. And Moira, too. She would have loved this.

After dinner, Brody showed me Mr. Leeds's library. It was amazing! There were books from the floor to the ceiling, and he was right. Books did have an aroma of their own! I took one book out of its place on the shelf, opened it and smelled the pages, then closed it and smelled the leather that bound it. Brody chuckled at me for smelling them.

"What are you doing?" he asked.

"I'm smellin' the books. I don't care what ya think. I want to remember this moment. The fire crackling in the hearth, the books surroundin' me, the big, comfy chairs, and the loveseat. This is like a story from one of Jane Austen's books." I told him.

He smiled. His mother loved Jane Austen.

As I was looking through the books, there was a knock on the door. Betsy answered it and brought in a young lady. Brody's whole demeanor changed. He was thrilled. It was Miss Abernathy. This was the young lady he had talked about. What he hadn't told Ma and me was that she was his age. Hmmm?!

Lost in asking each other questions, Brody didn't even take a breath to introduce me. I ignored them both and found a book to sit down with and read through. When I accidentally sneezed, Brody remembered I was there, and introduced me to her.

I could tell she liked Brody because she seemed so interested in every word coming out of his mouth, except when he introduced me. She didn't give me much attention, and took his hand and directed him back to her to focus on her again.

I fell asleep reading in the chair, and it was late when Brody woke me up and told me to go to bed. Miss Abernathy had gone when he woke me up and I had no idea what time it was. It was late and Betsy was nowhere to be found. The fire was down to its last embers and wasn't giving off much heat anymore.

Brody and I went upstairs and he turned down the lanterns as we went upstairs. "Brody, may I sleep in your room?" I asked.

"You have your own room, Allie, don't be ridiculous!"

"But I've never slept alone."

"You will be fine. Betsy lit the fire in your room, so it is warm and ready for you."

"Please?" I asked one more time.

"No! You should be thrilled to have your own room and bed to sleep in. Now go to bed."

We had spent months in the same house, sleeping next to one another, and right now it seemed so strange to be sleeping in separate rooms. I obeyed him and went into the bedroom. On the bed was a sleeping gown, with lace up by the collar and at the end of the sleeves. It was so soft, and fell all the way to the floor.

I put on the gown, and then stared at the bed. Almost like the bath, I had never slept on such a bed. It was high up off of the floor and had so much stuff on top of it. Why would anyone need so much to sleep on?

I slipped in between the sheets and under the down comforter. I remember Brody telling Ma and me about this, too, but no one could imagine the feeling unless you had slept in a bed like this before. Japers, it was like being on a cloud. It was fanciful.

Brody was also right on his explaining the feeling of guilt you have knowing your loved ones are not sleeping or living like this. Ma was at home, sleeping on the hard ground, and had probably gone all day without much to eat. She worked for people who lived like this, but had never slept on a bed like this in her life, either. I wish she were right here with me, sleeping next to me. I would sleep so much better if she were here.

It is hard to believe, but I couldn't really sleep. Oh, the bed was the most fanciful thing I had ever been on, and the fire was warm and soothing, but I just couldn't sleep. I rolled out of bed and slipped into Brody's room. He was asleep and sleeping soundly enough that he didn't hear me come in. I couldn't even see him because of all of the covers surrounding him and the height and softness of the bed, but I knew he was there. I could hear his breathing and I knew the sounds he made while he slept.

I brought my comforter into the room and lay on the floor in front of the fireplace. I was more accustomed to the floor, and being by Brody was more comforting than being in the other room. I knew it didn't make any sense, but now I could sleep.

I dreamt my whole family was back together. Ma and Da, Moira and Quinlan and we were having dinner and laughing and telling stories. We were telling stories all at once. The three of us were trying our best to get our stories out for Ma and Da, and they were enjoying the ri-ra of it all. We were having colcannon which was cabbage, kale and butter, and Ma was going back and forth from the pot that sat over the fire. She was smiling and enjoying the family being together. Da eventually quieted us down so we could eat without choking, he said. We could all tell our stories, but one at a time, so we sat down and said a blessing so as to begin our eating.

Ma looked happy and young, without a wrinkle on her face. Da looked strong and loving. We were all clothed. In clothes not wrinkled or torn, and they fit. Moira had on a dress like Ma. She looked pretty in her dress and had on a pair of Ma's old shoes like boots, and she was excited about wearing them.

Her story was about coming home from town and a young boy she liked, Curran Adair. He stopped to talk to her and walked with her on her way to deliver some yarn she had for a seamstress in town. He walked her back to the road that led home. She was so excited. She talked about the way he looked in his knickers and shirt and vest. His red hair was pulled back, but many of his curls were loose around his face. He had a square face with a strong jaw. She said he had grown over the summer and he was almost a foot taller than she, or so she thought. She was beaming, but I thought she was being silly.

My story was about Brody and Patrick and watching them ride their horses. I was hiding up in a tree by their property and could watch them easily. They rode two beautiful horses, one gray and one a deep, deep brown. Both of the horses looked huge, bigger than the boys, but the boys rode well and could handle their horses. They would canter and jump over brush and logs laid out like a course.

They seemed to compete with one another even though there was no judge or teacher for them to compete for. They both wore short, beige knickers and tall, black boots made of shiny leather. They had on navy jackets that hung down below their waist and split in the back to lie by the back side of the saddle. Their white shirts had ruffles down the front and went all of the way up to their necks. Even the times I couldn't see where they were, I could hear the beating of the horse's hoofs on the ground.

It looked like so much fun and I so wanted to learn how to ride. Ma reminded me the Farradays were gentry and one day I could learn to ride, but it would be for a different purpose. I looked down at my cabbage to take a bite, but it was so hot I burnt my tongue.

Burning my tongue woke me up. I don't think Brody was up yet because I could still hear him with his usual sleeping noises. I was still comfortable and safe on the floor and decided I should probably sneak out and go back to my bedroom before anyone caught me in Brody's room, so I crept out and slipped into the bed in my room. I slipped down under the covers and the sheets and this time I fell asleep.

Betsy came in to wake me up. She had cleaned my clothes and ironed them so even though they were still old and ragged, they were clean.

She brought me a brush and asked, "Could I brush your hair?"

"Of course, but it's tangled."

I slipped out of the bed and sat on the vanity chair placed in front of the vanity mirror. I hadn't really seen myself in over a year, so I looked different. I looked tired and ratty. I looked like the waif everyone talked about when talking about the Irish in general, but I didn't feel that way. Funny how you look different than you feel about yourself. I wonder if other people felt the same way.

Betsy talked while she brushed my hair, "Brody left after he had breakfast this mornin'."

"Really?" I asked, "Where did he go?"

"He went to meet Miss Abernathy at the Library. I think they like one another. Isn't that fun?"

How dare he? I wanted to see the Library he had talked about and while I could care less about seeing Miss Abernathy, the Library would have been a treat. I would have to get on him later and ask him to take me with him next time.

Betsy kept talking and telling me what was downstairs for breakfast and when Mr. Leeds was to be returning. She had a very strong accent that made her more endearing to me.

"He should be home by mid-mornin', so ya have about an hour and a half."

"Do I need to do anythin' before he gets home?" I asked.

She didn't acknowledge that and went on, "I have a little boy 'bout three years younger than ya. I've always wanted a little girl so brushing your hair is such a delight."

As I looked in the mirror, I couldn't see brushing my hair as a delight. It was a ratty mess, but she was quite gentle with me and brushed through the tangles and knots and pulled it back and braided it. She even put a ribbon on the end. When she was done, she told me to get dressed and come downstairs for breakfast. She would make sure I had as much jam as I liked.

I hurriedly put on my clothes, spending a few moments looking at myself in the mirror. I really did look wretched. I felt clean, but my clothes were so shabby and this was all I had for my trip to America. I was going to have to act better than I was to make sure people did not think I was so destitute.

Well, I was destitute, but I didn't want to be treated that way. I wanted to be like the Farraday's were, or like Mr. Leeds, and I haven't even met him, yet.

Betsy was waiting on me downstairs and sat with me while I ate. She noticed my improper way of eating and sitting, because she ever so kindly pushed my chair in to the table, help me sit up straight, showed me the proper utensils, and how to eat over my plate. Just like Brody had tried to do.

"It's a good thing I pulled your hair back so it isn't falling off your plate and into your food." She said.

We both chuckled. I liked Betsy. She knew I wasn't the same as Brody or Mr. Leeds, and she took the time to tell me about Mr. Leeds and her working for him.

"Mr. Leeds is an Englishman, but moved to Galway almost thirty years ago. He sells items to and from Ireland and chose Galway since it was a seaport. He has never been married, but has always loved children and is most kind to everyone he deems respectable. That doesn't mean only those with money, because he is kind to those who respect others, whatever their station in life.

"He ran in to me, literally, on the way home from work one day and I dropped the eggs I was carryin'. The eggs broke and I was distraught knowin' I didn't have any more money to buy more eggs. I wasn't upset with him, and I told him it was all right. I was rushin', too, and accidents do happen.

"He must have liked me, because he offered me a position in his home. At first I only did menial tasks for him in the home like coal shuttlin' and runnin' errands. He had a staff of four, then, and I rounded out the fifth person. I think he only hired me because he felt sorry for me, but now it is only me. He had to let everyone go because of how difficult things are right now, and I am honored and grateful that he kept me as his housekeeper. My husband has no job. With our little one, we need the money he gives me and the extra food he allows me to take home. My husband takes care of our son."

"It sounds like my family with the Farradays. Well, they lost everything."

"I couldn't imagine somethin' like that happenin' to Mr. Leeds."

"I couldn't believe it happened to the Farradays either," I said, "but it did."

It was nice talking to Betsy and listening to her story, but she told me she had duties to do and I could wait in the study or go back to my room. I wanted to go back in the study and look at the books again.

I helped Betsy take the food back to the kitchen. As I looked around, it reminded me of the Brumleys and I thought of Ma. What was she doing? She would be at the Brumleys right now. Was she in the kitchen, too? I helped Betsy rinse the dishes and wiped my hands on my clothes to go into the study.

Betsy handed me a hand towel and told me, "Don't wipe your 'ands on your clothes, they are clean. Ya should use a 'and towel to dry them."

I shrugged my shoulders, wiped my hands, and headed into the study. Once again I was amazed at all of the books. Betsy had made a fire in the hearth and the curtains were open and it was a beautiful day.

The sun was so bright it warmed the room, but the fire helped take the chill off the openness of the room. The wood surrounding the walls was dark which made it a peaceful place. Perfect, I thought, for reading. One day I would want a place just like this to be able to read in, in private. However, I thought back on the knoll and the Mulberry tree that shaded it. I had always thought that was such a perfect place. This was different and would be a new memory for me.

Chapter 8
The Fire Room

I didn't have a chance to pick a book when Mr. Leeds walked in. I was startled at his size and demeanor. He was a large man with quite a big belly. He had a beard and was wearing a tall hat that made him look even larger. He yelled for Betsy without saying a word to me. He stepped out of the room for a second to talk to Betsy in the hallway. I know it must have been about me, for when he turned back towards the open door, he stepped in and held out his arms.

"Where's Brody?"

I stood there, motionless, while he boomed more questions at me and walked towards me. I stepped back not knowing what was to happen next. I stumbled on the carpet and fell back into a chair. He laughed loudly and stopped, realizing, I guess, that I was startled at his openness.

Betsy came in and shuttled up to me holding my shoulders and introducing me to him. She must have felt my discomfort, also, and didn't want me to come across badly.

Betsy told Mr. Leeds, "Brody is visitin' Miss Finola Abernathy at the Library."

"Oh," he smiled and took off his hat and coat and sat down across from me.

Looking at me, he said, "Finola is a nice young lady and I am glad Brody found a friend. Maybe having her as a friend will cause him to come back and visit more often."

Mr. Leeds spoke fondly of Brody so I eased up on my stiffness a bit and was more at ease at his lack of shyness towards me.

He went on to ask me, "How was your trip? And, how is Thorn Farraday?"

I remembered now that Brody had said his first night at Mr. Leeds's was spent with his head swirling at all of the questions Mr. Leeds asked of him. I understood now and was hoping Brody would walk in at any minute.

"Betsy, will you bring us some tea?"

I must be dreaming. I was having tea, in a study with a room full of books, a fire burning lively, and the thought of all the awful things happening in my real world, world's away. She brought in little cakes with the tea.

"Would you like some sugar for your tea, Allie?" Betsy asked. I shook my head vigorously up and down, as if to say yes!

My reaction made Mr. Leeds laugh again. "Don't you think we should go shopping to buy some new clothes for our young lady here?"

Betsy smiled and shook her head up and down, the same way I had just done.

"I've never bought clothes for a young lady," Mr. Leeds said. "We should all go and buy something nice for her travels."

"That would be wonderful!" Betsy jumped at the suggestion.

It is such a generous offer, I thought to myself, but the only thing that came out of my mouth was, "but Brody is not back and shouldn't we wait for him?" I really didn't want to go without Brody and while I felt comfortable with Betsy, I wasn't sure how to act around Mr. Leeds.

"We'll leave a note for Brody, but we should go before it gets too late. I'll buy Brody something at a later time. Anyway," he said, "young men are much easier to buy for. I was a young man, once myself."

I giggled at the thought of him being a boy, or from nervousness, but either way my giggling made both Betsy and he smile.

He grabbed his hat and coat, "Let's go everyone! Betsy get your hat and coat, and Allie you get yours."

"I don't have anything else but the night clothes Betsy gave me." I said.

"All right then, you can't wear those, so we better get you something else! We do have some shopping to do."

Out the door the three of us went. Betsy held my hand and we walked about two steps behind Mr. Leeds. We all walked at a brisk pace, and I noticed that Betsy kept her head down just like Brody told me to do.

Mr. Leeds didn't keep his head down. He stood up tall and straight, looking forward at all times. That's what I wanted to do, but Betsy took my chin in her hand and turned my head down. We looked towards Mr. Leeds's feet, and followed closely.

We came to some kind of store that had clothes for all ages, and for both men and women. They knew Mr. Leeds in the store and even called him by name. They also knew Betsy, but spoke first to Mr. Leeds. They jumped at any word he said. Not from fear, but quickly like jack rabbits, like he had something they all wanted - quickly!

Betsy let go of my hand and I wandered aimlessly through the store looking at everything they had. This must have been the best store in the world. There were clothes everywhere. Some were hanging, some were folded, and some were on hooks. And, there was every type of item you might need to dress yourself head to toe; knickers, shirts, coats, stockings, socks, shoes, and even pants. I might have been embarrassed had I not been so dumbfounded by it all.

One woman came up to me and took me by the hand. She had not seen me come in with Mr. Leeds and she must have thought I didn't look like I should be there. She was right. I didn't look like I should be there, and she started to walk me to the door. She had a good grip on my arm and had it twisted up at a sharp angle.

In a second I heard Mr. Leeds bellow out, "What do you think you are doing?"

She stopped abruptly and turned around looking ever so taken aback. Before she could answer Betsy scurried over to get me and bring me back to Mr. Leeds and the ladies attending him.

"Start bringing her clothes." He said, and motioned for Betsy to take me somewhere.

She took my arm and pulled back a curtain and said, "Go in 'ere and the ladies will bring ya clothes to try on."

I stared at her with a blank look because I had no idea what she meant. I was always just given clothes that Moira had, and put on what I was given.

Betsy told me, "Here's what ya do, as they bring you things, ya put them on and step out so Mr. Leeds can see them on ya."

I stood there blankly, still, but she pulled the curtain closed and I stood there staring at the back of the curtain. Within second the ladies brought me undergarments, stockings, skirts, shirts, dresses, and more. I had no idea what to do with all of this and continued standing there staring at it.

One of the ladies noticed I had not moved. She looked under the curtain and saw my feet not moving a step. She came in to help me dress. I was mortified. No one but Ma had ever seen me without my clothes, and I didn't know this woman and she was undressing me as if I was on fire, and getting naked was going to put the fire out. She changed me so quickly I didn't have a chance to object. As soon as she was done, she threw the curtain open and pulled me out into the open room.

I wasn't naked, but I felt that way. Mr. Leeds, Betsy and three of the helpers were staring at me.

Mr. Leeds said, "Now turn around, walk up, walk back."

It was all happening so quickly, the only thing I could think of was how mad I was going to be at Brody for leaving me in this situation. They didn't like this outfit, so the lady took me back into the room and did the fire drill again. It must have been a race, or they were about to close, because she had me in and out in such a short time period. Everyone seemed to like this outfit much better. Yes, Mr. Leeds said we would take this one.

I thought to myself, "thank heavens, we're done!" Then before I knew it, he said, "Next!" And there we went again, back into what they called the dressing room, but I called it the "fire room" in my head.

By the third outfit, I caught on to the process and told the lady I could do it myself, now. Anyway, it was just a dress, how hard could it be? I slipped into the dress, pulled on the stockings and stepped outside the curtains. Mr. Leeds was very enthusiastic about this dress and said I must have some shoes to go with it.

"What do you think about this one, Allie?"

"I hadn't looked at myself, yet, on any of them."

He laughed and motioned for me to go to the mirror. I stepped in front of the mirror, and stopped. This was fine-looking, and I looked so much better than before. I now understood what Brody meant by thinking he looked handsome. The clothes can make such a difference, and with my hair clean, brushed, and braided I almost looked like the pictures I had seen of Ma as a young girl.

"Mr. Leeds, this is a most lovely dress, but it isn't practical for me. I am goin' on a long trip. It will be fall and the weather will be quite chilly. Could I please try on some knickers?"

He laughed at that, saying, "But you're not a boy. You should start dressing as a young lady."

A young lady, the statement caught me off guard. Could I really be a young lady? I know I was a girl, but a lady? What a dream that would be.

He must have thought about my comments on my voyage and the conditions I might be in, and agreed and sent me back in to the "fire room". The ladies brought me some travel clothes and a coat. I put these items on and felt much more comfortable and stepped out with a smile on my face. I was much happier with these and told him so. He agreed and asked the ladies to bring me scarves and hats to try on, oh, and don't forget boots and shoes, he said. This was all too much and I didn't realize how exhausting trying on clothes could be.

When we were finally done, Mr. Leeds asked, "What would you like to wear home?"

"My clothes, of course."

He laughed, from deep in his belly. "They are all your clothes now, so which ones did you want to put on?"

"The clothes I came in with."

He looked rather disappointed. I glanced at Betsy and she shook her head and motioned for me to pick something else. I chose the traveling outfit, but asked him if I could please keep the clothes I came in with, anyway. He smiled and said Brody had done the exact same thing. It made me think he did not know about the attack on Brody and what had happened to him. I would let Brody explain that one to him later.

Mr. Leeds told the ladies he wanted the clothes delivered tomorrow, to his house. I asked if I could please carry my old clothes with me, so he asked the ladies to box them up for me so I could carry them, and we headed out the door.

We walked the same way back, just as briskly, and with Betsy and my head's down. The streets were more crowded and Mr. Leeds said we had to be more careful since it was getting closer to sunset.

"I hope Brody will be home when we get there," said Mr. Leeds.

"Of course he will be," I said.

"Well," Mr. Leeds said, "Finola might have his interest more than us, so he might not be home, just yet."

I couldn't imagine why, but he was correct, Brody wasn't there when we arrived home.

I was no longer mad at Brody for not being there when I went to breakfast this morning. Nor when Mr. Leeds came home. Nor was I mad at him for not going shopping with us. It had all turned out all right, after all, but not being here when we arrived home, how selfish of him.

"Allie, I think I shall bathe before dinner. You can too if you like."

"Thank you. Taking a bath every day would be fine with me," I said, and tried not to look too excited at the thought of being so pampered again and smelling the wonderful aroma of lavender in the warm water. However, this time I was going to get in.

"Now, Brody better be back by the time we are done," said Mr. Leeds, "or I will have to send someone out looking for him. It just isn't safe to be out at night, especially by yourself in a strange place. Finola knows the area, but she herself would have to be home by now."

I started to worry and by the time I slipped into the bath, I was mad at Brody for making me worried about him. If he was hurt, what was I to do? I couldn't go back to Ma by myself? What would I tell her and his father? This day was full of continual bouts of anger at Brody. I didn't realize he could make me so mad. I knew he could annoy me, but anger me so much? And for so many different reasons? I didn't enjoy my bath at all because I spent the whole time worrying, going back and forth between being mad and being worried at Brody.

I finished my bath and slipped back into my new travel clothes. I brushed my hair with my own, new brush tonight. I felt so good about being clean and feeling better about the way I looked.

I checked myself out in the full length mirror and headed down to the study. No one was in there, but I could hear talking in the dining room. Maybe Brody was back and he was with Mr. Leeds. I hoped they weren't waiting on me.

They didn't seem to give me much notice when I came in and sat in the seat Betsy pulled out for me to sit in. The table was beautifully set and there were candles lit with food already sitting on the table. I guess they had been waiting but they didn't say anything to make me feel as though they were waiting on me to eat.

I kept looking at Brody hoping to get his attention and give him an evil squint so he would know I was mad at him. That didn't work so I tried to break into the conversation, but they were so focused on talking about what Brody and Finola had done all day that my rudeness at interrupting them didn't work at all.

They were still talking as we started to eat, so I ate with pleasure thinking I could eat faster and then they would be busy eating and I could talk. There was so much food compared to what we were used to eating. I don't think I had ever had so many choices, even before the famine. I tried my best to eat politely and like a young lady, but I was focused on getting through the meal so I could ask Brody some questions.

Brody looked strangely at me a couple of times, and fumbled as he talked, but did not stop talking with Mr. Leeds. The two of them did not have any problem running out of things to talk about. They talked about Finola, the library, Mr. Farraday, what kept me from getting on the June sailing, and more. I finally had enough and broke in asking,

"Brody, have ya told Mr. Leeds about your trip home last time, and what happened to the new clothes he gave ya?"

They both stopped talking! It worked. They both looked at me, then at each other, and Brody fumbled some more with his words while trying to tell the story. What a silly boy! I knew the story so I decided I could tell it much better. Let's see if Mr. Leeds would be upset with Brody, now. They were new clothes and Brody talked such a big game and acted like such a man when he really wasn't.

I did not understand things sometimes. Not only was Mr. Leeds not upset with Brody, he told him he would get him some new ones tomorrow and he was sorry they had been the cause of any trouble. He also told Brody he was the smarter one for keeping his old clothes. He was happy that Brody was all right.

"What would Brody have done without the old clothes? Run home stark-naked?"

They laughed as I just stared at them, rolled my eyes and turned down my mouth.

Mr. Leeds finally told Brody about our day and the shopping we had done. He told him about all the items we purchased and that I, too, had asked to keep my old clothes. He said Brody was obviously a good influence on me since I had taken to heart his opinion and done the exact same thing.

Why was Brody getting the credit? I'm the one that had done the asking, and I had given him my explanation about my travels and the importance of having my old clothes.

I didn't know why and for that matter, didn't care, but for some reason I was steaming at Brody, silently. I knew it would be very rude of me to show it in front of Mr. Leeds, so I kept it inside. He had been so kind and generous to both of us, and he was the one coordinating my trip to America. I gave Brody every hint of my being disgruntled, but he either ignored it or didn't realize what I was doing, which just made me angrier.

All three of us retired to the study and Mr. Leeds had a pipe which he lit. I've known many people who have smoked a pipe, but not in such close quarters. Oh, the house was big enough, but the windows weren't open and there wasn't any fresh air to blow the smoke away. I was getting sick to my stomach. Neither of them noticed my turning green for they were back into their endless conversation, but this time it was about the next few days and what we needed to do to prepare. I was most interested, but turning greener by the minute.

When I could take it no longer, I ran out of the room and up the stairs to the bathroom. I wasn't sure where I needed to throw up; the tub, the commode, the sink? Yikes! I chose the bathtub just as Betsy was coming up the stairs to check on me. She held my hair back as I continued to be sick.

I kind of sank over the side of the bathtub like a wet rag and she grabbed a wash cloth, soaked it with cool water and wiped my face. I didn't move because the room was spinning. She told me I would feel much better if I prepared for bed and lay down for a while with the wet washcloth over my eyes.

She helped me change out of my clothes and get into bed, and then placed the washcloth over my eyes. It did feel better, and the coolness of the washcloth and the blocking out of the light helped to stop the room from spinning. She opened the windows to let some fresh air in which helped, also.

Then, she brought me some milk and toast and told me, "You might feel a little better if you could get some of this down."

I couldn't eat much of it, but I was starting to feel better.

"Pipes, cigars and tobacco can cause many people to feel nauseous, so ya shouldn't be embarrassed about gettin' sick." She said.

"I feel horrible about runnin' out on Mr. Leeds when he did so much for me today. Please apologize to him. I will make an apology myself, tomorrow."

"No need to worry. Try and get a good night's rest. Tomorrow will be another big day."

I lied flat and thought only of being calm and quiet as she slowly shut the door and said goodnight.

I couldn't get to sleep. I just lied there and listened to the noise on the street outside and to the crackling of the burning wood in the hearth. I heard Brody come up the stairs and go to his room, and then a few minutes later I heard Mr. Leeds come up and go to his room. I listened as they both shuffled around their rooms, getting ready for bed, stoking their fires, washing their faces. Then all was quiet except for the noises from the street and my own fire, again.

I felt better, now, but I still couldn't go to sleep. Why was that? This was the perfect place to go to sleep. It was safe and warm, and very comfortable, but still I couldn't get to sleep.

Whether I was mad at Brody or not, I waited long enough to make sure he was asleep, and then I slipped out of my room, and back into his. He was asleep as by his own noises coming from his bed. So with me and my comforter, I lied on the floor, again, by his fire, and fell asleep.

The next morning I was awakened by the light changing above me. It startled me until I opened my eyes and saw Brody leaning over me. He was about to poke me, when I sat up and quickly gathered my covers. I stormed out of the room, mad at myself for not waking up early enough to get up and out of there before he woke up. He didn't say anything to me as I left, which aggravated me more. He was plainly ignoring my feelings on everything these last two days.

I put on the skirt, shirt and vest Mr. Leeds bought me the day before, and fixed my hair. This time I only pulled back the upper half of my hair, and left the lower half hanging. I used the same ribbon Betsy had brought me the day before and tied it in my hair. I checked myself out in the long mirror and headed down for breakfast.

"Good Morning! You look very pretty this morning." Mr. Leeds stated loudly.

Brody said nothing. He only smiled and rearranged the napkin in his lap.

Betsy came over and took me into the kitchen. "Ya 'ave your skirt on backwards. Let me turn it 'round. There, that's fine."

How was I supposed to know which way the skirt went? I had never worn a separate skirt, or at least, I couldn't remember ever wearing one, and I never paid much attention to Ma getting dressed. I was embarrassed and knew why Brody had smiled, or was that a smirk, to himself. Why couldn't he have been as polite as Mr. Leeds and just said hello? This new Brody was rude and thoughtless. What had come over him?

Despite my embarrassment, we had a lovely breakfast with scones and jam and tea with cream and sugar. It was so yummy. I think I ate three scones all by myself.

"If you continue to eat like that you'll outgrow your new clothes," said Brody.

I ignored him and looked the other way.

Mr. Leeds chimed in and said "She could never do that, and anyway" he said, "look at me!"

We all stood up from the table to go into the parlor. The windows were open this morning and it was a crisp, fall morning. The windows being open reminded me that I had run out on Mr. Leeds last night and not apologized, yet. I went right over to him and expressed my regret for running out, and for forgetting about it this morning and not mentioning it as soon as I saw him. I was quite remorseful. He hugged me and told me to forget about it. He had disregarded the fact I was young and the smoke might affect me that way. He said he was sorry he had made me sick, and he would open the windows from now on if he were to smoke.

Mr. Leeds should have been married and had children. He was such a generous man, and so good with Brody and me. He would have made a good father. I was curious as to why he had never been married, but knew it would be rude of me to inquire. Maybe I could ask Betsy later on? Maybe she would know.

Mr. Leeds talked of our day and what we needed to do.

He reminded Brody, "We need to buy you some more clothes."

"That is not necessary, Mr. Leeds."

"Ah, but if you are to continue to see Finola, then you have to compete with all the other young men who are interested in her, too."

My eyes darted to Brody. He was interested in Mary Knapp back home, and now Finola Abernathy? Japers, I guess Brody fancied girls quite a bit right now! Mr. Leeds seemed to be approving of the idea. Finola was quite pretty, but I didn't have a very good opinion of her when I first saw her. She seemed to be too flirty and obvious. Quite unladylike, I thought.

"I would like to try and see Miss Abernathy later this afternoon, but I will do whatever you think is necessary."

"I think we can get everything done by mid-afternoon," said Mr. Leeds, "and then you should be free by three o'clock or so."

Brody smiled and sat up straighter. What was that about?

Mr. Leeds looked through his paper, "We should be able to find something in here to give us more specifics on the ship Allie is to take to America. I believe its name is the *Kate*."

I jumped at the name and Mr. Leeds asked, "What in God's name is wrong?"

Brody spoke up, "That's her Mother's name."

"Well, that's a good sign, isn't it?"

I agreed. "A ship that has my ma's name must be a wonderful ship!"

This ship, the *Kate*, was to take me to America. It would be like Ma carrying me there and being with me. It was a good sign. I couldn't wait to see this ship.

"Can we go by and see it before I leave on her?"

Brody spoke up again but to reprimand me this time. "Mr. Leeds does not have time to grant your every wish, Allie. We will do what Mr. Leeds tells us to do, not the other way around."

Mr. Leeds reached out and motioned to Brody to stop his admonishing of me.

"It's all right, we can see the *Kate* without cutting into our time. Anyway, you and I are going down to the ship dock this morning. We'll just take Allie with us."

Brody gave me a stern look, and I wanted to give him one right back but didn't want Mr. Leeds to see me do it, so I held it in.

"We need to see the ship's Captain and Allie can tag along and meet him and see the ship. We'll leave in about twenty minutes, so if there is anything you need to do, go ahead and take care of it so we can leave shortly."

I didn't really have anything I needed to do, but I ran upstairs anyway so I could be excited all by myself. I looked out my window hoping to be able to see the port, but all of my windows faced houses behind Mr. Leeds's.

I could see laundry hanging, and fencing, and windows of other houses. Some had their linens hanging out on the window sills, while others were closed. I looked up at the blue sky which was scattered with white puffs of clouds. I thought about being on the *Kate*, and being able to see wide open skies and stars at night. I bet it will be beautiful on the ocean. Within days I will be able to see as much sky as I wanted.

Betsy came in to check on me and tell me how to act, and what to do properly. She told me how to walk, how far to walk behind the men, and what not to say. Well, I really wasn't supposed to say anything unless it was Brody, Mr. Leeds and me. If anyone else was there, it wasn't my place to speak. I didn't really understand but I knew she knew more than me in this world and I should respect what she tells me to do. I promised her I would try my best.

Mr. Leeds called Betsy to bring me down. He and Brody were waiting at the door when I joined them. I followed them out and stayed as close to them as possible on our walk to the docks. It was about three blocks away, so we didn't have too far to walk, but as the street opened up on to the docks, the ships and activity of the port was in full view.

I looked around and saw sailors and workers and fishermen and maids and people of every sort. They were all going about their business, but as to what I wasn't sure. It was a loud and noisy area. I could hear talking, and laughing, and then sounds of the sea. There were horns, and birds, and flapping of sails, and ropes being pulled against wood and iron, and there was clanging, and waves hitting against the pier. This was much more than I ever expected. I never dreamt that so much would be going on.

It frightened me a little even though I did not want them to know it, so I stayed closer to Brody and Mr. Leeds. I worried that if I faultered, I would never find my way back. People were coming up to Mr. Leeds and asking him for offerings or to buy things, and he just walked on by. He didn't take the time to answer each person and I understood why. There were so many.

I can now see why one would keep their head down and walk with a purpose, if you stopped, even for a moment, you might get swallowed up in this chaos. One might slip away and be lost forever in this sea of mayhem. I grabbed Brody's hand and held on tight. I didn't want to be lost.

As we walked down to the pier, I was worried about getting pulled into the masses. I had not been watching for the *Kate*. I knew the reason I was being brought along, but I hadn't expected the situation to be like this.

Before I knew it, Mr. Leeds took my hand and stopped. When he did, I looked up, and there she was, the *Kate*. She was enormous, with three different sets of sails wrapped around her masts. She was long and sleek looking, with crew working on her deck.

We walked up the ramp slowly, and a gruff looking man asked Mr. Leeds, "And just what are you doin' on the Kate?

"We have business with the Captain. Please direct us to him right away."

The man grumbled something and motioned for us to follow him.

We stepped down a few steps and behind some slatted doors into what looked like a small room with a single bed and a desk. The sailor grumbled something to this man, and he stood up and cheerfully greeted Mr. Leeds.

They must have been friends for they hugged and were jolly to one another. Mr. Leeds introduced Brody and me. Right away the Captain came over to me and bent down so as to sit back on his heels and look at me.

He took one hand and said, "I was expecting you in June, but I'm glad you're here. You will enjoy America and it will be a great adventure."

I smiled at him and looked up at Mr. Leeds for support.

"Can she sit up on the edge of the ship and watch everything going on the deck while we talk?" Asked Mr. Leeds.

"Of course," the Captain said.

"Brody," said Mr. Leeds, "take Allie up to the outside deck and find her a good spot to watch everything while Captain Kiper and I talk."

I followed Brody and obeyed, but as we stepped outside I told him, "I really don't want to be up here alone."

"We'll come and get you before we leave. I promise."

"Well I hope so!"

"Don't be ridiculous. No one is going to get you or hurt you. Why don't you enjoy watching everyone and seeing all of the ships?"

I did not let go of his hand, so he shook my hand loose and went back down into the Captain's room. I sat there stiff at first; worried someone would come up and grab me or start begging me for something.

I finally started to relax when I realized everyone went about their work as if I wasn't even there. I leaned against the ropes that were strung along the side of the ship and watched the world around me. It was chaos, but maybe I was looking at it the wrong way. There were people who were begging, but there were also people obviously doing their jobs and going about it as if it was normal for them. I guess it was just new to me.

A sailor on the ship came up to me and asked, "Are ya sailin' on this ship?"

I was frightened at first, but he told me, "I have a lass like ya and this would be quite a journey for anyone, especially a young lass like yourself. She wants ta go wit me, but I told her it was too dangerous and I would worry 'bout her too much."

"What do ya mean?" I asked him.

"The seas are rough, and many times people die on these ships because of diseases."

"Why do ya sail on them then?"

"I am a sailor," he said, "and it is my job. I love bein' on the open seas and travelin' and bein' in new ports. It is high adventure and it is in my blood."

The first man who grumbled to us earlier, yelled at him to get back to work.

He leaned over to me and said, "Ya can call me Skully."

I shrugged my head as if to say why, and he showed me a tattoo on his arm of a skull and crossbones. I smiled as he turned to get back to work.

He looked back and told me, "The other side of the ship has a totally different view. Ya might enjoy lookin' out over the ocean from there."

I stood up, walk over, and stood on the opposite side of the ship. I looked out over the vast blue water. There were seagulls and fish jumping out of the water. The seagulls would swoop down towards the fish at times. I laughed thinking of the opposite side of the ship and how they kind of looked the same in a way, but it was people swooping on the other side, not birds.

I looked back out over the ocean and wondered what happened to you when you get to the edge of the horizon? Do you fall off? Do you see America, then? I couldn't see any land towards the horizon. I looked up and saw the beautiful sky again with the same puffy clouds, and thought about Ma. I wish she could see this. I wish she was here with me. We could both be standing here anticipating our journey to America, together.

The grumbling man hollered at me to get back to where I was sitting before. He said he didn't want me to fall overboard because he would have to go in after me. I wanted to roll my eyes but was afraid of his saying something to me if he saw me do it. I went back to my original spot where Brody had placed me hoping he would say no more.

I leaned back into the rope and continued watching the hustle and bustle of the people below. I noticed a group of people with luggage and trunks and waiting in a group. I wondered if they would be on this ship with me. I looked them over, trying to guess their ages. I watched how they interacted with one another and what they did.

They really seemed like the people I knew back in Knock. They were talkative. They were dressed in clothes like Brody and I had on when we arrived, and they spoke in the same strong Gaelic accent I was used to. I hoped they would be on my ship, because I would feel better knowing we were much the same, or at least I expected us to be that way.

Brody, Mr. Leeds, and Captain Kiper came on deck and were animated with their talking. Mr. Leeds slapped the Captain on the back in an enthusiastic gesture and they all laughed. They looked at me, and Brody motioned for me to get up and come over to them. I did as I was asked and joined them by the ramp.

They weren't talking about my journey but about cutting back on the vegetables and meats being exported. The Captain and Mr. Leeds must have agreed on the issue, but the Captain said he didn't know what they could do to change the situation.

They weren't in a serious discussion because neither of them looked that way in their facial expression. They looked like Mr. Farraday did at our house a long time ago when they were discussing anything and everything all at once. I wondered if Brody was reminded of his father during this exchange. I would never know because we headed off to our next stop and I forgot about it almost as soon as we left.

The Captain directed us to the document office and told Mr. Leeds to make sure we had all of our paperwork in order. Fortunately Brody brought all of my paperwork and had it out and ready by the time we arrived.

As we walked in we saw there was quite a line for the permits. Mr. Leeds placed us against the wall and walked up to a person behind a counter. The person left his post and stepped behind the counter and into another office.

When he came out, a man followed him and motioned for us to come back to his office. Mr. Leeds nodded at us and we followed him into the man's office. They shook hands and the man asked Mr. Leeds if he would like a seat. He did and sat down in front of the man's desk.

We stood at the back of his office, trying to be as quiet as possible. Mr. Leeds was making a case for me and trying to make sure I would be taken care of in getting to America. He told the man he was friends with Captain Kiper of the *Kate* and we had just been with him discussing my journey, but he wanted to make sure all of my paperwork was in order for me and that there wouldn't be any issues.

The man asked to see my boarding and travel documents. Mr. Leeds pulled out the papers the man needed to see, and told the man, "We've already paid Captain Kiper."

The man took quite a long time looking over the paper work to see what we had.

He told Mr. Leeds, "It is going to take more money for her to travel on this requested date."

"Like I said, we've already paid the Captain for the amount due."

"If you want her to be able to go to America in the next couple of days, you will have to pay extra for her to gain passage."

"I'll be back tomorrow with the extra money." said Mr. Leeds, "I want you to have all the paperwork in order for her to be able to go, and I better not be double crossed. I am going to hold you personally responsible."

I had not heard Mr. Leeds speak in this tone before. He stood up and we followed him out the door. As we walked back towards Mr. Leeds's house, I could tell he was frustrated with the man and said the man was taking advantage of our situation. He told us the best thing for us to do is pay the man whatever he's asking to ensure I would be able to go.

We went into the house and Betsy met us at the door. She took Mr. Leeds's coat and hat and hung them on their hooks. She must have been able to tell Mr. Leeds's mood because she scurried about to make him tea and to make him comfortable in the parlor.

Mr. Leeds looked over the paper work, "Brody, I will take care of this, and tomorrow we should be all set. If you like, you go on to the library now. Finola is probably waiting for you and she shouldn't have to wait on you any longer."

"If you're sure, Mr. Leeds? I would not want Miss Abernathy to be disappointed."

Mr. Leeds was lost in the paperwork and motioned for Brody to go on.

Brody stood up and went into the kitchen to tell Betsy he would be back by dinnertime. He left out the front door in a very happy mood. I sat opposite Mr. Leeds, quietly, while he reviewed the paperwork.

"I apologize for the situation, Allie. I need to go out right now and see someone who can ensure you leave day after tomorrow." said Mr. Leeds.

"Betsy," he called out, "I need to resolve this issue so it means I need to go out. I will also be back for dinner."

Betsy gathered his hat and coat and helped Mr. Leeds put it on. I wished Mr. Leeds good luck, and headed into the study to read. I heard the door shut and listened to Betsy's footsteps as she walked back into the kitchen. I heard the sounds of pots and pans and her moving about in the kitchen.

I took a book by Nathaniel Hawthorne, *Twice - Told Tales*, from the shelves and flipped through the pages knowing I had some time before both men returned.

The book is a collection of stories, and perfect I thought for being able to read in small amounts of time. I knew I didn't have more than 2 days before my ship left, so the stories were short enough for me to be able to read through and get finished before I had to leave.

I chose the *Hollow of the Three Hills* to start. Then I was able to read through two more. The author of these stories is American, but he wrote much like I was used to, and his places seemed more like places I could relate. They might not have been as exciting as the *Last of the Mohicans,* but they were still interesting. I liked that. I could finish a story in one sitting. And I guess, in this circumstance, I had enough time to finish three stories.

Chapter 9
Items To Treasure

Three stories and the men were still not back! I went into the kitchen and asked Betsy, "Can I help ya with dinner?"

"I almost have all of it finished, but ya can help me set the table and pour the drinks."

She thought it would be a good idea for me anyway to learn how to set a table properly. She came into the dining room with me and showed me how. She gave me new candles to place in the candleholders and brought me fresh fruit to place in the silver bowl in the center of the table. It did make it look nice, and told her so.

"The placement of things on the table helps in the enjoyment of the meal." She said.

I gave her a strange look, not really understanding, and she went on to say, "Not only proportion of food on a plate and the colors of the food placed on the plate, but the table setting itself needs to be pleasin'."

"I really don't understand that," I told her.

"Well, put it away in your memory and remember it anyway. Maybe one day it will make sense to ya."

As we were finishing up in the dining room, Mr. Leeds came home. Betsy left me in the dining room asking me to light the candles. She went to greet Mr. Leeds in the foyer and to take his hat and coat again and hang it up. He bellowed for me to join him the parlor, and asked Betsy to bring him a glass of Port.

I joined him in the parlor and asked, "Do ya feel any better?"

"I do," he said, "everything is going to be all right."

He was a little more at ease, even though he still seemed to have a bit more on his mind than he was letting on.

"I did some reading while ya were gone." I told him.

"Oh? And what were you reading?" He asked.

"Stories by Nathaniel Hawthorne."

"I enjoy that author. You should read *Mr. Higginbotham's Catastrophe* and *David Swan*, if you have the time. These are short stories but interesting ones."

He stood up and picked up another book. This one was from a higher shelf than I could reach.

He handed it to me, and said, "Here is *The Sketch Book*, written by Geoffrey Crayon, it has two wonderful stories in it, called, "Rip Van Winkle" and "The Story of Sleepy Hollow". The author's real name is Washington Irving, but he uses this name as a pseudonym."

"A what?"

But before he could answer, Brody walked in.

Brody was in a good mood, again, and was full of stories from Miss Abernathy and their afternoon activities. She had taken him to a garden in a private area owned by a friend of their family's. The gardens were changing seasons, but Brody said it did not keep them from enjoying it.

They appreciated the layout of the gardens and the use of design associated with the style of the house and its environs.

This explanation made about as much sense to me as the one Betsy had given me for the setting of the table, and the food on the plates. I had never taken the time to look at things in these ways and wasn't very interested in learning why it was important.

Betsy came in and told us dinner was ready. It looked delicious. I was hungry and her cooking was always delicious. She laid out the food in arms reach for all of us, but food was food to me and I tried to see if I could appreciate it the way she suggested, in a pleasing manner.

There was a pork roast, with red potatoes around it. There was yellow squash with onion slivers, orange carrots, and green cabbage. I guess if you were looking at colors, this was a nice variety, blended well. Well, didn't I sound lawdy daw! I was grateful there was food on the table, and I enjoyed Mr. Leeds's company.

He was fun to listen to in this short time; I had grown accustomed to his outgoingness. The men ate some of everything, and while I knew I should eat some of all, I really didn't like cooked carrots very much. I liked the crispness and coolness of uncooked ones, but boiled ones weren't my favorite, and squash alone was fine, but the onions were rather slimy. I didn't say anything about my personal tastes, but ate more of the pork, potatoes and cabbage. They were delicious.

We finished another meal and headed into the parlor. Mr. Leeds, Brody, and I discussed the next few days. We knew I would have to pack, and if I had my items organized and ready, I could take them to the ship tomorrow and place them on it. I could even get on the ship tomorrow and find a place for me to bunk, but I wasn't too sure I was ready for that, and fortunately, Mr. Leeds suggested I stay at his home another night. Brody and he would go back to the Foreign and Commonwealth Office tomorrow to insure my passage and finish my paperwork. I offered to go, but Mr. Leeds felt Betsy and I should finish packing. I agreed and excused myself for the evening, saying I wanted to take a bath and go to bed.

Mr. Leeds picked up the book he had suggested earlier and handed it to me, stating, "Maybe this would help you get to sleep."

I took the book and went upstairs. Betsy came in and helped me fill the tub with warm water. She told me that not everyone enjoys baths as much as I did, nor do they take them as often as I have.

She added the salts and the petals of lavender and I slipped in and actually enjoyed the relaxation of it all. I did have the guilt that Brody has spoken about, but I knew Ma would want me to appreciate what was being offered to me. And this was a moment I could easily appreciate.

I wasn't upset with Brody tonight, and I had the new book of stories to look forward to. I washed my hair and my body and slipped down with water up to my chin, and just lied there. My knees were bent slightly and my kneecaps were slightly above the water level. Most of me was beneath the water and it was quite soothing.

I hoped to remember this moment, because I really didn't think I would ever be able to have such luxury again. I knew Uncle Brennan would never be able to afford this and any boarding house we might live in wouldn't have a personal bath for me.

I dried off and slipped into my bed gown. Betsy came in and discussed our schedule for the following morning. Then she tucked me in. She lit the lamp next to my bed and reminded me to turn it down before I went to sleep so as not to burn it out. She turned towards the door and smiled at me as she slowly closed it behind her.

I picked up The Sketch Book and decided I would read "Rip Van Winkle" tonight. I turned on my side, holding the book against one side of the cover and began reading.

It was such a fun story. I almost fell asleep twice trying to finish it, but enjoyed it so much I had to make myself stay awake to finish the story. I finally fell asleep with the book closed on my fingers.

When I woke up in the middle of the night, the fire had burned out. It was kind of chilly in the room. I had forgotten to turn down my light, so I did as Betsy told me. I placed the book on the bedside table and turned the lantern down.

The room was dark until my eyes adjusted, and I realized this was my first night to be sleeping alone. And I was alone, and lonely, too. I was in a comfortable house, in a comfortable bed, with comfortable surroundings, and yet I wasn't comfortable. Yet, again. I didn't really understand why, it was just a feeling I had. I finally fell asleep, and slept through the night.

When Betsy came in to check on me the next morning, she had to wake me up. She told me Brody and Mr. Leeds had already had breakfast and left for their morning appointments. We were to pack everything and get me ready for the next day.

It was to be an important day for me, Betsy said. She gathered my clothes, the same ones I had worn the day before and helped me get dressed. She fixed my hair again and braided it all the way down the back. She re-did the braid twice, but I think she enjoyed braiding it more than just her thinking it was braided incorrectly.

When she was finished she told me to join her in the kitchen and she would give me some breakfast. I slumped over towards the vanity and sighed. I was excited about going to America, but it was so much to swallow. I missed Ma and I enjoyed being here. I was going to a place I had only read about and heard about, and to a person I could barely remember. I was going to be alone and feel lonely for quite some time, I thought.

My mind turned to Brody and how much I really wanted him to go with me. I was so much more at ease when he was around, even when I was mad at him!

I sat up straight and looked at myself in the mirror. In the reflection of the mirror I noticed a stack of items I had not brought, next to my bed. I stood up and walked over to them, perplexed at their being there.

I sat down on the back of my heels and on my knees, and looked through the items. Ma and Brody must have assembled these items for me to take to America.

I was taken aback by the assortment. There were letters from Uncle Brennan and a picture Moira had drawn of Ma, years ago. There was a scarf of Ma's that had been her Mother's. I knew she loved this scarf and rarely ever wore it because she cherished it so much and didn't want to ruin it. I felt a knot in my throat at the realization of what all of these items meant... Ma had folded the scarf neatly, but I held it close to my face and could smell Ma.

Memories flooded back of Ma, family, and of grandmother. I can barely picture grandma because she died when I was about 4 years old. I can see her sitting in her house in a chair by the fire. She sat their knitting or something, and told Moira, Quinlan, and me stories of her growing up and her ancestors. She had gray hair she pulled back from her face and always tucked it neatly in a bun, close to her neck. She didn't wear the scarf in this memory, but I knew I needed to remember her and cherish the scarf the same way Ma did.

I tried folding the scarf back into the neat square Ma had folded it for travel. I placed it in the stack with Moira's drawing, and looked to the other items. There were four books included in the pile from the Farraday family. They were: William Wordsworth's, *Lyrical Ballads*, Edgar Allen Poe's *The Purloined Letter*, Nathaniel Hawthorne, *The House of Seven Gables*, and Jane Austen's, *Emma*. I was thrilled they had included these books.

I would take such pleasure in them. They would entertain me for hours, and they would have their own set of memories, even though

I had never heard Mrs. Farraday read from all of them, nor had I read them myself, yet. I knew I would, and I looked forward to it.

I placed each of these books next to my sketch and scarf, and picked up the last bunch of items tied in another scarf. I didn't remember this scarf, but I untied it and opened it to find a surprising collection. Here in this bundle were items that must have been Mrs. Farradays. They were all very personal and the lump in my throat grew larger as I felt tears rolling down my face. I slumped over again. This

was too much. These items were her personal items and I felt as if she were sitting with me at this moment and giving them to me herself!

There was a brooch that had jewels in it. I didn't know what they were, but their colors were pink, and white, and clear. They were in the shape of a flower that was open. There was another pin with a side view of a woman and looked as if her face was carved and placed against the other stone. There were two rings. One was a gold band, and the other was a gold band with a white, single, round jewel placed on it so it sat up slightly from the band.

I looked at these items through my teary eyes. I was so taken aback, and I hadn't gone through all of them. They had enclosed some silver utensils, silver accessories, a silver frame, and an assortment of coins and paper money. I was overwhelmed!

Betsy called to me to come down to breakfast. I tried to collect myself. I washed my face and patted it dry so as not to rub it and make it look worse. I rushed back to the piles to wrap up the loose items again and place them next to the complete assortment Brody and Ma had packed for me. I realized Brody must have come in this morning and left these items knowing I needed to pack them. He hadn't awakened me, but I beamed thinking he had been there, and had kept all of this a secret!

I joined Betsy in the kitchen and after breakfast we went up to my room and packed all of the items I had. We packed the items I brought, those Ma and Brody had added, and the clothing Mr. Leeds had purchased for me.

"I'll have food ready for ya so we can pack it tomorrow," Betsy said. "I've heard not all ships have enough food for their passengers, and sometimes the trips take longer than they are supposed to. Sometimes they have more passengers than they are supposed to carry, too. One trip took three months instead of the regular one month because of storms in the ocean. Don't worry though, Mr. Leeds trusts this Captain and I know he would not place you on a boat he did not trust."

I felt a little better, but was reminded of Skully on the ship, who told me stories. Skully was a tall and skinny fellow, with muscle over bone. He looked as though he had only lived on the ocean and worked every day of his life. He was missing a few teeth, but his demeanor and actions showed him to be a better man than one might expect by just looking at him. He had that skull tattoo plus other ones that I hadn't looked at that closely. His beard was scraggly but trimmed closer to his face and his well-worn skin was as tan as leather on a saddle. He seemed to be kind in a rough seaman type of way. His being a father probably softened him around the edges a little.

I know he told me how difficult sailing could be, but I couldn't see how any of it could be bad. We were going to be out on the ocean with beautiful open skies, and birds flying around, and people to entertain each other.

Most of all, I would have the books Ma and Brody had given me. I looked forward to my time on the ship and being able to read those books. My time on the *Kate*. It was almost as good thinking about it as reading. I was going on an adventure. My own. And I was looking forward to it.

We finished my packing by lunchtime. Funny how fast time can go by. I didn't realize so much time had passed. It didn't seem as though I had that much stuff to pack.

Betsy and I went down to the kitchen and I helped her fix our lunch. She was going to make bread for dinner. She showed me how to knead the bread and let it rise. We hadn't baked bread at home in such a long time, I had forgotten the process. Or maybe, I had never paid attention to the process before. Making the bread took more time than I thought it did, too. Ma used to always make it, however it never seemed like it took so many steps, and time waiting. It was always worth it because just the smell of bread was worth the time waiting.

During the rising process, Brody and Mr. Leeds returned home. Betsy, once again, met Mr. Leeds by the door and took his hat and coat. While it was chilly and damp last night, today was a lovely day. Cool and crisp with the sun out and a clear sky. Mr. Leeds walked into the study as Brody and I followed.

"I'll prepare some lunch for all of ya," Betsy told him, "and then let ya know when it is ready."

"Thank you, Betsy." Mr. Leeds acknowledged, and then continued with his focus on my trip. "Everything seems to be settled, Allie, and you are ready to sail tomorrow. We tried to reserve you a place on the ship, but you would have had to stay there until it left tomorrow. Brody and I decided you should stay home this last night. If that's all right?"

I nodded yes, and he continued. "Brody, I've invited Finola to join us for a farewell dinner this evening."

Brody smiled and sat up alertly. I was bewildered. It wasn't Brody's last night, it was mine. Why was Miss Abernathy coming to my farewell evening?

Betsy came in and told Mr. Leeds that our lunch was being served. He and Brody stood up to go eat. I excused myself, and used the excuse I had some more packing to do. Betsy looked at me with a puzzled look. She knew we were finished and didn't know why I didn't join them for lunch. I really didn't know either, but I wanted to be by myself for a while, and my room was the safest place to hide.

I picked up the book I had been reading from last night, and started another story, *The Legend of Sleepy Hollow*. I was at the place in the book where the superstitious part of the story is told, when Brody knocked on the door.

He poked his head in, "Mr. Leeds wants you to come down to the study. He wants to go over finances and help you understand the currency system in America."

I hadn't really thought about it, even that it would have been different. I didn't want to get up from the book, but I knew I needed to respect Mr. Leeds's wishes and join him.

Brody had already started going down the stairs when I called to him, "Brody?"

He didn't come back up so I asked him, "Bro-dee, come back!"

He turned around and came back in. "I want to thank ya for the surprise ya left me this morning. Betsy helped me pack it."

"The jewelry and miscellaneous items are for you to be able to sell if you need to." He said.

I must have looked at him baffled, because he said, "Father wanted to make sure you were not left shorthanded. And, you will eventually need these items to sell."

"I could never sell any of them!"

He nodded his head and left the room. I didn't know what else to say. I followed him down the stairs and into the study.
Mr. Leeds sat me down next to his desk, and asked Brody to joins us.

"I think knowing about American money is an important thing for both of you to understand. The British currency and the American currency are used the same way, but look and are called different things."

He then explained it all in detail and tried to compare each piece to its American counterpart, or what was closest to it. Then he separated the American currency and he played us against one another in a game. We had to add up the amounts quicker than the other one. And get it correct.

I tried to be faster, first, but it wasn't always correct. Brody would take his time and be more correct, more often. It was a fun game, though, and we laughed and made light of our mistakes. We had a fun time and Mr. Leeds enjoyed coming up with some outrageous scenarios and math problems. I couldn't imagine ever having to use them, but laughing and learning was a smart way to learn currency. I wasn't sure if I had it down, but I understood the basics and how they were different.

We spent most of the afternoon playing this game, then Mr. Leeds reminded us we had other things to cover. He suggested Betsy bring us some tea, and he moved on to cultural differences and issues he thought I might not be aware of.

He took us in to the library and pulled some books from their shelves. "These books will help you understand the social differences you might face in America."

He pulled one book I already knew about, *The Deerslayer*. It was by the same author that wrote, *Last of the Mohicans*. "When people immigrated to America, the American Indian was already there. This book tells of the American Indians and their situation. It is kind of like the Irish and how the British took land from the landowners."

He explained it in more detail, talking about the prejudice that occurred because of religion and how people were treated differently because of their religion.

This took him to a collection of papers. He told us about the American slave trade. He explained how black people were taken from Africa and sold to Americans for cheap labor. They were sold by slave traders in Africa, who were often black, themselves, but were trying to make some money. They were transported by ship and brought to America. Most of the black families were split up when they arrived in America and sold to different owners. This was not only awful for the families, but it gave a stronger hold to the owners by weakening the family bond, or so they thought.

"These papers cover a variety of topics, but they are mainly about their strong opposition to anyone being a slave. Many of these authors have been arrested." said Mr. Leeds. "It is a very sensitive subject in America."

"Do you know anything about 'Free Blacks'? A letter from my Uncle Brennan talked about that."

"A 'Free Black' is a person of color who is no longer a slave or has never been one. Most have to carry papers that prove he was 'let go of by his owner's free will. This allowed him to work and travel like any other American, but that usually meant only in the northern areas."

He spoke of a collection of papers about America. He called them the Declaration of Independence and the Constitution of the United States. He also pointed to the Inaugural Address of the current President James Polk and his words on the strength of America and how after the Revolution and the War of 1812 America had repaid their debts to European countries. He shared the desire of Texas to be part of the United States. He read a speech by Patrick Henry, March 23, 1775, *Give Me Liberty Or Give Me Death*. He was so well informed on America.

He showed us a book by Cotton Mather, *The Devil in New England*, which talked about witches and puritan beliefs. He said it was important for me to understand the background of America and the stages this young country had gone through to understand more of what was happening now. There was prejudice for more than just people of color.

Any immigrant will face prejudice like the Irish, the Germans, the Italians, and most foreigners. He said I should be aware of this because I should be more understanding when things happen to me, and treat other people with respect and kindness. Whatever their religion or nationality, America was hope for all people to grow and find freedom.

I had so many questions swirling in my head, but I didn't know where to start. I would have to take in all he told me and hope I would learn the answers to these questions throughout my life. I just wasn't sure I could remember everything he had told us about.

"I think it is so fascinating about the Indians and America going west." said Brody. He liked the adventurous part of the stories. "Have you ever wanted to go to America?" he asked Mr. Leeds.

"I have been to America, but only New York and Boston. One day I would like to visit more places." He looked at me and said, "Allie, you can show me more of America when I come the next time."

"Indeed! It would be so much fun to show ya somethin' I might know more about!

He laughed as Betsy stepped in and told us Miss Abernathy would be here at any moment, and dinner would be served in an hour. Brody excused himself and headed upstairs.

Mr. Leeds said Brody was going upstairs to refresh himself for her. Why? I thought. She was all right, but if she really liked him, wouldn't she like him in his old clothes, too? As I was thinking about it, the doorbell rang. It was Miss Abernathy.

Betsy let her in and we joined her in the parlor for a drink. Well, Mr. Leeds had a drink, Miss Abernathy and I sat on opposite loveseats. She was cheerfully engaged in conversation with Mr. Leeds when Brody stepped in.

He had on some new clothes. I assume Mr. Leeds had purchased these clothes for him and had them delivered. They were quite smart looking, and I could tell by Miss Abernathy's response she was pleased with his entrance. The three of them discussed the day's activities, but Brody seemed to stumble when he talked. He seemed uneasy and said some ridiculous things. What was the matter with him? I giggled at one of his comments and he shot me a fretted glance.

We sat in the parlor until dinner was served. The two men sat at the ends of the table, and Miss Abernathy and I sat across from one another. We seemed so far apart from one another. The table was made for seating eight to ten people, so that length kept us apart. When it was just the three of us, Betsy sat us together at one end of the table and we were close enough to talk comfortably. This seating arrangement seemed humorous, but I would never have let on since it was Betsy who knew more about table setting and proper etiquette.

As I watched Miss Abernathy, she spent most of her time looking back and forth between the two men and giggling and agreeing with their comments. I don't think she knew or agreed with each comment, but that didn't seem to change her responses. Her body language changed, too. She leaned forward towards the table, didn't eat very much, and nodded as well as verbally responding. I ended up watching her more for her reactions, than for what they were saying to one another.

After dinner, we retired back to the parlor. The conversation changed to me and my journey starting tomorrow. I let go of my obsession of watching Miss Abernathy, and listened to them discussing our afternoon and my future plans. Miss Abernathy said she would love to be traveling to America and one day she hoped she could make the trip.

Hah! I had something on her, and, this trip was for me. I was the one leaving tomorrow and going on this grand adventure. I was going to be living the stories we had read about.

Mr. Leeds reminded me tomorrow would be an early day for all of us, and he and I should head upstairs and go to bed. I looked at Brody wondering why he wasn't going up with us. I noticed Miss Abernathy looked down and said she needed to go home and thanked Mr. Leeds for inviting her to dinner. Brody said he would walk her home and come right back. Mr. Leeds reminded him of the dangers after dark, and he needed to make sure and come straight home. Brody nodded, and Mr. Leeds and I went upstairs.

Betsy had already gone home for the evening, so Mr. Leeds came in and checked on my fire. Everything seemed to be in order, and he sat in the chair next to the fire.

"Allie, I have so enjoyed having you and Brody here. I always wanted children, and Brody and you have brought me so much pleasure, even for the small amount of time you have been here. I want you to take the two books I showed you last night. It would make me very happy knowing you enjoy them."

I ran over to him and gave him a hug. Intensely, without knowing why. He tried to comfort me, but I felt an immense sorrow even though I knew this would be a wonderful adventure. I was leaving Ma, Brody, my da, Mr. Leeds and Betsy behind. I was going to be on my own, I knew there was no turning back.

He hugged me once again and said, "Oh, you must not be sad. All of your loved ones will be joining you in America, one day. By your going first, you will give them hope and pleasure in knowing you are in a better place."

I know he meant well, but it didn't change my feelings at the moment. He kissed my forehead, stroked my hair, and left the room.

I slipped into my bed clothes and slipped under the covers. I continued to mournful. I tried to read some more of *The Headless Horseman*, but couldn't get past a few paragraphs. It wasn't a happy story, and was scary at times, so I guess I wasn't in the mood to read this tonight. I hadn't heard Brody come up the stairs and in my door. He came over to me and sat by my side.

"It's going to be all right, Allie, you need to be strong. The strongest person I know is your mother and she would want you to be strong, too."

He was right, I knew it, but it didn't take away my sorrow completely.

"I'll stay with you until you fall asleep. Will that help you?"

He turned down my lantern and went over to the chair by the fire and sat down. I could only see his shadow against the wall, but it was comforting having him there. I woke up once in the middle of the night, and his shadow was still there. I was comforted by his presence.

Chapter 10
Knots In My Throat

I woke up early and went over to Brody to awaken him. He had stayed there, in that uncomfortable chair all night, but I was grateful. I didn't tell him so, but I was. He stood up and said he would meet me downstairs for breakfast.

Betsy came in and filled my bath. She said I should enjoy one more bath before I take my trip. She added extra petals and lavender.

While I was in the tub, I could hear her finishing my last minute packing. She told me Mr. Leeds had purchased some new luggage for me and she needed to switch my items to the new set. I was anxious at her doing so and asked her repeatedly if she included everything. I told her these items were all I had. She knew that and said she added a few things of her own and I shouldn't worry. She did not leave out any of my items.

I stepped out of the bath and dried myself off. I put on my traveling clothes, and asked Betsy to fix my hair. I knew she would like that, and I liked it, too. She was taking care of me and I knew I would miss her. I had only met her and Mr. Leeds a few days ago, but it seemed as if I had known them all my life. They were both so likable and kind. I would write to them both, from America, and keep them informed of my travels.

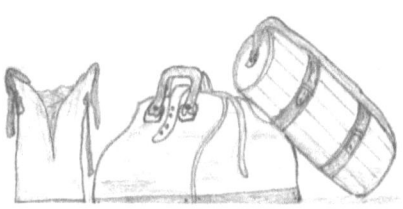

Before heading down to breakfast, I glanced at the luggage Mr. Leeds gave me. It was a beautiful set. It was made of leather and must have been quite expensive. With my new clothes and new luggage, I felt like a different person. I even looked more well-to-do than I knew

I was. I must act the part, I thought. I must do this for everyone sacrificing for me. I must make the best of it.

Brody and Mr. Leeds were waiting for me at the breakfast table. Mr. Leeds tried to make light conversation and keep it moving, but Brody and I were both quiet. Mr. Leeds went over everything I was supposed to do, and made sure I repeated it back to him. He had taken the time to write it down, just in case, he told me. He wrote down the names of people I could contact in America if I ever needed the help. He said I could always use his name as a reference.

The time was almost here. We had waited months for this time, and now today was the day. I had knots in my throat and in my stomach and I felt anxious. I didn't have a clear enough head to think through any questions I might have, so I just sat there.

Mr. Leeds asked Betsy if my baggage was ready. He asked her if she had packed enough food for me. He asked her if she had added the extra items. Betsy said yes to all of his questions. I guess he was rather anxious, too. He then asked Brody if he would go upstairs with me and help me bring my things down.

"Of course," he said and moved his head as if to motion me to follow, and we headed up the stairs and into my room.

Brody went in first and picked up two suitcases. I went in and backed up against the wall across from the fireplace and windows. Brody turned around, holding the suitcases, and stared at me.

I must have had a blank look on my face because Brody walked over to me, "Allie, are you all right?"

I shook my head, 'yes,' but I really meant 'no!'

"Come on and grab the other bag." he said.

I said, "yah," but stayed in the exact same spot staring at the far wall!

I must have stood there longer than I knew, because Brody came back upstairs to get me. He told me to look around to make sure I hadn't left anything and to come down. He picked up the last suitcase and went downstairs, leaving me alone in the room for the last time.

I looked around and tried to commit to memory this room, this house, and the people in it as long as I could. This would be a good recollection, I thought, and I turned and headed down the stairs. I had to move on.

Brody, Mr. Leeds and Betsy were all standing at the door with my suitcases and packages around them. I walked to them trying to seem as though I was happy and ready to go. I was not going to let Mr. Leeds down, and I knew it would upset Betsy if I did not seem happy.

Mr. Leeds pressed the moment and told Brody to get two of the suitcases and he would carry the other one. I was to carry the food bag. Betsy gave me a hug and stroked my head wishing me the best of luck.

She grasped my hand and said, "May the Lord keep you in his hand."

She then walked me to the door, and waved goodbye as we walked down the street.

We walked down the crowded street with our bags. Brody, almost angrily, yelled at me to stay close to Mr. Leeds and him People were pulling on us and trying to get the bags we were carrying. They were desperate.

I felt so sorry for the ones with children. I wanted to give them my food, but I knew if I was going to make it to America, I would need the food I was carrying. We pushed and forced our way through the streets until we finally arrived at the *Kate*.

She was docked in the same place I remember, but there were people lined up everywhere; on the pier, on the ramp, and even on the ropes along the side the deck. I looked up in amazement, and the three of us must have been thinking the same thing as we all just stood there, gaping. There were so many people on the ship. Were they all passengers?

Mr. Leeds collected himself and took my arm and motioned to Brody to come on.

"We must fight our way on!" he said.

We pushed our way up the ramp amidst those crying and jovial, angry and happy. There seemed to be every emotion. The sailor at the head of the ramp told us to check in with the Purser in the aft of the ship. We walked along the port side of the ship towards the back of the boat. There was a line, but not that long. We waited quietly until it was our turn, and then Mr. Leeds stepped up to the man checking passengers on board. Mr. Leeds gave him the paperwork and told him my name. The man looked down the list, checked off my name, and told me I could go down below and pick out a spot to make my own.

We picked up my belongings and headed back towards the middle of the ship where there were stairs to go below. We went down the stairs, weaving in and out, between the people standing everywhere. We found the deck where the bunks were, and walked around with my luggage trying to find a spot. There were none left, so Mr. Leeds went back upstairs to see what we should do next.

I sat down with my knees pulled into me chest, and placed my head down on my knees. I was silent. I really didn't know what to make of all of this. It was overwhelming.

Brody bent down and told me again, "Everything's going to be all right. You will make friends with all of these people and hear wonderful stories of their travels and families. You should write about it as often as possible, and we'll do the same. We'll let you know what is happening in Knock. You know your mother will love to hear about your travels. And you've always had a good imagination, so that should make for good reading!"

I smiled and put my head back down. He stood up again, and we both waited for Mr. Leeds to come back.

When he did, he said all of the bunks were taken. He said many had checked in the night before and taken spots. The Boatswain had told him I could go below and find a place in the Hold if I wanted. I looked up at Mr. Leeds not understanding what the Hold was. He said it was the place where they stored items like goods, and it was below the other decks. We picked up my items and headed to the stairs to go even deeper into the ship's hull.

As we came out of the stairs we turned the corner to see what the Hold had to offer. We all stopped and surveyed the scene. It was dark and musty, with crates everywhere. There were a few other people down here who must have signed in late, like us. Mr. Leeds said hello and moved towards the back to try and find me a private spot. When he stopped he motioned to us and we carried my bags to him. He showed me a spot between stacks of crates he said should be a safe spot.

"Don't worry about being down here. You will only be down here at nighttime when you are sleeping. All of the other time" he said, "you can be on the upper deck and outside seeing the ocean and the birds and visiting with other people."

After he told me that, I didn't feel as bad as I thought. He was right; I could spend all of my time outside, above, and maybe with other girls my age. This might be the perfect place.

We left my items in my new spot and headed back up to the sunshine. It was a beautiful day and the seagulls were here with us, swooping and chattering and adding to the liveliness of the whole picture. Some of the crew were opening the sails and preparing them for our journey. Before I knew it the Boatswain was announcing our departure and alerting those not ticketed for the ship to leave at once.

All of a sudden, and without warning, I was frantic. My heart began to pound. I didn't want them to leave me here. I was all alone. I grabbed Brody and begged him not to leave me here!

Mr. Leeds realized my anxiousness and took me from Brody. I looked back at Brody and noticed his worried look at me, but Mr. Leeds was turning me toward him and holding my shoulders tightly. He was trying to get my attention but I was focused on Brody, begging him not to leave me!

Mr. Leeds shook me and said I had to be strong. "Remember everything we talked about." He said, "You will have a grand time."

I yelled for Brody as Mr. Leeds told Brody to leave! I continued yelling for him, as I saw him turn and walk down the gangway! I continued but it was of no use now. I began looking apprehensive and Mr. Leeds tried his hardest to get me to stop.

"Allie!" He bellowed, "You must remember everything we discussed! I am placing your ticket in your pocket, and you must keep it close to you at all times! Do you understand?"

"Clear the decks!" The Boatswain called one last time. Mr. Leeds hugged me and told me he would write to me. I shook my head 'yes,' even though I was still fretful. He squeezed me one last time and headed down the gangway himself.

I ran to the stern of the ship, squeezing my way through, and fell down on the edge of the ship watching the *Kate* leave her docking! People were standing above me and around me waving to family members and friends. I looked down at the crowd and didn't see Mr. Leeds or Brody! I felt abandoned. How could Brody do this to me? Ma hadn't abandoned him when he was left all alone. I was furious and hurt at the same time. I leaned against the rope as the ship continued to pull out. I was devastated and overwhelmed.

I told myself I was going to stay in this spot until they made me leave. I didn't know what else to do. I could hear the sails popping as they caught the wind, and the ship moving through the water slowly. I could also hear the birds above, the people talking and laughing. I didn't understand their happiness at the moment. Especially at the moment I was so sad.

I was lost in mournfulness when I heard my name being called from the pier. I sat up and frantically looked over the edge of the ship towards the end of the docks. Looking for the person calling my name. I knew the voice but was afraid to believe.

There, standing at the edge was Brody. He was calling my name and was there for me as I searched. I jumped up and waved, crying at the same time! I knew it was him, but he was blurry. I was mad at myself because I couldn't really see him through my tears. I tried wiping them away, but the crowd pushed me away from my spot as they tried to see their own families better. I lost my spot and my last moment with Brody. We were separated forever, now, and I was all alone.

Chapter 11
The Hole

I ran down below to hide in the only place I knew I would have some privacy. I stayed there the rest of the day without getting anything to eat or going above. I cried the rest of the day. I was so alone. No one checked on me in my dark and private spot. I could be dead for all anyone knows and no one would know, I thought.

This couldn't get any worse. I missed my Ma. I missed our home. I know it was only a house made of mud and sticks, but when we were together Ma always made it the best she could. Even when it rained so hard outside and the water ran down my back at nighttime. It wasn't so bad when she was there. She would find a way to cover me or move me, and then repair the roof the next day. I really missed Ma.

I fell asleep thinking of her, but woke up when the ship started to rock. It was swaying so much I started to feel sick. I had never felt this way before. Why was it rocking so much? No one had told me about this and I couldn't think of anything else but the rocking and the way my stomach and head felt.

I jumped up knowing I was about to be sick. I didn't know where to go except up and out. I ran up the flights of stairs to the upper deck and leaned out over the ropes. It was an awful feeling being by myself and being sick, especially like this, hanging over the side of the ship unloading my insides. I had nothing inside to bring up, so I was trying, but nothing was coming out.

Before I knew it, Skully came over to me, "Aaah, how ya?"

I looked up at him, and his eyes brightened when he saw me.

"Why ya the lass I talked to a couple a days ago?"

I nodded as I leaned back over the ropes and tried bringing up again.

"You should try lookin' at the edge of the sea where it meets the sky and you will get used to the swayin' of the ship and the way she moves."

I truly couldn't imagine ever getting used to this feeling of back and forth, and back and forth. Ughhhh! I had to stop thinking about it because that didn't help me either.

He brought me some water and some bread and said I needed to stay up here a little while. Eat and drink this, and eventually I would calm down. I did as he said and by the time I saw the sunrise, I started to feel better.

I looked out over the ocean and couldn't believe I couldn't see a thing but the ocean. No other ships, no land, and only a few birds. The water was kind of choppy, and the waves had white foam on their tips. I started to feel woozy again and remembered what Skully had told me, "look at the edge of the sea", and so I did. I leaned against the ropes, again, and watched where it met the sky.

The Bosun's mate called out to everyone that breakfast was being served and tapped me on the shoulder to get me up. I followed the crowd of people into a room where they were handing out food and I looked around. There was a line for the food, and people standing everywhere, so there would be no place to sit unless you went outside.

I thought of doing that but was turned back at the door. The Bosun's mate told me we had to stay inside to eat because they didn't want birds attacking everyone and following the ship the entire time. I turned towards the wall and leaned up against it. I started feeling sick again and really couldn't eat. I asked a woman if she wanted my share and she immediately took it. I headed outside. I thought I might spend my entire time outside if this is the way I was going to feel the whole voyage.

I stayed on top deck most of the day, and another day not eating.

Skully found me up top again, "Ya have to eat somethin' or ya might get sick."

"I just can't, Skully."

"But ya must."

"I promise I'll try tomorrow. Sitting here is about all I can do, today."

He reminded me of Da. He was probably about the same age. He brought me his blanket as it started to get cold. The day turned to sunset. I thanked him and sat up another hour before I was just too tired to stay awake. I gave him his blanket and told him I was going below to try and sleep.

I walked back down the flights of stairs and to my spot. It really wasn't my spot I thought, but a hole, and that was what I was going to call it the rest of the trip, The Hole. I noticed it looked as if my items had been sifted through and that bothered me, but I felt so bad all I could do was fall down and go to sleep. I think I was out before my head hit the pillow. I remember worrying about my things, but I couldn't stop the urge to sleep.

The call to breakfast woke me up and I opened my eyes to see the crates that made up The Hole. There was light, but only a little from the stairway. You had to let your eyes get adjusted before you could actually see anything.

I looked around and noticed I was the only one down here. I realized my luggage was not safe at all. I could easily go through other people's items while they were gone, and that is probably what happened to my things. I frantically tore through my luggage to see if I had lost anything. The only thing I could find missing was some money. It had been on tap of one of the bags because Mr. Leeds thought we might need some before I left. I was lucky I guess. They could have taken much more. I would have to be more careful from now on. I would have to find someone I could trust.

While looking through the items I noticed some things I had not packed with Betsy. She told me she had packed some other things, so I thought maybe this is what she meant. I looked through them and found a small painting of her with her son. He looked precious. This was a wonderful item from her. I can see her with him and her joy of him. I was glad she packed it in my things. I also found a folded piece of paper. The light wasn't bright enough for me to read it. I placed it in my pocket to take it outside and read it there.

I rearranged my luggage so it would be harder for someone to take my most precious things, and then tucked my bags away from the open area. Maybe if they didn't see it sitting out, they wouldn't know it was there. I felt a little better and headed up the stairs to breakfast.

I was at the end of the line by the time I went upstairs, and there was only a little food left. I took what I could and ate it this morning. It felt good to eat something. Maybe I was going to make it, I prayed. I looked around the area and tried to start making sense of my surroundings and the people on this voyage with me. I remembered the Captain and wondered why I hadn't seen him. I would have to ask Skully about him later.

I finished my breakfast and went outside to take in all I could. Today I would watch the people. There were quite a few families, and not too many people seemed to be alone like me. I thought it strange and wished I wasn't alone.

I started feeling sorry for myself and wondering what I was going to do on this trip, when I remembered the paper in my pocket. I reached in to my pocket and pulled it out and opened it. The handwriting was Brody's, but it started with words from Ma.

Her words were sweet and loving. She told me how proud she was of me and she would miss me dearly and hoped I wouldn't be angry with her for sending me away. She tried to explain herself. I knew what her reasons were, and I knew she loved me. I understood what she was saying, but I still felt sorry for myself as I read.

I started to tear again and one of my tears fell on the page. The words ran and I quickly rubbed my eyes and held the paper away from my face. I didn't want to ruin the few words I had from her. If I ruined this letter, it would be like I was getting rid of her forever. I couldn't do that. I needed these words, because as I read them I could hear her saying them to me. I will read this over and over again, I thought. I will wear this paper out. I knew that's what I would end up doing.

As I looked back at the words, I noticed Brody had written something from himself. He must have added these words after Ma dictated hers to him. It caught my attention that he would do this and so I skipped down the page to see what he said.

He talked about his sorrow at the death of Quinlan and he was sorry he had not shown my mother or me his sorrow. He said he could not have survived without my mother, and he was so grateful to her for her kindness and acceptance. He said she didn't have to bring him into her home, and he would try harder to appreciate her.

He wanted me to know that, and that he would take care of her and make sure she joined me in America one day. They would write regularly, he promised.

I had to stop again and keep the paper away from my face. Would I ever stop crying, I thought? I tried to look up and out into the ocean hoping the sea would take my mind off the letter and my sadness.

While doing so I overheard a family talking to Captain Kiper. I stood up and went over to him to wait my turn to speak to him while putting the letter in my pocket and taking my sleeve to wipe off my face.

When they were done, he started to walk to another family when I called out to him. He turned towards me and held out his arm and waved. I walked up to him and gave him my name and that I was a ward of Mr. Leeds's.

"Of course, I remember now." He said. "How are you Miss McCreary?

"I've been seasick since my first night and not had that much to eat because of it."

He told me the same thing Skully had, "You have to watch the horizon. You have to make sure you keep up your strength. You must try not to get sick because there isn't too much we can do on this voyage and everyone has to be healthy to be allowed into America."

"I don't want to get sick anymore. Tis an awful feeling."

He agreed, "Some people never get used to it, but hang in there and be strong. Where are you sleeping? Do you feel safe?"

I told him about The Hole and why I called it that.

"I like your sense of humor. I'm sorry you are down in the Hold. That can be an awful place, but you can make it more of an adventure by accepting the privacy of the spot. However, it does worry me about some of your items. Why don't you bring them up at sunset, and I will place some of your valuables in my cabin and keep them until we arrive?"

"I would feel so much better if I could do that. I have some things that are too important to me and I don't want them to be taken. I will go and organize them right away and bring them later. Thank ya ever so much." I said

He smiled and patted me on the head. There were other people waiting to speak to him, so he winked at me and said he would see me later.

He was a handsome man, weather worn, and very strong looking. His hair was starting to go gray and had a rough look to it as if he was in the salty ocean too long, or in the wind for too long. I smiled to myself and how long he must have been at sea. His uniform was clean and looked very good on him. I think he was German by his accent. He seemed a few years younger than Da. I hadn't thought to ask Mr. Leeds about it before, but maybe I would have a chance to ask Captain Kiper directly. He looked much better than most of the other sailors on the ship, especially Skully. But I liked Skully, however he looked.

I ran down the stairs to The Hole and rummaged through my things getting out the items I wanted the Captain to keep. I rearranged them so I could put them in my smaller bag and leave that one with the Captain. I repacked the other things and pushed them back into my hiding spot, away from prying eyes. I sat there then, waiting for the time to pass.

When I heard the call to dinner, I picked up my small bag and went upstairs. I walked past the line for dinner and out onto the deck and towards the Captain's cabin. He was heading out and just happened to see me. He welcomed me in.

"You can put your things right back here." He said, and showed me where he would be hiding my bag.

"I am truly grateful, and feel so much better about their safety."

"They will be just fine, here. Why don't you go on to dinner and enjoy the voyage?"

I went to dinner and stood, once again, to eat my share. I was starting to feel a little better about the trip, and seeing some of the same faces added to my secure feeling.

As I was finishing dinner, I remembered I had not finished the letter from Ma and Brody. I ran outside hoping there was a little light left for me to read the letter. It was too dark on deck, but there were a few lanterns lit that I could use for light. I went over to one and opened my letter.

I reread the section of Ma's I had already read and found the place where I had skipped. She talked about Moira, and Quinlan, and Da, and that I should always remember my family and that they all loved me. 'We want a better place for you, Allie. We hope you take every advantage that is given you, and not feel guilty about it.' She told me to help Uncle Brennan and learn as much as possible. She ended her section with a blessing.

Always remember to forget
The things that made you sad.
But never forget to remember
The things that made you glad.
Always remember to forget
The friends that proved untrue.
But never forget to remember
Those that have stuck by you.
Always remember to forget

The troubles that passed away.
But never forget to remember
The blessings that come each day.

I looked out over the ocean and waited for my eyes to adjust. I could see stars and the reflection of the moon over the ocean. It was a beautiful sight. It reminded me of some of the poems Mrs. Farraday read to us. This is what they saw when they wrote about the stars and the ocean and the moon. This was beautiful.

I thought of Mrs. Farraday and thought maybe I wasn't as deprived a situation as I thought I was. I still had my life, and one day I would be together with my family again. She didn't have that option. She wouldn't be able to see her husband or her boys again. Yes, maybe I was lucky.

I decided I wouldn't make myself sad or wallow in my own pity. If I was going to make it, I would have to make it on my own. I was only twelve, but…wait, I thought. I had a birthday six months ago, and none of us had remembered! I was thirteen now! How strange none of us had remembered. I guess it really didn't make a difference…I was thirteen! I felt older just thinking about it. I wish I had remembered my birthday so I could give Brody a hard time. I was thirteen!

Chapter 12
Unscrupulous Characters

I started feeling better about the trip around the third day, and would take a book with me to the upper deck and read in between meals. I finished *The Headless Horseman,* and had to start another book right away. Not because I was necessarily anxious, but because the previous one had scared me. My mind imagined scary things from the story and I hoped reading something else would help me think about something else.

I was still sad and mournful at times, but holding the books in my hand helped me get through the days. This book was William Wordsworth's, *Lyrical Ballads.* I could read his poems and not get caught up in a long story, and the romantic thoughts helped me get my mind on other things.

On the fourth day, I heard the Captain was not feeling well. I went up to Skully and asked, "May I check on him?"

"I don't think so, but I will ask the First Mate for ya." He said.

"I just want to see if I can help. I could be his cabin boy, even though I am a girl!"

Skully laughed, "Yer a good lass for offerin', wait near the bow of the ship, and I'll get back to ya as soon as I can."

I took my *Lyrical Ballads* book and started reading. *The Yew Tree.* I thought I might have found memories reading this poem. There was a Yew tree close to the Mulberry tree on the knoll back home. It sat below the knoll and had another Mulberry tree next to it.

I didn't have to wait long, when Skully returned. "The First Mate said, 'No' and said 'if he let ya see the Captain, then everyone would want to see 'im."

"I promise not to tell anyone. I just want to help."

"I'll try and talk to 'im directly, if I get a chance. I can't promise ya anythin'.

"Yah, thank ya." And returned to my reading.

The Yew Tree wasn't exactly what I thought, so I moved on to another story, *The Complaint of a Forsaken Indian Woman*. It was about a woman who is left to die because she is too ill to carry on with her tribesman. It is not a very happy story, but it started me thinking. What if the Captain needed my help and his crew was not taking care of him? I told myself this was probably a crazy idea, and pushed it out of my mind.

Two more days passed and I did not see Captain Kiper, still. I asked Skully about him, again, and he said he had not seen him either. I decided to take matters into my own hands and sneak into his cabin and check on him myself. I knew I might get into a lot of trouble, but he had been so nice to me. This was the least I could do. If he told me he was all right, then I would let it go and leave him alone.

That night, when I thought everyone was asleep, I slipped back upstairs and into his cabin. He was lying in bed when I slipped in and quietly shut the doors. No one else was there, and I hated to wake him up, so I hid behind some trunks, waiting for him to wake up.

I fell asleep back there, and only woke up when I heard the call to breakfast. I peered over the trunk and saw Captain Kiper still asleep with his back turned towards the center of the room. I was greatly worried, but dared not move. I needed to wait for him to wake up.

I missed the call to breakfast, but he still had not awakened. He moved and groaned, but did not get up. I toyed with the idea of going to get someone, because something didn't feel right. I slowly rose to go and check on him and tried to rouse him, but I heard footsteps outside his door. I jumped back behind the trunk.

There were two men talking as they entered his cabin. They were pleased the Captain was still out, and talked about their plan on trying to get rid of him. I peered out to the side of the trunk to see if I could see who it was, but I couldn't and I was too afraid to peek out anymore. I pulled myself back in and waited, listening to them and what they were doing.

The men cackled at their ability to trick the Captain so easily and drug him with his drink. They pushed on him and he still didn't rouse. One sat on the bed next to him and the other pulled the chair out next to the Captain's desk. It was awfully close to me and I was afraid to breathe. If they heard me, who knows what might happen.

And if they did, who was going to take my word over these two grown men.

I wanted to see them. I tried to get a look at the man sitting in the chair by the desk. The only thing I could see was his back. It was a uniform in dark blue with a tail almost like the ones Brody and Patrick had for riding because it split in the back, and it had a high white color sticking out at his neck. I could also see a triangular shaped, dark blue hat sitting on the desk, and he played with it as he talked. He had dark red hair that was messy, but flattened down on his head.

I was trying to pay attention to what they said, at the same time I was trying to get as many clues as possible as to who they were. I didn't have anything on the other man, but I figured I had enough to at least know who one of them was, now.

They discussed who would come back to check on the Captain, and who would bring him his food so no one became suspicious. The man sitting closest to me in the chair said it would be no problem. He had the Captain covered for the journey, as long as Captain Kiper didn't get out of his cabin.

I wasn't sure what they meant by that, but they eventually stood up, checked on him one more time, and walked out the doors pulling them closed. I waited a few minutes, making sure they were gone, and then I stood up and went over to the Captain. I figured if I could wake him up before they brought him his lunch, I could let him know what was happening.

He had some fresh water in a bowl where he would wash his face, so I went over and wet a washcloth. With this cloth I wiped his brow and face hoping to stir him from his sleep. He did start to move, but he was groaning and I was afraid someone might hear him.

I placed my hand over his mouth trying to keep it closed, and kept telling him, "Shhh! You must be quiet!"

He continued making guttural noise. I didn't really think he understood what was going on at all.

An hour must have passed before I finally roused him to a stage where he could listen. He was groggy, but seemed to understand what I was saying. I told him of what I had heard, and that I was worried about him.

"Allie, we can't take a chance on your getting caught. I can take care of myself and know how to deal with this situation."

I nodded, but I wasn't sure of his ability to help himself.

"Who else can ya trust?" I asked, "And, who else can tell ya who one of the people are?"

"You must trust me. I can't have you at risk, too."

"Can I at least try and bring ya food? That way ya can get somethin' else in your stomach besides the food they bring ya."

"I don't know how you would be able to pull that off. Don't take any chances, all right? Now, help me get moving. I need to try and get this out of my system."

I helped him get up and move towards the chair. He leaned on the chair and told me, "You need to go. You won't be safe if anyone else finds you here with me."

I nodded and walked out the door. I looked back at him as I shut the door, and he smiled at me. I walked out on the upper deck and moved to the starboard side to look out over the ocean.

I stood there thinking about what I should do next. I looked side to side at all the people standing on the deck. As I looked at everyone, I knew I needed to find the person I saw in the Captain's cabin. There were so many people on the boat, my wandering around would not be obvious to anyone.

It was almost lunchtime, and I thought I could stay on the upper deck and see who took the food into the Captain. But then I thought if I waited, he might get drugged again. If I waited, what if they gave him too much? I needed to find the sailor who was sitting right in front of me in the Captain's quarters. He shouldn't be too hard to find.

I began walking around the ship. I saw Skully who called to me, but I was afraid to even speak to him, right now. What if he was the other person? It didn't really sound like him, but I didn't know.

What I did know was he wasn't the one in the dark blue coat with the high collar. That's who I needed to find. I continued walking around the upper deck, but saw no one dressed like that. As I looked around, I tried to make a mental note of the sailors and their uniforms in case I needed the information later.

The call to lunch came and I had not found the person I was looking for. I ran back towards the Captain's cabin knowing I had missed his food delivery. They always served him first. I went to his door and knocked lightly. There was no answer so I called his name. There was still no answer so I opened the door slightly and peaked in. He was back on his bed. I stepped in quickly and ran over to him to check on him. I said his name, but no movement. I shook his shoulder, but no movement, again. How did this happen? Why did he eat or drink whatever they gave him? I reached towards his nose as I laid my head on his chest. He was breathing, so maybe he was all right. This made me more determined to figure out who was involved so I could get help for him.

I left the Captain's cabin and started searching the ship, again. I went down to lunch to see if I could see anyone there. This would be a perfect time to see everyone in one spot. They would all be together, standing around, eating. I waited in line, picked up my serving, and stood against the wall eating, and yet, mainly looking.

I saw many passengers, but only a few sailors. It made me think maybe the sailors ate at a separate time, or in a different area. I knew Skully would tell me, so I would ask him later. He would only think I was being inquisitive.

I didn't see anyone in the dark blue jacket, or in a triangular hat, or with red hair like I saw earlier. Where could that person be? I knew they wouldn't let me in to all the crew cabin areas, or the Purser's office, so I had to find another way to see everyone.

I walked around both decks of the ship. I asked if I could walk through the galley.

The Cook said, "You can't come in because you might steal somethin' from the galley! If I let you in, I would have to let everyone in."

What was up with this crew? Does everyone say the same thing about every question?

Skully walked by just as the Cook was shutting the door on me. He took me by the hand and said, "Come on. I'll take ya into the galley with me. Listen, Chefy I'll be responsible for the lass."

The cook wasn't at all happy with me and showed me a disgruntled facial expression. Skully walked me around and told me about the big pots and pans, and how much food it took to feed all of these passengers for 6 weeks. The galley didn't seem that big, so the cook must be cooking all the time to feed so many people.

"So the sailors all eat in one place?" I asked Skully. "Do some eat in a place different from the passengers?"

"They do, follow me." He took my hand again and walked me into another room. It was a room with a table and chairs for about twelve people.

"Is there anyone from the Crew who doesn't eat in here?"

He gave me a strange look. I was scared he might catch on, so I asked him, "Do the officers eat with the crew?"

"Only the Captain can eat in his own room. Everyone else eats in here."

"Thank ya for showing me. Ya must be busy. I don't want to bother ya anymore, or get ya into trouble."

He walked me out to the upper deck and told me to enjoy the sunshine. I acted as though I was going towards the stern of the ship, but I slipped into the Captain's cabin to check on him. He was still passed out on the bed. I went over to him and nudged his shoulder. This time he tried to move and say something, so I knew he was coming out of his stupor, again; however I realized he wasn't alert enough to understand me, so I left him there hoping to come back later and check on him.

I went back out to the open deck and looked around. Why hadn't I seen the man in the dark blue jacket? I sat outside towards the front of the ship and looked backwards at everyone on deck. People were talking, and playing games. There were even people singing. Amidst this happy crowd there was a crime occurring and all these people didn't even know it. What was I to do?

I looked around some more and noticed a man in a triangular hat near the center of the ship and to the side of the Captain's cabin. He was standing by himself looking towards the back of the boat. I went down the port side of the ship and slipped around the back to see if I could sneak a peek at this man. This had to be the man. There was red hair poking out from under his hat.

I was nervous as I rounded the last corner of the ship. As soon as I turned this corner, I would see the man, face to face. I had to be calm. I had to walk right past him as if I was going somewhere else. I took a deep breath in and turned the corner.

I was looking up, but he caught my eye as soon as I turned the corner so I looked down towards the boards and walked towards him. Before I passed him, I looked up and took a good look at this man. It was the Boatswain! I was shocked. This was a trusted individual. No wonder the Captain had eaten his food at lunch. If the Boatswain brought it to him, he would have trusted him. I had to let the Captain know. Then I had to find out who his traitors were!

I walked past the man and sat back down in the spot I was at before. I watched the Boatswain and realized he must have been standing there to make sure the Captain didn't get out in case he woke up. I looked around again trying to see who might be doing this with him. Skully came up to him and my heart dropped. Surely it wasn't Skully? I watched him talk to the Boatswain but their mannerisms with each other didn't seem familiar. They didn't seem like two people working for the same cause. The Boatswain bossed Skully more than just talking to one another.

Skully moved on and returned to work with the ropes on the sails. I was hoping it wasn't Skully. Besides the Captain, he was the only other person on the ship that had taken some time with me. My eyes were drawn back to the Boatswain who was standing with the Purser. I didn't think much about it, so I continued to watch. They did look familiar with one another, and their body language was much more closed and private looking, as if they were trying to hide something and not have anyone hear what they were saying.

I knew I must be obvious; however I couldn't take my eyes off of them. Fortunately there were people moving everywhere, so they didn't notice me watching them. I sat there as they talked. I noticed they would stop talking as someone passed or stood too near. I wondered if anyone else was involved. I could at least give the Captain this information, and he could do with it what he wanted.

I needed to get in to see him, but I didn't think the two men would leave him alone tonight, and I was scared at the thought of them catching me. Maybe I could get close enough to them to hear what they were talking about and what their plans were. I needed to think about my options and how I could get near them.

I stayed up on deck for the remainder of the day, trying to think of ways to help the Captain. Besides the Captain, Skully was really the only one I thought I could trust, and even then I didn't know if he would believe me. I had to think of something.

For some reason, only Brody came to mind and I figured it must be because he would have thought of something to do. What would Brody do under these circumstances? I wished Brody was here with me. He would know what to do.

I tried to get him out of my head. He wasn't here, and if I was to get anything done, I needed to focus on my own situation and what I needed to do. As the sun set, dinner was ready and I headed down to the mess to eat.

Dinner was stale bread and potato soup. It was a familiar meal to me, yet not as good as Ma used to make years ago. She always knew what to do to make a plain old soup made of potatoes, tastier. I still missed Ma, of course, and started thinking about her now as I waited in line.

I should have waited a little longer for the line to be shorter, because everyone pushed when the meal lines were first opened. I hated that, and they often pushed me aside as people pushed me out of the way. I would always have to find my way back in the line, so waiting seemed to be the easier thing to do. But that had its drawbacks, too. When you waited, there wasn't always enough food, so my portions were often smaller than the first people in line. I didn't mind too much, though. I was used to not having too much food, and sometimes the more food in my belly, the sicker I felt when the boat swayed heavily.

I ate the bread and soup, and sat against the wall and watched everyone eating. I looked up at the lanterns hanging, and watched them sway slightly with the rocking of the ship. I didn't like watching them too much because I would get woozy again. I focused back on the people surrounding me in the mess. When I was done, I placed my bowl on the table by the kitchen door where the cook picked it up for cleaning.

I walked down to The Hole. Only one lantern was lit below, and I couldn't see my things very well. I lied down and tried to think of things to do for the Captain. I could tell Skully. I could try to make friends with someone on board and ask them to help. I could tell the Captain, or I could face the Boatswain and the Purser and tell them I knew what they were doing. No, that wouldn't work. They could easily do something to me since I had no one on ship with me, and there was no one to account for my whereabouts.

I lied there and found myself listening to the boards creaking as the ship swayed. I was beginning to feel that the sounds of the boat were becoming comforting sounds and the creaking had an almost rhythmic rock that lured me to sleep. Maybe I was going to get over that awful nauseous feeling after all.

I woke up and realized I had fallen asleep without deciding what to do. The Captain needed me and I needed to get to him and tell him I was willing to help him in any way he needed. I grabbed at my pockets and felt through them for my letter from Ma and Brody. I picked up one of the smaller books that would fit in my pocket, William Wordsworth's, <u>Lyrical Ballads</u>. I could read some of these as I sat outside. Yes, that would be good, so I dropped it in my pocket.

I loved my travel clothes, but I was starting to feel dirty in them. I remembered the wonderful bath at Mr. Leeds's. I wondered if I would ever get to take another bath like that again. I crinkled the side of my mouth and started up the stairs to go above deck.

It was still too early for breakfast. I was hoping I might be able to sneak into the Captain's cabin and talk to him. As I reached the outer deck, I looked around and didn't see anyone. It made me rather nervous because I liked it when there were people everywhere and I could hide easier amidst the crowd. I decided to go up front and sit for a while, watching for anyone coming and going.

I was going to read. It was such a beautiful morning. The sky was perfectly clear except for some very dark clouds way off on the horizon. The ocean was calm right now and there was a slight breeze pressing against the sails which moved us along easily. I looked out towards the horizon and saw fish jumping from the sea.

My attention was drawn back to the door of the Captain's cabin. The Purser was going down to his room and carrying a tray of food. Probably his breakfast. I worried and watched as the doors closed. I figured the Captain had no idea who was trying to deceive him and keep him from commanding his ship. I didn't have anything to tell him about why, nonetheless I could at least tell him about the two I thought were involved.

I pulled out my book on ballads and held it on my knees, playing like I was reading it. I was sitting on my bottom with my heels toward it and my knees up by my chin. That way I could hold the book above my knees and the Captain's cabin would be at my eye level as I looked at the book. I read a little and then glanced up when I noticed movement. More people were getting up and wandering around, so I began to feel more comfortable with being up and watching.

I read almost four poems, when I noticed the Purser step out of the Captain's cabin. I waited for him to be out of site. I waited a little longer, watching for anyone else to come by. When no one did, I stood up and slowly walked towards the cabin door. As I approached, I noticed the Boatswain walking by. I don't think he noticed me, but I slipped in the door quickly in case he was heading this way. I shut the door and glanced at the Captain who was on his bed, again, and facing away from me. I ran to the trunk I had hidden behind before and dropped down in case the Boatswain came in to see what I was doing.

I was breathing heavily and my heart felt like it was pounding out of my chest. I looked up slowly and saw a figure coming towards the door. I could hear my heart beating and I was afraid anyone in the room could hear it, too. The shadow stayed there for a moment, and then went back up the few stairs to the main deck.

I sat there a few moments to catch my breath and calm down. I was scared I might get caught and I had no one to protect me. For some reason I felt protective of the Captain, and I knew he would help me if needed, so I kept telling myself I was doing the right thing. I was reminded at this moment of all the people that told me this would be an adventure. They were right, but this adventure is not exactly what I wanted to be doing. And alone?

When I felt it was safe to come out, I stood up and went over to Captain Kiper's bedside. He was groggy, hence I shook him hoping to get him to wake up a bit. He rolled over and looked at me. I knew he was awake and he looked all right, now. I grabbed him and hugged him. I don't know why, but I was glad to see he looked all right.

"I know there are people trying to drug me. Unscrupulous characters. I'm trying to go along with it until I can figure out what to do."

I told him what I knew about the Boatswain and the Purser. "The only person I think ya can trust is Skully."

He nodded, "I agree with you, nevertheless I don't want you involved in this, at all. Do you understand? I am afraid they might hurt you if they are planning on taking over the ship. This is not something you should be concerned with. Allie, I will be all right."

"I don't have anyone else on the ship."

"Try not to worry," he said as he reached for me, "Keep your distance from this situation. I will take care of them when we get to New York. You must understand that I am going to have to play their game for a while until I can figure out the state of affairs."

"I still feel all alone."

"I am sorry about that. Be careful as you leave the cabin. Had anyone seen you when you entered the cabin?"

"I don't think so."

"Still, be careful as you leave and sneak back in to the crowd of people outside."

I hugged him and held on for a while. He did nothing to push me away, but stroked the back of my head as I hugged him and told him to be careful.

"Don't you worry about me. You are a considerate, sweet girl to think about me, but I need you to go."

He let go of his hug. I reluctantly let go and stood up. I looked towards the door, then back at him as he motioned me to go with his hand. I knew he was right, but I felt if I left his cabin, I might never feel safe on the ship again. I aroused my courage and stepped towards the door.

"I'll find you when this entire situation is over. I promise."

I nodded and opened the door slightly. I glance out and saw no one, so I waved goodbye to him and walked out the door.

I was saddened by the moment and had my head down lost in my melancholy as I walked up the few stairs to the upper deck. Wrong thing to do! On the last step up, I was grabbed by my shoulders and pulled up to the upper deck. It was the Boatswain who was calling to another sailor to take me down below.

I was so startled I didn't say a word. I was shocked! He must have been waiting for me while I was in with Captain Kiper. Had he heard our conversation? I wasn't sure, but right now I was in trouble.

The sailor was rough and forceful as he pushed me around and down the stairs past the mess. I thought he might be taking me to the Hold. It was close to The Hole, but we went down to the other side. It was a separate room in the bow of the ship; completely dark except for some spaces between slats in the door. He threw me in and told me to stay quiet and wait here. I heard him drag something like a box towards the door, and then I heard him push it into the door.

I felt around the room and didn't feel anything but damp wood, everywhere. There was no chair, no box, no blanket, just an empty room. I was scared. No one would know I was here, or even miss me. No one. This was what I was afraid of and now it was coming true.

I sat against the back corner, pulling my knees into my chest as I began to cry. The smell was stale. I could hear the waves hitting the ship, and the regular creaking of the boards as the ship sailed along. Right now these sounds weren't as comforting to me as I sat here in the dark and all alone.

Chapter 13
A Shortage Of Rations

I didn't sleep. I spent most of the night scared and worried. Worried because I didn't know what they were going to do to me. Had the Boatswain heard my conversation with the Captain? What were they going to do with the Captain now if they *had* heard? What were they going to do to me?

My imagination went wild. I thought they might throw me overboard, or leave me down here to starve. I even thought they might let rats in run over my face and eat me. I couldn't get my mind to stop wandering. It was racing, and I was getting myself more worked up not knowing what was going to happen.

I tried to calm myself and remember my favorite spot, the knoll. I tried to think about the Mulberry tree and the gentle breezes that swayed through its branches. I tried to think about the creek down below it that trickled over stones and earth. I tried to think of the folktale about the Mulberry tree and the couple who made the berries turn red. None of these thoughts were working. I kept coming back to where I was and how alone I was.

No one came to see me. It must have been an entire day. I couldn't see any outside light, and the lanterns burning were my only gauge of time. They were lit at nighttime, so when they came on the next night, I realized a day must have passed, and no one had come in to see me.

They must be leaving me here, I thought. I had no more tears to cry, and even though I was still scared, I realized I must do something or I would die in this dark and damp room.

Another night passed. I only knew this because the lanterns were turned off. My eyes had adjusted to the darkness and the cracks in the door offered me a direction to the outside. I tried the door, pushing, pulling, and even kicking it, but it didn't budge. I tried yelling, but the people staying in the Hold with me must have gone to breakfast or gone outside for the day.

The ship was rocking heavily and the motion of it was making me sick. I had gone two days without any food and I was starting to feel sick again. I lied by the door hoping to hear any sign of movement out there so I could yell out for help.

The waves against the bow of the ship were very loud and I could hear thunder and pounding rain on the boards above me. Maybe that would bring people back down below, I thought. Maybe they would hear me and help me.

I felt awful. I couldn't stand up because of the dizziness. I stayed by the door. Eventually I could hold it no longer and began an awful cycle of heaving. I didn't have anything in my stomach and my stomach was twisting like the wringing of clothes when you are washing them. Nothing was coming out and my head felt as though it would burst.

Finally I heard people talking and I began to yell for them. I yelled as long as I could. No one came to my assistance. Another day passed, and no one came to check on me or help. I was downhearted. Was the same thing happening to Captain Kiper? Had Skully wondered where I was? Had no one noticed that I hadn't returned to my spot in the Hold?

Everyone I knew told me this would be an adventure. I needed to look at this as an adventure they would say. Well, this was an adventure, but not one I would have wanted to have, or wished on anyone. An adventure isn't always a positive thing. I hoped I would make it through this one.

I was so exhausted I fell asleep against the door and unknowingly rolled in my own waste. Twas awful. I had not cleaned myself in fourteen days and the smell in this space was nauseating. It didn't help at all with the way I was feeling.

The ship had not stopped its violent rocking and had become so fierce I could not stop myself from rolling back and forth on the filthy floor boards. I tried scooting over to the corner hoping the two sides would help me remain still, but the heaving and dropping of the bow was too strong for me to halt.

I made it through the night, but was only more exhausted and sickly. I wanted this to end and was no longer worried about what they were going to do to me, because this must be it. *That* was it. They were leaving me here to die.

On the third day, I realized I should try and mark my name somewhere. I should also scratch marks in the wood to keep count of days, so when they found me, they would know who I was and how long I had been there. Ma might not ever know what happened to me, but then again, maybe Uncle Brennan would be waiting for me when I arrived in New York and if I wasn't there, maybe he would track me down and collect my body.

I felt so sickly I resolved this was to be my fate. I might try one more time to get someone's attention, and if not, I would just lie and wait for the inevitable. I crawled over to the door and reached up to the latch on the door. It was still locked, however this time as I pulled and pushed, there was some shifting of the door. It did not sound like there was anything against it now. Maybe it had moved during the rocking of the boat. I might have a chance! Before it had a chance to slide back, I had to give it everything I had and try and get someone's attention.

I pulled the door as hard as I could and pressed my face against the opening. It was only open about as wide as the width of my hand, but my mouth and nose squeezed through and I yelled as loud as I could. I yelled every 'please' and 'help' I could think of until I ran out of breath.

No one came, again. I lied back down, still holding the door at its crack. I continued begging for help. I no longer had the energy to yell, but I tried to keep talking, hoping the noise would interest someone and make them come over.

Finally, a girl about my age came over and asked what I was doing. I wasn't sure if I was dreaming or hallucinating, but I tried to sit up and talk to her. I had to trust her. She was my only chance at getting help. I explained to her what had happened and asked her if there was anyone else with her so they could go for help.

"Do ya have some water or any morsel of food I could have?"

"I don't have any on me, but I will try to find ye some and be back as soon as I can."

My head dropped back down to the floor and I let go of the door. She was my last chance. I didn't have the energy anymore to cause a raucous.

I waited for the girl to come back and drifted in and out of sleep, losing time in the process. I wasn't sure how long it had been when I felt the door being push against me. I was lying in front of it like a doorstop and whomever was pushing on the door kept banging it against me until it was open wide enough for them to get in. I couldn't see who it was and it wasn't until they spoke that I figured it out.

"I heard ya tryin' to bring attention to ya. It's of no use, girly," said the Boatswain.

His laugh was evil. I tried to get up, but was too weak to stand so I tried to sit up as he pushed me with his foot. I still couldn't see very much and I don't know how he could see, but he seemed to know where I was and where to push me.

"I've brought ya some bread and water, and a blanket. Be glad I brought ya anytin' at all"

"What are ya going to do with me?" I asked weakly.

"We haven't decided what to do. What did ya squeal to the Captain? And, who else do ya think is involved?"

"I don't know anythin' else, and I was just checkin' on the Captain since I hadn't seen him in a while."

"We are takin' care of the Captain, and pretty soon we will be in charge of the ship. If ya keep quiet and don't cause any trouble, maybe we will let ya live."

"What are ya goin' to do with the Captain?"

"None of yar business! And if ya had any sense, ya would be worried about yarself!

I didn't want to let him know I was scared, but I began to make some noise and he grabbed my hair.

"Be quiet!" He barked. "Need I remind ya to stay in here and be good? Ya do want to live, don't ya?"

He dropped the bread and water jug on the ground and threw the blanket at me.

As he walked out the door he yelled, "Stop yar bloody bawlin'!" Then he slammed the door.

I heard a chain slam against the door, and a box being pushed back into the door. I was going to be here for a while and once again, I passed out.

When I woke up, I remembered the bread and water and crawled around the floor looking for either. I was dying of thirst and had a headache that was splitting my head in two. I was achy and weak, and thought it must have been the kicking and pushing from the Boatswain.

As I felt for the bread or water, I felt a squishy, wet floor. I was afraid of what it might be, but my hunger and thirst overrode my feeling of disgust. The first thing I felt was the bread and as I reached for it with both hands, I felt something else on it, moving. I shrieked and jerked my hands back. I heard a familiar noise and I realized what it was – rats! There were rats in this room with me. I was terrified. I scooted back hoping they would eat the bread and not me.

My mind was totally focused on the squeaking. I figured there must be at least three of them. It sounded as though they were busy nibbling on the bread. Pushing myself back against a wall, waiting for the sounds to change as though they were finished.

Finally, I could hear them scurrying about looking for more. I was scared to death that they would think I was their next course, and as weak as I was, I found myself swishing my arms and legs back and forth trying to scare the rats enough to keep them away.

After a while I no longer heard them. It must have worked. I summoned enough courage up to start feeling around the floor boards again for the water jug.

As I was crawling and feeling, the ship began rocking heavily and I could hear something rolling around. It must be the jug. I tried listening for it to see where it rolled next. It was rolling everywhere and I was afraid I wouldn't have enough energy to stay after it.

My luck changed. The next rocking motion, the jug rolled right into me. I grabbed it as quick as I could and felt for the stopper. I pulled it off and put the lip of it up to my mouth, gulping as much as I could. I swallowed some, but lost the jug as quickly as I found it. I could hear the water pouring out on the floor boards and I rushed to the sound of the pouring, grabbing it and trying to stop it from pouring out completely.

I was afraid to open it again, not wanting to repeat what I had just done. I was going to have to be smarter about this or I wasn't going to have any bread or water. I had lost the bread and now I had very little water. I had to hold on. Ma and Da would want me to; I had to be there for them when they came to America. I was living their dream and I had to make it come true.

I lied down in the corner and tried to bunch the blanket up enough to make a place for the jug so it wouldn't roll away from me. The ship was still pounding the waves, and while I tried my best to stay still against the wall, I had nothing to hold on to.

I decided I had to hold the jug, if it was going to stay with me. I made sure the tap was tightly in it and I bunched up the blanket again to use as a wedge to keep me from rolling. I fell asleep, but was awakened by the girl who came to my door and tried to help me, before.

I was startled at her being there and didn't understand how she entered. Everything seemed so murky and I was too exhausted and weak to question her.

"We can't be too loud." She said. "There are some bad men out there. They have taken over the ship, and some of the crew have died."

"Did the men kill them?" I asked.

"No, not the mutineers," she said, "disease. The men have locked up the Captain and are barely giving any food to the passengers, so people are weak, and sickness has overcome them. The mutineers throw the dead bodies overboard to get rid of them. Others," she said, "have been separated so as to keep the sick ones separate."

"What about your family?" I asked her.

"I have two sisters and my Ma and Da on board, and they are all right. My name is Kerry. What's yours?"

"Allie"

"Allie what? Mine is Kerry Duffield."

"Mine is McCreary, Allie McCreary, but I am. My Da is in a workhouse in Ireland, and my Ma is back in Knock. She wasn't able to come with me on this trip."

"You are all alone? That's terrible. I would hate being alone. How old are you?"

"I am 13."

"Me, too!"

She was quite talkative and I enjoyed her talking to me even if I couldn't talk back to her. She picked up the jug for me and lifted my head. She placed the lip of the jug on my lips and told me to take a sip, then grabbed some bread she had brought and broke off a piece and placed it in my mouth. I was almost too tired to chew but I was so hungry and she encouraged me to eat it.

She said I had a fever and she heard her Ma say anyone who was sick needed to keep their strength and stay strong. Everyone tells me that, but I don't have too many choices right now.

She suddenly stopped talking and told me to be quiet, someone was coming. She jumped up and must have run behind the door to hide, for when the door opened, the light of the lantern only showed the man bringing in my bread and water.

I couldn't see her anywhere, and he must not have known she was there because he turned around and slammed the door shut again. I heard him lock it and push the box back up against the door.

When it was clear that he was gone, she knelt back down next to me and said, "That was the Bosun's Mate who brought your ration for the day. You're lucky he brings you some"

I strained my eyes to see her and only saw a slight glow around her from the slats letting the lantern light peak through. I could only see her outline. She sat with me for a while and told me more stories of her family and how they had come to make this journey to America.

I didn't want her to leave, but she said she had to. She said she did not want others to question her whereabouts, and promised me she would be back the next day. I barely blinked and she was gone. I had no idea how she entered. I figured I would ask her tomorrow when she came back. Maybe I could get out and hide somewhere else.

I slept better that night knowing Kerry would check on me tomorrow. I could hear the rats rustling about, but Kerry had hidden my food in the blanket and then tucked it under my legs. I knew they were sniffing around, but I really didn't mind anymore. They needed food, too, and they entertained me, even it was because they were one of the only things to take my mind off my situation.

The next morning I awoke to Kerry by my side. She was sitting there quietly. She was humming something.

"What is that?" I asked her. "It sounds familiar to me."

"It's an song Ma taught me called, Give Me Your Hand."

"Do you know the words?"

"Of course!" And she cheerily sang it to me.

I actually didn't know it, but it was a wonderful song of friendship. When she finished I asked her about the happenings of the ship and if she had heard anything about Captain Kiper. She said she hadn't, but she would try and get more information today. She said I was still running a fever and I needed to rest and get stronger. She was worried about me and told me I had to make it.

She was right; I was so tired and felt horrible. I hurt all over and was constantly sick to my stomach. If it wasn't for Kerry, I would probably not eat at all. She kept me company all day and told me more about her family. I seemed to be going in and out and not really following her stories. I asked her about her family and she laughed and said she had already told me their names and all about them. I asked her to please tell me again.

"Oh, all right. My parents are Brian and Ena. My sisters are Kassidy and Kelly. Ma wanted all of us to have names that started with the same letter. She had first wanted a boy, and Kassidy was the chosen name for the first born. Kelly and I always give Kassidy a hard time since she was given a name that was for a boy. We call her Kassy, and that nickname fits her perfectly."

Kerry was patient and kind. I was glad she found a way into this room. I didn't have the energy today to ask her how she entered my room and I really didn't care. She was here and she entertained me and took care of me.

I remember something about her family being from a town called, Meath, and her father was much like mine. They lived as tenants. But the situation did not sound quite as bad as in Knock. Meath was in the eastern part of Ireland by Dublin, which is a big city. She said they decided to travel to America to join other family members who had already immigrated there.

"I have never been out of Knock except to travel to Galway." I told her.

Kerry seemed so worldly already and she had so many stories. She talked about Meath and its history. I don't remember everything. I felt so poorly and dizzy. My head was spinning and I was fluctuating between sweating and freezing. I asked her if I could lie here quietly for a while. She made sure I was tucked in snuggly and she lied next to me.

The next thing I remember is Kerry moving around the room and singing a song. I opened my eyes and saw her image in the darkness. She was spinning and twirling and singing, As I Roved Out. It was a joyous song and she was having so much fun.

I flashed back to a memory I had of a dream, long ago. The one with my family and friends. They were dancing and singing, too, and this was the song. Of course, that dream ended with water washing down my back, but the song made me smile and think of my entire family. It was a long time ago, and only a dream, but we were together as a family. It seemed like one hundred years ago.

I glanced back at Kerry as she danced and sang, "Kerry?"

She jumped with joy; almost jumping on top of me. "You've been out for more than a week! I've been worried, but I have been with ya every day and made sure ya drank water and ate soup or bread."

"Thank ya. Can ya help me sit up?" I still felt very weak.

"Here. Let's get ya up against the wall." She said. "Now tuck the blanket around your legs." She grabbed the water jug, "Try to drink some of this."

"I can't," I said.

"Well, let me hold it! At least ya should wet your throat," she said. "You've missed so much in regard to the ship and all of its activities. The mutineers are keeping the Captain in his cabin, but they are allowing him to roam around the ship at times. I'm just glad he's alive."

I nodded, "What are they planning on doing with him?"

"They told the passengers the Captain swindled them and took their money without having enough rations and medicine on the ship to take care of them. Most of the passengers believe them since so many people are dying.

"It's awful up there. The ship is overcrowded. Disease is spreading and many more have died. There are no clean places on the ship and no place for the well people to stay anymore. Most families are now half of the number they boarded the ship with. I am worried the Captain might be hurt by the passengers themselves because the bad men have convinced them of the Captain's guilt."

I was disheartened, but not surprised. I knew the Boatswain and the Purser had something terrible planned. Kerry was right. At least Captain Kiper was still alive. Because of Kerry, I now had hope. She was watching over me, and for the first time since the trouble started, I felt like it might be all right. I knew there was nothing I could do, but maybe, just maybe someone else could help the Captain out of this.

Kerry lifted a bowl. She said it had broth in it. "Try some of this," she said, "it will be good for ya. Just taste it."

Umm. It was good and I tried to eat all of it. She also brought me some bread. I was going to get my energy back and get well I told myself. Kerry asked if I wanted to hear about Meath and its history. I told her I would love that.

She started by telling me it was a lush and green land with Castles and Churches and Celtic monuments. She said it was very old and Kings of Ireland had lived there. She stood up and continued with her story, acting it out as much as she could. She said there were many sacred places there, but one of the most famous was a hill called Tara and people settled there believing the hill had mystical and temporal powers. And, it was Saint Patrick that began his travels there to convert the Irish to Christianity.

One of the most famous events in County Meath was the historic Battle of the Boyne which began the struggle between Protestants and Catholics in Ireland. The battle was in the Valley in 1690. A very long time ago.

She sat down by me again to check on me. I told her I was just tired and wanted to lie down but also wanted to keep listening if that was all right. She understood, but rather than going on with her history of Meath, she began to sing me a lullaby.

This time it was one I had heard my grandmother sing to Moira, Quinlan, and me when we were babies. A lullaby, soothing and sentimental. I closed my eyes and envisioned my family. Kerry sat up by my head and continued singing the song until I fell asleep.

I woke up to Kerry's singing, again, but this time it was a song called The Cliffs of Doneen. I knew this one, and smiled as I tried to sit up.

"What day is it today, Kerry?" I asked her.

"You've been out another two days," she said, "hopefully we are going to get ya better." She took my hand and we felt the boards next to me on the back wall. "This is where we have been marking your days. I used a button to make marks and scratched away each day hoping to keep a record."

I couldn't see the marks, so I had to feel the marks and count them. I don't know if it was accurate, but I counted four weeks and two days.

"Has it really been that long? Where has all the time gone? I can't believe so much time has gone by." I told her

"Yesterday was an awful day for the ship. The weather was terrible and it was a good thing ya were out for the day. I didn't mean to, but I laughed at us rolling around, from wall to wall, not being able to control our own movements."

"Well, I'm glad I was not awake for that! It must be better today since I can only hear the ocean rushing by against the bow and not crashing sounds against it."

"It is a beautiful day outside and I wish they would let ya out! They did not bring ya your daily rations yesterday, and I thought something might be up with the ship and the crew. There are only about one hundred passengers left of the three hundred."

"That's all?" I asked her. "I can't believe it. Only one hundred? Is your family all right?

"Yes, my parents, Kassy and Kelly are lucky enough to be alive."

As the day wore on, Kerry fed me some dried beef she had hidden in her pockets and gave me some water. I hadn't had dried beef in so long. It was tough to chew, but tasted very good. She wanted me to eat more bread so as not to upset my stomach very much. I couldn't eat much, but as the day wore on, I tried to stand. I was weak and wobbly and Kerry laughed at me as I tried to stand. She teased me saying the ship wasn't even rocking. Then she said maybe I had been drinking and started singing the song, The Irish Washerwoman. I laughed and we sang together as she held my hands and went around in circles. I couldn't do it very much because I was weak. I fell down laughing and watched her as she twirled by herself.

When she finished she plopped down next to me and asked, "Would ya like to play a game? If you feel better, maybe we could play some games to spend the time?"

"I'm not sure how well we could see them, but it would be fun to do something else besides sit on this hard floor and listen to the rats."

She laughed, "Ya need to make friends with the rats. I named all three of them since they have shared this space with us. Especially during the times you were out. I played with them and watched them scamper about! Sometimes they were all I had to talk to!"

Kerry was so lively. She was a good friend and I wondered where her family was going to live when they arrived in America.

"Ya named the rats?" I asked her.

"Of course I did! We're all good friends, now! Their names are Brady, Brody, and Broody."

I laughed out loud. If I had food in my mouth, I would have spewed it. She thought I was laughing at the words and their similarity, but I told her Brody was a friend of mine from home, and he would hate it if he thought we had named a rat after him. She smiled and danced around saying their names. I heard the rats scurrying about and I wondered if they knew their names and were coming out to join her in her merriment.

The next couple of days, we spent playing, talking and singing, Kerry brought strings to play with on our fingers, cards and spinning taps. We could only see when we sat very close to the door and the lanterns were lit.

They seemed to leave them lit most of the time, now, so it helped with our being able to see what we were doing. Kerry said it grew dark out much earlier than when we started the journey and I would be surprised how long the nights were.

"Has anyone said anything about our arrival?" I asked her.

"I thought I heard them say about another week. I know they told us it had taken longer than expected because of the weather. I also think since the Captain has not been in charge, the mutineers do not know how to sail the ship as well as he does."

Our days passed much better as we sailed closer to America. I felt better and the sea was calmer. Kerry woke me up one morning.

"Allie! Allie! You won't believe what is happening on the ship! There is bedlam above!"

"What's happening?" I asked her.

"Captain Kiper gained support from some loyal sailors on board and they have taken the First Mate, Boatswain, the Purser, and their accomplices and tied them together on deck!"

She was out of breath and excited at everything happening.

"Skully sided with the Captain and helped him gather other sailors. These loyal sailors conspired to take the ship back from the ones that swindled the passengers and drugged the Captain."

"That's wonderful!" I was pleased. "Maybe I can get out of here, now! And be free again!"

"We are within two days of arriving in America, I think." Kerry said.

"Two days! This is wonderful news! I am going to see my Uncle Brennan. We are going to see America. I am going to see the sunshine, again!"

"There is so much confusion above that the passengers are being told to stay below and at their sleeping areas and wait for word on being able to come above. Captain Kiper and the other sailors are busy regrouping."

"Kerry, will ya ask your family to talk to the Captain and let him know where I am?"

"I will, but I don't know when they will be able to see him. Captain Kiper has not updated the passengers about the situation."

We were so excited we danced and sang and talked about living in America! We played with the rats and gave them some of the crumbs we had left over. This awful journey was almost over and Kerry and I would be in a wonderful new land experiencing things we had only read about.

Since the Captain didn't know I was down here, and the bad guys had been detained, no one knew to bring me food. Kerry said even the passengers were not being fed tonight because they were not allowed out of their living spaces, yet. We didn't care, we were too excited to eat, or sleep for that matter.

We stayed up most of the night. This time I talked more and told Kerry about my family and the Farradays. She laughed when I told her about Brody and said she now understood why I laughed at the thought of one of the rats being named Brody. I went on and told her about the items I had brought with me and I hoped they were still in 'the Hole.'

I had totally forgotten about the Hole and wondered if I had anything left. I would hate it if I had lost the special items I had been given. They were my only connection to home, except for my memories, and I wanted desperately for those items to still be there when I was freed.

We stayed awake as long as we could. Talking until we dozed off. When I woke up, Kerry was gone. I felt my pockets to see if I still had the letter and the book I had stashed in there weeks ago. I felt them, but the letter was crumpled. I hoped they were both going to be all right. I knew they must have gone through terrible circumstances with my rolling around and being sick and all. At least they were still in my pocket. I had not been robbed of them and I would check on them as soon as I could.

I lied there thinking about this ordeal and being grateful for Kerry. When she appeared by my side, she was always so quiet. I appreciated her being so cautious. I was sure it was why I was still alive. Had they caught her, too, neither one of us might have made it. And then her family might be in trouble, too.

"Kerry, I need to thank ya for taking care of me. I would never have made it if it weren't for ya. I could never repay ya," I told her, "I always want to be friends...always."

She took my hand, but changed the subject, "Captain Kiper called the passengers up to the upper deck and explained the situation to them. He said the First Mate, the Purser, the Boatswain and some other sailors stole everyone's payment for passage and tried to steal the ship, but the money had been retrieved and the ship was back in the Captain's hands. Everyone cheered!

"Captain Kiper then told us he knew it had been such a difficult journey for everyone and he apologized. He knew many had died, and the First Mate and Purser had allowed more people on the ship than was acceptable so he knew the passage was a miserable one for most. However, he said, we will be in New York tomorrow and we must plan accordingly. That meant everyone was to get their articles together and prepare their paperwork for disembarking."

He warned us, "Anyone who is sick, or looks as though they were sick might not be allowed off because America would not allow sick immigrants into their country."

"I'm worried about that for ya, Allie, since you are still weak and pale."

"I am a little weak," I told her, "but I am going to be all right. Surely they wouldn't keep me from disembarking if I have Uncle Brennan waiting for me? I will pinch my cheeks and act as well as I can. Maybe if I walk out with your family they won't notice me."

·"That's a great idea! I'll see if we can do just that!"

She talked me through the items she heard Captain Kiper say we all needed and impressed upon me I needed to have my things in order for everything to go smoothly. She was almost like Moira in her ways. I was still excited but tired from not sleeping much the night before.

As Kerry left, she said, "You're going to be all right Allie. We will see each other again soon."

"What do ya mean by that? Aren't we going to see each other tomorrow?"

"I think so, but what if they organize families for disembarkment? We might be separated for a while. Ya are my best friend, Allie."

With the excitement of almost being in America, I was surprised I fell asleep. But, I fell asleep knowing we would have this trip to connect us for the rest of our lives and the journey was almost over. We had made it, and we would always be the best of friends.

Chapter 14
The Mystery of Kerry

America! A new land. I no longer heard the ocean crashing against the bow, the boat felt still. It sounded as though there were horns going off and dragging or walking above. The loud noises were probably trunks and suitcases being pulled across the upper deck.

We were in New York! We were there! I didn't understand why no one had come to get me, yet, but my excitement overrode any bit of skepticism I might have of being left.

As the day wore on I started to worry something had happened. Kerry didn't come by and no one had come to my rescue. I didn't even hear anyone below in the hold. It was just me and my new friends the rats. I listened to their playing and scurrying around. Someone had to come down here, sometime, I told myself.

By the end of the day my worries increased. I had not had food for three days and I wondered if this would never end. I didn't want to make it all the way to America and then be left here for them to find me lifeless.

I continued to remind myself Kerry would never leave me if she thought I was not going to be all right. Her family must have left the ship. I clung to the fact she would not let me die down here, and I lied back down.

I was starting to feel woozy again from having no food. At least the boat wasn't swaying, but the smell of the room was adding to my feeling of nausea. I heard crates being moved and men talking loudly. I crawled over to the door and tried banging on it. I was so weak I couldn't bang loud enough. I tried yelling, too, but no one came to the door as I called out.

Finally, I heard them move the crate against my door. I kicked at the door. After such a long wait - it worked! A sailor pulled open the door and hollered for another soldier to come quickly. They bent over me and asked me if I was all right. I nodded, but lied there, limp. It must have been the relief of knowing I was found that made my body give up, and I fainted.

The next thing I remember was waking up in Captain Kiper's cabin. He was kneeling next to me with a glass of water. He lifted my head slightly and helped me sip the water.

"Allie, I thought you were one of the passengers that died since I had not seen you these last few days."

I was too tired to talk. I wanted to ask about Kerry and her family, but nothing came out. I could barely move my head when Captain Kiper asked me questions.

"You must try and eat something. We need to show the officers doing the final check of the ship you are all right and able to get off the ship. We have one more night to clear immigration before they will send you to a Ward. That would not be the best of circumstances for you. Please, Allie, let's try and pull yourself together so I can meet your Uncle."

I nodded, but drifted back to sleep.

Captain Kiper brought me a tray of food and the smell of it woke me up. Skully came in and checked on me and I was glad to see he was one of the loyal sailors. I really wanted to hear about everything that happened and about Kerry, but Captain Kiper asked me first about my Uncle.

"Do you know what he looks like?"

"No. I really can't remember what he looks like." I told him. "I was hoping he would find me."

"No one has been waiting or asking for you. If they allow you to leave, and no one is waiting, they'll send you to an orphanage."

I felt distressed by this and anxious at the thought of my being left in an orphanage.

"They can't do that!" I told Captain Kiper, "They can't take me to a Ward or an orphanage. Please, I begged him; please don't let them do that!"

I looked distressed, and he said, "We'll think of something."

The next day I felt a little better and was able to sit up. Skully brought me breakfast and sat with me while I ate.

"I can't believe ya made it! Ya are such a strong young lass. Ya must be destined for somethin' very special after all yuv gone through.

We need to get ya up to stand and walk." He said. "Yuv come this far; ya have to make it off this ship and get to your Uncle."

"Has anyone heard anythin'? Or seen my Uncle Brennan?"

Helping me to stand, he said "No, but the Captain will think of somethin'."

We walked a few steps and I asked to sit down.

"We really need to keep ya movin', missy. We must keep going and get yar blood flowin'. Within the next few hours, them officials will come aboard to see the few people that are left and considered too sick to leave."

I thought that was a rather strange statement.

"Even if I am well, won't they wonder why I am still on the ship? They won't let me go unless I have a good reason to still be here."

I started thinking my situation was hopeless. Skully didn't know what to say. He must have realized what I said was true.

He told me to continue trying to walk and showed me the wash bowl in case I wanted to wash my face. He told me he was going to talk with the Captain, and then headed out the door.

The thought of washing my face made me realize I had to get my things from down below. Vigor came from somewhere deep within, so I gathered enough energy to make my way out the door and down to 'the Hole'. There were sailors working with the crates and boxes, and some people lying around in different spots on the ship.

One of the sailors was one of the ones who found me and asked, "Are you feelin' any better, lass?"

"Yes, thank ya" I said, "but I need to find my items that were left down here. Do ya know where they might have been put?"

He took me to a spot behind the galley where they had placed items that were left by the passengers.

"Ya need to hurry, though, because the officials will be here shortly and they will have to destroy all of these items before they clear the ship."

I started rummaging through the things and easily found my suitcase and bags. Everything looked intact and I was reminded the Captain had held my most precious items in his cabin. I was relieved I had my things. I didn't have time to inventory everything, but it looked like I had everything.

I grabbed my things and lugged them back to Captain Kiper's cabin. I had to have them with me, whatever my consequences were. I pulled them in to his cabin and plopped back down on the bed to catch my breath.

I was wide awake and ready for Uncle Brennan to come and get me. Captain Kiper came in and said my uncle had not shown up, yet, but he had come up with an answer to my problem, if I wanted to go along with his suggestion. He had my curiosity up, and I turned my head towards him, waiting for his plan.

He took a deep breath in, "We will tell the Immigration officials that you are my daughter. That way they won't question if you are sick or not, and you will have a reason for still being on the ship."

I sat straight up, shocked. "What? Don't they know ya? Won't they know the truth? What if they figure out I'm not your daughter?"

"It isn't without consequences, so that is why I want you to agree to it. Either way, we are taking a chance at your going to a Ward or Orphanage. I would rather you be with me, than be sent away and end up in a worse place. I can't promise I can protect you if they take you away. This way, I can help you try and find your Uncle, and you will be safe at my home."

What he said made sense, but there was so much to think about and absolutely no time to think about it. I had to trust his judgment

"Please don't think I don't appreciate what ya are offering. It's just so much to think about, with no time to actually think about it. Would you really try to help me and take me home?"

"It's the least I can do after you tried to take care of me, and help me when I was being drugged by the Boatswain and Purser. I owe you for your caring about me and your loyalty."

I leaned over towards him, and then very determinedly said, "What do we do now?"

He went through the story, telling me not to say anything; he would tell the other sailors about it so they could corroborate our story.

Then he would bring me with him as he left the ship hoping the immigration officials wouldn't think twice about it. They would play like they were doing something they had done before when a daughter had sailed with her father. It sounded all right to me.

He told me to wash my face and put something else on so I didn't look like I was a stowaway on the ship. He said he would be back in a while, so I could take my time and wash my face and get dressed. I nodded and he walked out the door.

I grabbed my suitcase and opened it, pulling out the first thing I saw. I turned to the mirror and stared at this dirty, messy waif. I looked dreadful. I barely recognized the person in the reflection. I was filthy. My hair was knotted and matted in places, and I actually had dirt on most of my face. I looked down at my hands and didn't know where to start.

I figured they were only going to see my hands and face, so I washed those, thinking I could clean my entire self at a later time. I had to present myself like I was the Captain's daughter, so I was going to have to do something with my hair.

There wasn't enough water to wash my hair, and I couldn't get my brush through it, so I sat down in the chair by the desk wondering what I was going to do. As I sat there, my eyes wandered over the desk. Towards the back of the desk lay a pair of scissors. I looked back into the mirror, and realized I was going to have to cut my hair. I cringed at the thought of it, but I didn't know what else to do.

I brought the scissors up to my neck, held out a section of my hair, closed my eyes, and…cut. The cut section fell in my hand and I laid it on the desk. I grabbed the next section and cut again. I followed through with each section until my hair was completely cut. As I looked in the mirror, I saw a girl with hair to her jaw line. It was now at a length I could brush through.

Starting at the bottom and slowly working more hair through the brush, I worked out the welters. I couldn't help the dirtiness of it, but it was brushed and neat. I grabbed the ribbon Betsy had given me and pulled up the front right into a section, and tied the bow. I looked in the mirror and thought, I can do this!

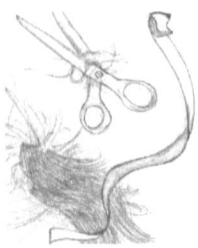

I repacked my things and waited for the Captain to come back. As I sat there, I thought about what I would call him. I didn't know, but I did think I really shouldn't say anything, because I would have a different accent than him. I needed to remind him of that. He would have to tell anyone that asked that I was a mute. I wasn't going to be able to talk or they would surely figure out our plan.

Captain Kiper came back and with eyes wide open, gasped, "You're hair! Did you do that yourself? You look so different. Good job!"

He then went on to tell me the Immigration officials had completed their search and he had told them everyone was accounted for. They were off the ship, but we still had to be careful as we walked through the immigration area. He asked me if I was ready, and then acknowledged my hair, again. He said I looked very nice and quite different with my hair short. I reached up to it and felt the length. It felt so strange, but I had to play the part and get me past the officials.

We picked up my bags, and placed them outside, up on deck. He went back in to get his, and joined me on the deck. We looked at each other, took a deep breath in and turned towards the gangway.

Skully was there waiting for us and smiled at me as we approached. He said I looked quite smart with my new haircut, and he would see me soon. We walked past him and down the gangway. He spoke to me as if we were used to one another. We smiled and went on past the gangway towards the immigration area.

Captain Kiper spoke to other Captains and sailors as we passed. No one paid any attention to me until we were almost out of the area. An immigration official stopped us and asked about the Kate's schedule. Captain Kiper said she would not be going out again for another three months and they were moving her to her assigned berth in the next couple of days.

The official looked down at me as I stepped closer behind Captain Kiper, hoping he wouldn't talk to me. He asked the Captain who this young lady was, and Captain Kiper told him I was his daughter and he needed to get me home because I was tired. The official nodded and let us pass.

I thought my heart was going to jump through my throat, and I think I held my breath the entire time. When we passed the gates, I let out a huge sigh of relief. Captain Kiper picked me up and swung me around.

"We made it!" he said.

My insides no longer churned and I immediately felt a sigh of relief. He was right, we had made it.

Chapter 15
The Kindness of Strangers

Captain Kiper had a five level home right on the wharf. It was a beautiful home stacked neatly between other ones much like his. He could look out and see his ship he told me, and it was a perfect spot for him.

We walked in the front door, and then another door and we were inside his home. It was warm and reminiscent of Mr. Leeds's home. We placed our luggage down and a woman greeted him, taking his coat and hat and welcoming him home.

She was a whirlwind of words and I could barely keep up with what she was saying. She also had an accent, but I wasn't sure what it was. I needed help in understanding her. Captain Kiper had to stop her to introduce me to her.

Her name was Rufina and she was a large woman with white, flaxen hair. Later on I found out she used to have dark red hair, and thus her name Rufina stood for just that. She was older than Ma and reminded me of some of the older women in Knock.

She seemed quite excited by my being here, but didn't stop talking for very long for me to say anything. She barely let Captain Kiper speak. He looked at me, smiled and showed me into his parlor.

She had the lanterns lit and the fire going. I looked around as she was talking and tried to take it all in. He had pictures of ships and maps everywhere. Even the things on his side tables were from or about the ocean and ships.

Rufina was still abuzz with movement and talking when she left the room.

"She's going to prepare your room," Captain Kiper said, "and then dinner will be ready in about an hour."

"I don't mean to be ill-mannered, but I barely understood a word she said."

"She's from Italy and eventually you will learn to understand her. She is a very loyal housekeeper and when you get to know her, you will enjoy her."

We could hear her upstairs and she would yell down at us still trying to talk to us as she worked. We laughed with one another and he offered to show me through the house. There was a parlor, an office, a dining room and the kitchen on the first floor.

We went upstairs to the next floor and there were two bedrooms both with baths and sitting rooms. We went up to the third floor and he showed me what he called the ballroom. It was a very large room where the stairs went through it. He said he didn't use it very much, but the family before had a large family and they would play games up here and have dances. I told him that sounded like so much fun and he agreed.

The fourth floor was two more bedrooms, a bath and a storage room.

"This is the floor where Rufina lives. She doesn't have any family in America and she lives here with me and takes care of my household."

"The fifth floor is an open room we don't use," he said. "It has a window overlooking the harbor and sometimes I come up here to watch the ships and read, or smoke a pipe."

We walked back down the stairs hearing Rufina talking to us even though we were not conversing back with her. She was on the second floor fixing my room she said and getting it ready for my stay.

We picked up our bags and took them back upstairs to our rooms. Captain Kiper helped me carry mine and took them in to my bedroom. Rufina was just finishing fluffing my pillows and telling me about the down in them and how cozy it would be. Or at least that's what I thought she was saying.

She went straight for my bags and opened them. I jumped and grabbed them from her. She was startled for a moment, and it actually stopped her talking. I apologized and said I would take care of it myself. I knew it was not polite, but I was overcome with emotion and protective of the few things I had.

Captain Kiper told her I had been through quite an ordeal and it was all right for me to take care of my own things. She waved her hand like she was making a wish over me, and moved on to talking about getting dinner finished and ready for us.

"First," she said, "I'll draw you both a bath. You are filthy. It might take two for each of you!"

She wandered off to the bathrooms telling the Captain what dinner was and how much he was going to enjoy it. She had found a new butcher and baker. Their old butcher was charging them too much and she wasn't happy with the cuts of beef he had been giving them. She told the Captain she let him know of her displeasure and we would not be back unless he improved his services.

The baker had his own bakery, Busto's Bakery, and was a man who had just opened his bakery around the corner and carried many of breads and pastries that reminded her of home. He even brought some of these breads to the house, and she liked his way of business.

Captain Kiper leaned over and whispered to me, "She probably just likes the fact that he brings the bread here."

"I did not hear what you said." Ruffina humphed.

"Oh, it was nothing, Ruffina."

She hummphed again, turned, and told us our baths were ready and she would be downstairs preparing dinner. We looked at each other and smiled. He made sure I felt satisfactory with the circumstances and then told me I could take my time.

He shut my bedroom door and I was alone again. This was such a difference from where I was two days ago. It all seemed like a dream. I went into the bathroom and undressed. The clothes I had on had been clean, but I was so filthy dirty, I had soiled them in the process of just wearing them from the ship to Captain Kiper's home.

I hated the fact I was so filthy, so I took a washcloth and tried to remove most of the filth from my body. Then, slipping into the warm, safe bath was unbelievable. There were no smelling salts or lavender petals like Betsy had put in the bath for me, but the clean warm water felt so good.

Even though I had taken the time to remove the grunge, I was still so horrid I spent the time cleaning myself rather than relaxing in the water. There was no time to daydream because I had some major scrubbing to do.

Fortunately, Rufina had placed a pitcher of warm water next to the bathtub and I used that to pour over my head to wash my hair. The water in the bath was not clean enough to do both now, so I appreciated her thoughtfulness at supplying the pitcher next to the tub.

I was clean, but I really didn't feel clean. I wanted to scrub some more, but didn't want either Captain Kiper or Rufina to wait on me. I pulled out another set of clothes and put them on to go down to dinner.

I went over to the vanity and looked in the mirror. I was startled as I looked at my hair, but took a deep breath in and brushed it. I didn't put the ribbon back in because the ribbon was dirty now, too, from being in my hair.

I took all of my dirty things and placed them in a pile in a far corner. They smelled. They were dirty in more ways than one. Dirty from dirt, and dirty from memories of my situation on the ship. I hated my entire journey and those dirty clothes in the corner reminded me of what I had just gone through.

I didn't know where to sit and I didn't want to get the bed dirty, so I leaned up against the wall and covered my face beginning to snivel. I tried to be quiet so no one would hear me. Forcing my face into my hands was the best way I knew how to keep quiet.

After a few minutes, I pulled myself together. I looked back in the mirror, and then walked out of the bedroom and down the stairs.

Captain Kiper hadn't come down yet, but Rufina caught me coming down the stairs and pulled me into the kitchen to help. She was talking fast again and I ended up nodding to her hoping she wouldn't ask me a question and I would have to ask her to repeat herself. She was going on and on about the Captain and his life, I think. She called him the Captain and seemed to be very fond of him.

As she was talking, she handed me items for the table. I wasn't sure if she wanted me to take them out to the table or just hold them, so I just stood there until she motioned with both hands in a type of shooing motion and opened the swinging door towards the dining room. There were three places set and I didn't know if someone else was joining us.

Rufina must have noticed my blank look and told me to set the table for the three of us. She said she often joined the Captain when he was alone, and she loved to hear about his travels.

As quickly as she put the items in my arms, she pulled them out and placed the things on the table. It was perfect timing for Captain Kiper turned the corner at the exact same time and joined us in the dining room.

Rufina motioned for me to follow her and I jumped towards her trying to keep up. We went back through the swinging doors and she handed me two drinks to carry in. One must have been ale for the Captain, and mine looked like milk. I hadn't had milk in ages, but I carried both drinks through the door with Rufina right on my heels. I don't know why she was in a hurry. It was almost comical.

I waited for Captain Kiper and Rufina to sit down first, and then I sat at the open chair. We were having something for dinner I wasn't sure what it was. I stared at it and Rufina thought I might not eat it so she told me about the meal.

It was pork covered in flour and fried. She said it was quite tasty and even better if I put gravy on it, so she stood up, walked over and poured some on the pork. She then told me about the noodles that were cooked in butter. The other vegetable were beans.

I stared at the plate and decided I needed to try the food and be polite. Rufina turned her attention to Captain Kiper and asked him about his voyage.

Before he could answer, she said, "I heard about the mutiny. Grazie cieli! I am most grateful to hear everything turned out all right. I can't believe the First Mate and the Purser turned against you! The Boatswain is another story. I never felt good about him and told you so years ago!"

The Captain agreed with her and looked at me. "I think Allie had a much worse go of it, than I had." he told Rufina.

I shook my head, no, and kept my eyes looking downward.

"I haven't heard the whole story from Allie, and want to hear about it so I can add these charges to the men who were responsible for my kidnapping and confinement." The Captain said.

I was silent and continued to look down.

"Well," said Rufina, "she must not want to talk about it, yet," and looked back at the Captain. "Tell me about the circumstances of your getting the ship back and who helped you?"

"Skully was the most helpful and he found other sailors to support me and rally around me to get the ship back. But, Allie was very brave and was the first to notice something was wrong." He said. "She tried to help me until the mutineers grabbed her and put her in a room in the Hold."

Rufina gasped, and looked at me. "How long were you kept in that awful place?"

I sat there for a moment, then, "I think about three weeks, but I'm not sure. I was sick most of the time and if it hadn't been for Kerry, I would probably be dead."

The Captain looked at me and asked, "Who?"

"Kerry Duffield." I said "she nursed me through fever and nausea, and brought me food and water.

"How?"

"I don't know," I answered and looked back down at my plate.

I ate what I could. The meal tasted delicious, but I wasn't able to eat much of it. I started feeling nauseous and Rufina realized maybe the food was too rich for me. If I had been sick, and not been able to eat very much, fried food and butter was not the best thing for my stomach. She stepped in to the kitchen and brought me some crackers.

"Would you like to go in to the parlor and lay down on the sofa?" She asked me. "The fire is going."

She guided me into the room and placed the pillows on one end of the settee.

I curled up on my side and she placed a quilt over me. The fire was burning strongly and I watched the flames flicker in the fireplace. Captain Kiper came in the room and sat in a chair beyond my head. I couldn't see him, but I knew he was there.

Rufina went back to the dining room and started cleaning the table and taking things to the kitchen. I could hear her doing these things without really looking at her. No one said anything else, and I felt comfortable enough to fall asleep.

They let me sleep on the settee the whole night, and Rufina slept in the chair across from me. I didn't wake up until I heard her getting up and folding the quilt she had over her. She was shuffling around and I opened my eyes and sat up slowly, stretching my arms above my head.

She noticed and asked if I would like a little breakfast. I nodded, and she told me to join her in the kitchen and we would have breakfast together.

I folded the quilt that laid over me and placed it on the arm of the settee. Rufina was already in the kitchen and I could hear pots and pans banging. She called to me as if it had been hours and I hadn't come in, so I smiled and pushed the swinging door open from the dining room into the kitchen. As soon as she heard the door swinging she started talking.

She was off and running with chatter about my clothes and personal items and I could put them away in any of the drawers I wanted to in my room. She also asked if I had any dirty clothes and told me I could bring them down and she would wash and iron them for me. I barely had time to nod before she moved on to the Captain's schedule.

He must have heard her talking about him because he called out to her that his schedule might change now since I was here.

He stepped in to the kitchen and told Rufina, "We'll have to rethink our normal schedule."

He looked at me and said, "We had a routine we've been used to, but that was before you came into the picture. We need to try and find Allie's Uncle, Rufina. He will make sure she is taken care of. Oh, and this is a change of subject, but I've promoted Skully to Boatswain and given him orders for the ship. That gives us the next couple of days free to help Allie. We have to find the right people to help track her Uncle Brennan."

"Thank ya," I said, "but I have no idea how to find him, or what to do."

"I know of some people who can help us, and I plan on contacting them this morning. Rufina, will you go to *the Kate* and talk to Skully? Maybe Skully has word on Uncle Brennan's whereabouts, or maybe he stopped by trying to find Allie."

I hoped that had happened. Maybe he was just late in getting here and would wonder where I was if I wasn't on the ship.

I had crackers for breakfast, with milk and tea. Captain Kiper and Rufina talked more about the day as I sat there and listened to them both. My mind wandered off to the room I was in where I was held captive, and I stared out the window in the kitchen. I could hear them talking, but I wondered about Kerry. She was the only reason that horrible situation was bearable.

Rufina rose up from the table and it caught my attention. I looked back at both of them and they were still talking. Now, talking about what had happened while he was gone.

She told him about a group of investors who wanted to discuss a possible business venture with the *Kate*. There were also letters and inquiries on his desk. She then told him she would be in his room shortly to gather his dirty clothes. She looked at me, and I said I would go and get mine right now. She barely stopped while I told her so and she moved on without a blink of an eye.

I took this as a sign it was all right for me to leave the kitchen and go upstairs to get my stuff. They stayed in place and continued talking while I went up the stairs. They were muffled, but I thought to myself I was starting to understand Rufina without even knowing it. I hadn't asked her for clarification, and figured she talked so much it was forced translation.

I left the door open to my room as I went inside. I had not put anything away and everything was in the exact same place I left it when I went down for dinner last night. I glanced over at my pile of dirty clothes and was disgusted at the thought of picking them up. I knew I needed to take them to Rufina. At least she wasn't making me clean them. I would probably have burned them. That's what I really wanted to do with them. Burn them.

I bunched up the pile and carried them down to the kitchen. They were still engaged in conversation and she continued talking while she walked with me to the back of the kitchen and pointed where I should put the clothes. I dropped the pile, and realized they didn't even notice me as I walked back up the stairs and into my room.

This time I shut the door and looked over the room I was in. The bed was a plain wooden bed, but it had fluffy pillows on it and a quilt. The other furniture in the room did not exactly match, and the pieces looked like they were made of different woods. There were no pictures hanging, and no items on any of the furniture. It was a rather plain looking room. I don't know what I was expecting. My family had never had anything like this, but I guess I was comparing it to Mr. Leeds's home and his belongings.

The bathroom was mostly white. It had a wooden floor, but the sink and the tub were white porcelain, and the wooden walls looked as though they were painted white. There wasn't running water, yet, but I heard there were parts in New York that actually had indoor plumbing. I couldn't imagine such a thing, but what a wonder that would be! Just like Betsy in Mr. Leed's house, Rufina had to heat the water and bring it up to the bathtubs.

I went back in to the bedroom and unpacked my items. I wasn't sure where to put everything so I randomly chose drawers to place items, and hung the few outfits I had on pegs in the wardrobe. Everything was wrinkled, but I figured they wouldn't be there very long once Uncle Brennan arrived and we packed up my things again.

I grabbed the skirt and blouse I was going to wear for the day and went into the bathroom again. I wanted to take another bath. I knew this time I would have much cleaner water and I could scrub myself and try to feel cleaner. I would have to tell Rufina about my love of baths and Betsy telling me about not everyone loving it in the same way.

I used the same towel I had last night, which didn't help with my feeling cleaner. I would take it down with me when I went downstairs and add it to my dirty pile. Maybe tonight I would feel completely clean with a new towel and clean clothes.

There wasn't a mirror in the bathroom, and it wasn't until I went into the bedroom that I glanced at myself in the mirror. I had the towel wrapped around me, but as I caught a glimpse, I slowly opened the towel and looked at my body. I was emaciated. You could see each of my ribs and my hip bones. I had no shape, but only skin on bones.

I was never heavy, but this past year had been such a hard one, and this trip completely depleted any extra I might have had on my body. As I looked, I was amazed I had made it. I had nothing more to lose and if I had not had Kerry, and the voyage had not ended, I would not be standing here today. I wrapped the towel back around myself and turned away from my reflection.

I dressed myself and brushed my hair. I parted it on the side again and tried to make the best of it.

As I was finishing, Rufina knocked on my door and said, "The Captain has gone to talk to some of his contacts about finding your Uncle Brennan. Will you be all right staying here by yourself while I go over to the *Kate* and talk to Skully?"

I ran to the door, "May I go with ya? I really don't want to be left alone. I'm afraid what might happen and I know no one else here in case something does happen."

"Angel, nothing is going to happen to you here. Why don't you finish your dressing and I will be waiting for you downstairs."

I grabbed my dirty towel and rushed down the stairs after her. I ran to the back of the kitchen, dropped the towel in my pile, and ran to the door where she was waiting.

She laughed at my rushing and grabbed one of her scarves and a hat to place around my neck. While it wasn't freezing, she said she didn't want me to get sick again. I agreed with her so I didn't argue with her about adding any clothing to keep me warm. I didn't want to be sick ever again.

We walked outside and into the street. The sky was overcast but it felt good to be on steady ground and in fresh air. We could see the Kate down the way, so we didn't have very far to walk. The gangplank was still down and we could see sailors still on board.

Rufina grabbed my hand as we walked up the gangplank to the ship. We walked around until we found Skully who was lashing a sail to the main mast. She shouted for him and he looked around while still lashing the sail.

She went in to her fast talking mode, "Any word on her Uncle Brennan?"

"Woman!" he yelled, "stop yer yappin' so I can get a word in! Ya talk so fast I can barely understand ya!"

She humphed, but obeyed his request.

"No one's come around askin' for her, but someone did bring some letters for the Captain. I put 'em in the Captain's cabin."

Before he was finished with his sentence, she pulled me, turning towards the Captain's cabin. I glanced back at Skully who had not stopped his work, but was shaking his head. I assume at Rufina's actions while he was still talking to her.

We went below to the Captain's cabin and Rufina let go of me long enough to find the pile of correspondence on the Captain's desk. She grabbed my hand again and we headed out his cabin door. We walked towards the gangway and she shouted at Skully to let him know we were leaving. He barely took time to wave, but did acknowledge her. He winked at me.

As we walked back to the house, she showed me the spot the *Kate* is normally docked during repairs and maintenance. It was only about the fifth berth down the pier, and it was closer to where the Captain's house was. He could keep an eye out for it just by looking out the window, and she often cooked meals for the crew, so this was a convenient place for him to dock her, she said.

When we returned to the house, I glimpsed out the window and saw it was starting to rain. The day was so dreary. Rufina stoked the fire in the Parlor and told me I could wait in there for the Captain to come back. She was going to the kitchen to wash my clothes.

I went upstairs to get a book. I chose the *House of Seven Gables*. I hadn't read any part of this book so I headed back downstairs and into the parlor to begin reading it.

The parlor was warm with the fire going, and I had the quilt over my legs and had myself perched against the arm of the settee. I was comfortable, but then again, I wasn't. I stuck my finger in the book to mark the page and closed the book on my finger. I walked in to the kitchen and sat at the breakfast table.

Rufina was in the back wringing and washing clothes. She didn't notice me come in, nor did I get her attention so she did know. I placed my book on the table and began reading. I was much more comfortable reading here, and I fell asleep with my head against the table. The book fell to the side with my hands still holding it.

I woke up when I heard the Captain come in. I glanced up and saw Rufina wipe her hands on her apron and step out of the room. I could hear them talking as they came towards the kitchen. Rufina told him about the letters she retrieved from the *Kate* and asked him what he had found out from his connections. She started cutting bread which I assumed was for us, and asking the Captain repeated questions. He waited for her to take a breath and jumped in.

Captain Kiper said his acquaintances would be able to help him find Uncle Brennan, or at least get information on him. Rufina asked him if he would look through the letters she brought from the ship and see if there was anything in them about me and my Uncle Brennan. She pushed the pile his way and resumed making sandwiches.

He opened what he had and started reading through the pages briefly. After a few minutes he made a noise, and both Rufina and I looked at him waiting for word of some kind. He continued looking at this one piece of paper.

Rufina and I looked back and forth between each other and the Captain. We waited, but neither of us were very patient. She pulled a chair up closer to him and tried to look over his shoulder. He turned away slightly and held his finger up as if to say, "one more minute."

Finally, he said, "Hmmm," and looked up at me. I was anxious now and couldn't stand the waiting but didn't want to be rude.

Rufina spoke up and said, "So? Is it from her Uncle Brennan?"

He nodded, and bowed his head. It must not have been good, I thought to myself.

My eyes were wide open and Rufina asked again, "So? Don't make us wait."

The Captain said, "As much as I can tell, your Uncle Brennan is not able to come and retrieve you. He has taken a job which took him out west. The letter says the last letter he received from your Mother said they weren't sure if they had enough money to send you, so he thought going out west would be best for him to make more money. He will try to send money to your Mother. If you made it, he was sorry he was not there for you. He isn't sure if he is coming back to the east coast since there are so few jobs. Out west offered so many more opportunities, he says."

I was bewildered. Ma expected him to be here for me. So now what was I supposed to do? I looked at Captain Kiper, distraught.

"I'm going to be sent to an orphanage, aren't I?" I asked him. "I can't believe it. I want to go back to Ireland, but I can't make another voyage like the one that brought me here."

Captain Kiper reached towards me with his hands and held mine. He looked in to my eyes and said, "I won't let you go to an orphanage, Allie. If you still want to go back to Ireland when I journey back in February, you are welcome to go with me, but you don't have to decide now. For now, you can stay with Rufina and me."

I was unhappy even though I knew he meant well. I really didn't know what else to do. Both of them were so nice, and he had opened his home to me without asking for anything.

I said nothing, and surprisingly, neither did Rufina. I put my head down on my arms. Captain Kiper was still holding my hands. Not forcefully, but with comfort and care, and I knew he meant what he said. The final decision was not to be made, yet, but I could stay here until I had made that decision.

Rufina brought us our sandwiches and we sat there most of the lunch, quietly. When Rufina couldn't take it anymore, she brought up the subject of my needing to go to school.

"All girls Allie's age should be in school and there is so much to learn. I don't think she should get behind."

I looked up at her in astonishment.

"I can't go to school. I've never been to formal school and I would be so ashamed by it all. I would rather help ya around the house and work in the home. I'm used to that. I can help ya."

"Nonsense," she said, "you are going to have to go to school and the sooner you start, the better."

"We have plenty of time to figure all of that out," said Captain Kiper.

He changed the subject to discussing my room upstairs. I was so relieved he changed the subject. I really wasn't ready to discuss my going to school. I hadn't even decided if I was going to stay here or not.

"I think the room you are staying in needs some decorating. Why don't you decorate the room any way you want? It needs a change and it's not very welcoming for a young lady. Rufina can help you with it?" he said. "You can pick out fabric for curtains. You can choose a rug and anything else you need."

Rufina jumped on that, "That sounds wonderful! We can get to it right away! I have some wonderful ideas!"

"This room is for Allie, Rufina, not for you."

She quickly agreed, but I think both he and I knew she had her mind set on an idea already.

"That sounds lovely, and I appreciate it, but could we wait a few days? This is all so new to me, and I have so much to take in and think through." I said.

"Of course. I have business I need to take care of with the *Kate* and that will take about three days to resolve. Then," he said, "if you are ready, we can all go shopping and buy you some things. It will be a nice escape for all of us."

I spent the next three days thinking about home. I was disappointed with Uncle Brennan and missed my Ma and Da very much. I missed Moira and Quinlan, too. And the Farradays and Mr. Leeds and Betsy. Yah, I was feeling pretty sorry for myself and missed everyone I loved, it seemed.

I would go down to meals and follow Rufina to the Butcher or on her errands, but most of the time I sat in the kitchen with Rufina and read my book. I finished the *House of Seven Gables*. I think it was supposed to be a romance novel, but I found it to be very dark and tragic. The judge who builds the house has had a spell put on him and his family experiences trouble for generations. It is an interesting book and as we walked around New York, I could see many similarities in the homes and the people.

I had not put much thought in my situation, except for feeling sorry for myself. I knew as the third day arrived, we would be discussing it again. I knew I needed to direct my thoughts as to what I wanted to do.

I was too afraid to venture out on my own. An orphanage would be lonely and scary, and being in a ward would be no better. I don't know why I was apprehensive about agreeing to stay here. Maybe I was afraid of cutting all ties to my family in Ireland, or to the possibility of being with Uncle Brennan if he ever came back for me.

Silly, I know. Captain Kiper had not made me feel that way, nor do I truly believe he would keep me from anyone I loved. Of all the people that must have hardships coming to America, he had opened his home to me. How could I say no? We had opened our home to Brody and considered him family and this was basically the same thing.

I looked through my items I brought with me to America. Ma's scarf, Mrs. Farraday's jewelry, the books from everyone, and the letter Ma and Brody wrote. I was so glad I had not had to sell Mrs. Farraday's jewelry for money. One day I would give it back to Brody, I thought. He deserves to have it. I would treasure it and take care of it until that day.

I had not closed the door to my room this afternoon, and Captain Kiper walked by and saw me sitting next to the vanity looking at these items. He knocked on the door and I invited him in.

He looked down at the things, "Will you tell me about these things, Allie?"

They were so important to me, I was glad to let him in my world and tell him about each thing. He pulled a chair up next to me, and we spent the rest of the afternoon talking about my things.

It's not like there were that many, but I wandered off subject and told him about myself and why these things were so important. He said he wished he knew my parents and the Farradays, they all sounded like such nice people. He then said my mother had done a wonderful job with me under such difficult circumstances like the famine, and it must have been such a sacrifice for her to let me go. I agreed with him and gently restacked the books and placed the other items back in their drawer.

He suggested I show these things to Rufina. He said, if she could stay quiet long enough, she would enjoy learning about me and knowing what is important to me.

As we walked down to dinner, I realized this afternoon made me feel assured of the fact I needed to stay here. I went in to the Kitchen and helped Rufina bring items to the table in the Dining room.

We all sat in our places at the table and I felt at ease. I looked at them both and smiled at their discussing the baker and his daily deliveries.

Without realizing what I was doing, I broke in and stated, "I would like to stay here, please, with you both! I don't want to be sent away! That is, if you will still have me."

They both jumped up. Captain Kiper grabbed me from my chair and lifted me up spinning me around. Rufina stood in place, but clapped her hands and shouted with joy. It felt like a weight had been lifted from our shoulders and we could now plan on what to do next.

After we calmed down, Captain Kiper was now the one talking the most and listing off everything he thought we needed to do.

"We should write to your Mother, first thing, tonight, and let her know of your situation and that you are all right. She will be worried about you and want to know all about your trip and what is happening to you, now. Well, maybe not all about your trip."

He sounded somber for a moment, so I agreed with him and said, "I would love to write her. She would be so excited to hear about me and how I'm doing."

We finished dinner quickly and headed to his desk to write to Ma. He had a stationery set with a beautiful feather quill. It felt so formal. I asked him to write it because I was too nervous with excitement. He generously agreed and we sat together forming our words and putting them down as my first letter home.

We decided we would limit our story to accomplishing my voyage and not tell her about my captivity. We both agreed Ma would worry more than she needed, and everything was all right, now. One day I could tell her about it, but not today. I asked him to tell her about the new friend I made on the ship. She would love to know I had made a good friend. Especially one who liked to sing songs we all knew. I could also tell her about where Kerry and her family were from and I hoped to remain friends with her here in America.

Captain Kiper stopped for a moment as I was talking. "I don't remember a family named Duffield on the passenger list."

"You must have forgotten. Kerry was there every day I was locked up and sick, so you must have forgotten their names. You were sick most of the time, too, and it must have been such a traumatic time, maybe you didn't remember everyone."

He nodded, and continued with his writing. He wrote down everything I asked. It must have been five pages of stories.

"Ma will be so pleased with this," I said. "I know she will be disappointed with Uncle Brennan, but Brody knows you and he can tell her what a nice person you are and that Mr. Leeds trusts you."

He smiled and sealed the letter. He did it by taking a candle he had on the desk and holding it under a wax-like stick. The wax dripped down and sealed the envelope. He then took a small brass item with a flat bottom and told me to press it down on the warm wax. I did, and when I lifted it from the wax, it had the initials, HK, imprinted in the wax. He said it was his initials. This would seal the letter and keep it private until Ma opened it.

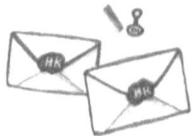

"How long will it take to get to her?" I asked him.

"Probably a month, or so."

"I am sure she has been wondering what happened to me."

"If she trusts in God as much as you say she does, she will have to draw on her faith to get her through your journey until word arrives."

I nodded and thanked him for writing the letter to her. I was so grateful.

I told him I was going to go to bed, and hugged him goodnight. I ran in to the kitchen to hug Rufina good night. She was finishing cleaning the kitchen. She spanked me on my behind as I turned around to go upstairs. I wasn't in trouble; I think it was her way of being excited for me and sending me on my way.

As I ran up the stairs, Captain Kiper said we would have an early morning. Tomorrow we start our planning for my staying with them. I said all right and continued up the stairs.

I ran in my room and still felt the excitement of the past hour and our writing Ma a letter. I knew Brody would read it to her and I wished I was there, sitting with them when they read it. Of course that was a silly thought because if I was there they wouldn't need a letter. Silly me! I laughed and flopped on the bed!

I needed to get into my bed clothes so I dragged myself off the bed and went into the bathroom to change my clothes. When I washed my face and changed my clothes, I headed back to bed. On my way I took a quick little detour and grabbed my letter from Brody. I wanted to think of home and be reminded of his words. The story didn't matter tonight, I just wanted something to read and calm me down.

I slithered into bed and held the letter to my chest. I was on my back with the letter above my chest and my eyes looking up towards the ceiling. The fire flickered and made shadows on the ceiling. I remembered my dream again. This time there were only shadows of furniture, but I smiled and began reading. I randomly chose a section, then another. I finished the letter completely, just not in order. My! I was full of thoughts and I had a big day tomorrow.

Chapter 16
Shocked and Bewildered

Captain Kiper knocked on my door the next morning. I couldn't believe I had not awakened beforehand. Especially since we had so much to discuss.

I jumped up and told him I would be down to breakfast as soon as I could. I wanted to take a bath, but that was going to have to wait. We had to get going and I knew if I didn't hurry, Rufina would have covered what I needed to hear without my even being there.

I ran down the stairs and plopped down at the kitchen table. The Captain and Rufina were having coffee, and she asked me if I would like some tea. I said "yes" and leaned into the table waiting to hear from Captain Kiper.

"First things first." He said, "What are you going to call me?"

My eyes widened and I looked at Rufina. She said nothing and so I looked back to the Captain and shrugged my shoulders.

"Well, my first name is Henry, would you like to call me that?"

I twisted my mouth up and to the side, and shook my head vigorously.

They laughed, and he then asked, "Well then, what?"

I shrugged my shoulders again and said, "I like 'the Captain', or just 'Captain'."

He thought that was too formal, but I told him after hearing Rufina call him that, and having lived here for a few days hearing that, it seemed to be very endearing and I really couldn't think of anything else to call him.

That's what I wanted to call him, so he said all right, and we moved on to twenty different things.

We talked about schools, and my room, and activities he thought would be proper for a young lady like me. Maybe a musical instrument, or etiquette classes, or singing lessons. It all sounded agreeable to me. I had never had anything like this, so while I was nervous about getting involved, I was excited about trying.

These were all things I read about. He asked me if there was anything I wanted to do. I told him I would like to learn to ride horses, and to grow my hair out again. He told me both of these things were quite acceptable and they would spend the next few days finding out what was available.

When we finished breakfast, Rufina picked up our dishes, but we remained at the table most of the morning. He told me about the *Kate* and how she was his ship. He had worked long and hard for her and he was using her now for transporting immigrants from Ireland to America.

He said he originally imagined being the Captain of a ship taking goods to and from America, but right now this paid a good income. This past voyage was his first taste of mutiny, and he hoped it would be his last. He usually took two trips a year which keeps him at sea roughly three to four months at a time. He would be gone during those times and it would just be Rufina and me at the house.

I hadn't really thought about his being gone for such long periods, but of course he would have to sail and be gone. I was getting more comfortable with Rufina every day and I didn't think there would be a problem with it being just the two of us.

I told him I didn't know how he enjoyed sailing. I felt sick most of the time I was on board, and he laughed and said it grows on you. I told him that's what Skully said, too.

We had a pause in the conversation and Captain Kiper said he needed to make sure our letter mailed this morning. I asked Rufina if I could take a bath and be back for lunch. She said, of course, and I bounced back upstairs to take a bath.

This time I was going to enjoy it, and be clean, and dry off clean. My mind had been on so many things these past few days this was the first time since I arrived in America I could enjoy my bath.

I lied there in the warm water and fanned my hands back and forth and caused little ripples on top of the water. I really was so fortunate. I thought about Kerry and how I needed to remember to ask Captain about her whereabouts and see if we could find her. I would love to let her know I was staying with the Captain and what our plans were. Maybe she was going to go to a school, too.

I finished my bath and dressed again. I headed back down stairs and the Captain and Rufina were already eating lunch. I sat down but was surprisingly not that hungry.

I asked the Captain if we could try and find the Duffields. I told him I would love to see Kerry and tell her what was happening.

Before I let him answer, I then asked Rufina if we could get some powder or salts for the bath. I had enjoyed those at Mr. Leeds's in Galway, and they smelled so good. She seemed excited at the thought of buying them and added them to our list of things to get.

Rufina and I spent the afternoon going over my bedroom and talking about what we needed to make it more feminine. I didn't want it too fancy, but it was a little plain for such a nice house. She did have some good ideas and I supposed she would know much better than I what it needed. I had never had a choice and didn't even know what was available. I do not even think Ma had ever had a choice.

The next couple of days were spent on buying things and checking in to classes and talking to other housekeepers. Rufina and I were together most of the time and we really didn't see the Captain except for meals.

He was busy following up on Rufina's leads for schools and classes, and filling out paperwork and getting me registered.

The week went by quickly and if I looked back, I would not recognize it as the same time period as a month ago. I wasn't even the same person. Ma could never have realized anything like this. I had so much at my fingertips. I didn't know which way to turn or where to look.

Captain Kiper and Rufina had me enrolled in a private girl's school where you wore a uniform every day. There were almost twenty girls in the school, and we shared many of the same classes.

The school itself had about seven rooms, but we spent the majority of our school days in one with the same teacher. I was only a day student. Some of the girls lived there all during the school year, but I was lucky enough to live only ten blocks from the school. Rufina walked me there every day for a while, but I eventually felt comfortable walking to school and back by myself.

One of my classes was music. I was going to learn how to play the piano and Captain Kiper said we would have to get a piano so I could practice. Best of all, he had found a stable where I could take horseback riding lessons. He had to take me there by carriage and only when he had the time, but I was grateful for any time I had. This was all a dream come true. The horse I rode was a chestnut thoroughbred with a black mane and tail. His name is Sir Raleigh. I rode on the side of the saddle and hoped one day I would learn how to jump fences.

I was often melancholy. I had no right to be with my station right now, but the inability to share this happiness with my own family was at times, unbearable. Oh I could correspond with them and tell them, and I knew Ma would be pleased, but I missed being with them and talking to them.

Time went faster than a ship with the ocean breezes behind it and it was December before I knew it. Captain Kiper asked me what I wanted for Christmas and I told him I had never had a real Christmas before. At least not the way America saw Christmas. And, we had such tough times my last few years in Ireland, we didn't celebrate Christmas or holidays, or even birth days.

Rufina and he thought I must begin enjoying the holidays and experiencing Christmas.

I really only want a few things, and they weren't things he could give me. "I want my family in America, or at least a letter from them, and I want to see Kerry." I told him.

He sat me down in the parlor. "I have checked the manifest more than once, and the Duffields were not on the *Kate* for this voyage,

Allie. There was a family named Duffield on the previous trip and they did have a daughter named Kerry, but she passed away on that trip and only her sisters, Mother and Father made it to New York."

"That can't be," I told him, "I was with her almost daily, and she was on that ship. She saved my life. I want to talk to the Duffields and see if they have family who came on the same voyage as me, but used a different name. Maybe that was it."

"I'll check their current address and see if we could plan a visit, but it might not be what you expect." he said. "They might not want to see us."

"They must!" I said "Please make the connection with them and get them to talk to me."

I was in a state of complete bewilderment. There must be a very simple answer we just hadn't thought of. I racked my brain trying to figure it out. I talked to Rufina about it and she didn't have any answers either, except, maybe I was so sick I was hallucinating.

"How could that be?" I asked her. "She brought me food, fed me, played games with me. She told me about her family and about the town they all lived in before they immigrated."

"Very strange things can happen when we are sick, or very scared, and you were probably both of those things at once. It must have been a horrible, scary situation for you. I can't stand even thinking about it. You were all alone and such a bambina. You are a miracle for making it. You are blessed."

"You are right in one aspect; the fact that I made it at all was a miracle. And I owe that miracle to Kerry." I said.

I bugged the Captain every day about contacting the Duffields. He finally found them the next Friday and sent word to them he wanted to meet with them. He did not tell them about me because he thought it might be too awkward a situation and they might not even consider seeing him if they were told my story. I begged him to take me, but he said he would talk to them first, and then see if they were willing to speak to me. He reminded me they had lived through a terrible loss and for me to be talking as though I met and played with a Kerry Duffield might be very upsetting to them.

They agreed to see him on the following Sunday, in the afternoon. I was anxious for him and wanted to go so badly.

"I promise I will hide under the covers in the buggy and stay there. I won't let them know I am even there. What if they want to see me right away?" I asked.

"If that is the case, I will make an appointment for all of us to meet."

I was reluctant to let him go, but I had no choice.

I spent the afternoon in Rufina's room with her. She was doing some darning and ironing and I brought a book to read. I didn't end up reading it because Rufina and I ended up talking about things. We talked about her family and her trip to America.

"I was married," she said, "but he died in Italy before I traveled to America. I loved him dearly and was sad we had not had children before he died. I will probably never marry again."

I couldn't see that. She had so much energy and was such a agreeable person; I figured someone would want to share their life with her.

She went on talking about how he met the Captain. "I met the Captain in almost the same way as you. I was on his ship, traveling to America, and did not think his cook was taking good enough care of him. I stepped right in and took over management of his meals and cleaning of his cabin. At first the crew and the cook were angry with me, but as time passed and people sickened, they found themselves very busy. They welcomed the help. I have not traveled with him, again. I think once was enough."

I agreed.

"I was living in a boarding house and trying to find work. People can be very mean to people from other countries who do not speak English so well, so they stay together to support one another. I ran in to the Captain one day and he just happened to be moving in to this big house. He asked me if I wanted to live with him and work for him. I was quite excited, and I knew him to be a good man.

"Then, when I saw the house, I was elated. It is a wonderful house and I knew I was lucky to have been made such an offer. I believe it was fate. And now, I believe it is fate that brought you to us. I am old enough to be The Captain's mother, and your grandmother, so it was a perfect match."

"Has the Captain ever been married?" I asked her.

"Yes" she said, "but she left him for a wealthier man. Well, that was before he had his own ship and was doing so well. His heart was broken and he has not married again. Oh, there are many women interested in him, and he has socialized at times, but he has never found anyone to replace his first wife. I've tried to help him meet young ladies, but he has never been very happy with the women I introduce to him. He always knows what I am trying to do, and he shies away from the situation."

Rufina and I ate dinner alone that night and I was in bed when the Captain came home. I ran to the stairs to greet him. He looked up at me as he was taking off his coat, scarf, and hat.

"Well?" I was ever so anxious to hear what had transpired.

"Just a minute, I'll be right up."

By now Rufina heard us and she came out wrapping her robe around her and tying her sash. We all went in to my room and he pulled out a locket.

I reached for it, but before he let me have it, he said, "They want to see you, Allie. Tomorrow, in fact."

I was thrilled; I knew there was an explanation. He showed me the locket and I took it over to the lantern to get a better look at it. I opened it and saw a lock of hair and a tiny drawing of Kerry.

"This is Kerry!" I shouted, "I knew it. Where is she? Are they bringing her?"

He stared at me, saying nothing.

Rufina was happy for me and said, "We'll have to have her visit."

Captain Kiper stopped her abruptly. I had not heard this tone before. "This *was* their daughter all right, but she died on the *Kate* back in March."

"No! No! No!" I said, "This is her; t*his* is who was with me."

"It could not have been her. They took her body from the ship and buried her in a cemetery last April. She could not be the same person."

"But it is," I said, "this *is* her!"

I stared at the picture not understanding what was happening. I understood the words, but not the situation.

"They are coming tomorrow morning to see you. They were upset at first at my mentioning of her being on the ship. Then, the sisters said they believed it was Kerry. They said she had come to them and told them not to worry about her. She was going to be all right. The sisters had not told their parents because they did not think they would believe them, and they didn't want to upset their mother. When I was leaving, the parents changed their minds and told me they had to meet you and hear your story."

"How could I if it wasn't even true? How could I have believed it so profoundly?"

"It is true in your mind, and that's what they want to hear." The Captain said.

"Remember," Rufina said, "we cannot understand or explain everything that happens, and this was one of those times. You should tell them everything. Maybe there was an answer, maybe not, but there is no turning back now, you have to meet with them and tell them your story."

I had a hard time sleeping, and my thoughts of Kerry and our time together raced through my mind. I tried as hard as I could to see if there was anything I could grasp to understand what had happened. I fell asleep thinking of her.

I dreamt of her just as we were on the ship, but here she was with me in the Captain's house. In my room.

She sat on the bed with me and said, "I died on the journey over with my family. I'm sorry I never told you, but I had a mission to protect you and help you. You had no one and I was meant to be there for you. I will always be there for you." she stated.

It was Kerry all right, the same one in the picture. "I don't understand." I told her. "I truly believed you were real. I am so confused by all of this. What am I to tell your parents? Your poor family."

She tried to explain herself and our time together, but there were no words to truly make me understand.

Before she left, she said, "Please tell my parents and my sisters I am all right and will always be watching over them, and I love them."

One split second she was here with me, and then another she was gone.

I woke up realizing I would be meeting her family today. There were still so many things I didn't understand. I would tell them what she told me, and about our experience, but I had so many more questions unanswered. I told Rufina about it, and she listened quietly.

This time, she did not have any answers for me. Strange. She always has something to talk about, but she said this was different. This was a subject she knew nothing about and there might not be any answers. Her guessing for answers wouldn't help me or the Duffields.

The Captain came down to breakfast, "Are you ready for our gathering with the Duffields?"

"I don't think I would ever be ready, but I did push to see them and I must now face them."

"I think I remember a saying by Jonathan Swift that goes something like, 'real vision is the ability to see the invisible.' Maybe you have a gift and a purpose in life that is not yet defined." the Captain said.

We finished breakfast and moved into the parlor. Rufina lit a fire in every fireplace, so the house smelled of lovely cedar and had a warm glow in the room.

It was cold outside, but sunny. The mix of the inside air and the light coming in through the windows had a certain comforting haze to it. Almost like being in church with sunlight passing though the stained glass windows.

We weren't there long before the doorbell rang. The Captain and I stood up as Rufina walked into the room. Not a word was spoken, but we all knew the time had come. Rufina went to the door as the Captain and I stood together on the foyer. He placed his arm around me and I looked up at him. He smiled at me in a very comforting way and I was relieved knowing he would stand by me.

"Mrs. Duffield could not come." said Mr. Duffield. "When it came down to leavin', she couldn't bring herself to come. Please don't take it personally. It is still too hard for her, but she wanted the rest of us to come because she knew we needed to hear your story."

The Captain introduced everyone to me and guided us into the parlor. Rufina followed and asked if anyone would like some tea. No one chose to partake. I believe everyone was more interested in hearing my story and tea would delay the process.

The group was silent. Everyone was looking at me. I saw the yearning in the Duffield's eyes. I saw the resemblance of each of them in Kerry, and I began my story with remarks of their similarities.

"I can see Kerry in each of you." I began. "Her mannerisms, her voice, and most importantly the way I would think of her to be. She told me about each of you with such love and affection. She sang songs to me, and she took care of me."

They cried off and on. At one time I quit talking when I noticed the father put his head in his hands. The oldest girl, Kassidy, put her arm around her father, but told me to go on.

"Seeing you do that reminds me of Kerry telling me about the origins of your name, Kassidy. She told me about Kelly and her giving you such a hard time about having a boy's name."

They all laughed and Mr. Duffield looked up with amazement.

"I connect with and understood the look you have because that is what I feel. I don't understand why she chose me, but I'm glad she did. Had it not been for her, I wouldn't be here. Maybe she helped me so I could get to you and you would realize she is really all right. She is content and wanted you to know that she will always be with you and watching you."

There was a pause in my speaking because I didn't know what else they might want to know. I had told them everything I remembered. Rufina took this moment to suggest we all have some tea. This time everyone wanted to partake, and they started asking their own questions about her. What did she have on? Had she suffered? Is she with anyone else?

"I wish I could answer your questions. I can't answer the questions because I truly don't know. I only found out yesterday she was dead, and when she came to me last night, she didn't say anything about how she had passed on, or if she was with anyone else."

We had our tea and the Duffields fondly talked about Kerry. They knew their Mother would want to know all of this and maybe someday she would want to hear it from me, but they knew right now they would have to be selective about what they told her. They knew Kerry was with them, but they all missed her desperately. The girls asked me to tell Kerry to come back to them in a dream if she were to reappear for me.

It was a very awkward feeling. I could easily tell Kerry to let them know of her presence, but I didn't really know how it all worked, and if I would actually ever see her again. I promised them anyway.

Mr. Duffield and the Captain began talking about the Duffields thoughts on being in America. He spoke of the difficulty he faced in finding a job and the prejudice he had not expected here.

He told the Captain, "It's not a matter of upper and lower class but of being up a while and down a while."

The Captain acknowledged his situation, and Mr. Duffield stood up to leave. He motioned to the girls, and they in turn stood up.

As they were leaving, Mr. Duffield turned to me and said, "The most beautiful music of all is the music of what happens."

He said he had been told that by his grandmother, and he felt it today as I told him about Kerry and what she had done for me and told me. Ireland had wonderful memories for him, and now I have given him some wonderful ones for a new start in America for his family.

Rufina told the girls they could come by anytime to visit, and I agreed. I told them if I ever heard anything else from Kerry, I would let them know, but I believed she had done her calling and now she was at peace.

We stood at the steps of the Captain's house and waved goodbye. The Captain stood there, again, with his arm around me and holding me right next to him. He said I had done a wonderful thing, even if I didn't understand it completely. We smiled at one another, and walked back in the house. Rufina said lunch was ready, and we all sat at the kitchen table and discussed the whole event of their being there, listening to my story, and trying to process such an enormous experience.

Chapter 17
The Importance of the Letter

The next few days slipped by and Christmas grew closer and closer. I was excited about Christmas, but more so about receiving a letter from Ma. What could be taking her so long? Surely Brody had written it for her and sent it right back to me.

I hoped nothing was wrong. I waited weekly in hopes the Postman would bring a letter. I'm sure he thought I had nothing better to do than wait for him. On the days I wasn't there to greet him; I would run straight to the Captain's desk and check his letters. Rufina always put them there so I knew just where to look.

Two days before Christmas, the Captain announced he and I were going on a shopping spree on Fifth Avenue. I had never been shopping on that street before. I had heard about it from the prosperous students in my school, but I had never thought I would go there and go shopping. I knew it would be luxurious, but the Captain was quite enthusiastic about going, so I grabbed my coat, hat, and muffler, and away we went.

We had a wonderful day! We lunched, window shopped, and sat around talking. We actually didn't buy anything, but it was wonderful looking and trying things on. The day slipped by and his excitement never ceased. I felt like the time I had gone shopping with Mr. Leeds the very first time. I was getting exhausted, but not the Captain.

It took being with him the whole day before he let the cat out of the bag. He said we were going to have a party for New Year's Eve and I could invite anyone I wanted - schoolmates, friends from music or horseback riding. It was up to me and he would get the word to them and invite them.

As soon as we returned home, I ran to Rufina to tell her. She of course already knew, but listened to me politely while I hastily told my story of the party and who I could invite.

"You will have to have a new dress," she said. "Did you find anything while you were shopping?"

The Captain was silent and I felt bad he might think I wasn't appreciative, so I told her, "I don't need a new one. I can wear one of my school dresses. That will be fine."

"No, no, no" she said and scolded the Captain for not having bought me something.

She moved on, but I was afraid we made him feel badly, and I hated that. We were going to have a party! After Christmas! This was going to be a remarkable holiday.

I asked Rufina if I had received anything in the mail, and she said no as she worked in the kitchen doing laundry.

"Allie, you know I will let me know if something comes in." She said.

The Captain changed the subject and asked, "Is there anything else we need to do to the Christmas tree?"

"I don't think so." I said. "Rufina made everything look so attractive, and our decorating everything last week took care of the rest. I didn't know anyone could do as much decorating as we have done. The tree is lovely and the stairs both inside and outside are festive. Even the table setting has a beautiful centerpiece which is perfect for the occasion.

He smiled and I felt a lot better about his facial expression than when we were talking about my dress for the party.

"I want this holiday season to be very special for all of us." he said.

"It's going to be." I said.

"Is there anything you can think of that you desire?" he asked.

"You know there is only one thing I really want, and that was a letter from Ma. I really want to know what is happening at home and how everyone is."

"I'm sure you will find out any day now. You just have to be patient."

I knew he was right, but remember, patience is not one of my strong points.

On Christmas Eve we all took a wonderful carriage ride. There were lanterns lit on all of the streets and the downtown part of New York was so festive and lively. It snowed the last two days and children were out throwing snowballs and building men of snow – even if it was at night.

It wasn't too late when we returned home, so we sat by the fire, and the Captain and Rufina talked about Christmas's that they remembered. They both had some strong memories about different Christmas's they had experienced, and I remained silent.

All I could think about was how poor we were, and how Ma and Brody must be freezing right now, with only a little food to eat. Why hadn't they written?

Rufina went and picked up some sweets for me, but I wasn't in the mood for them.

"I know they must be delicious, but I am so happy and content, all I can think of right now is my family and how bad off they probably are while I sit here happy."

"Captain?" she asked, "Don't you think it would be all right if she opened one of her presents tonight?"

"Yes, Rufina, that is a fine idea."

"No, I can wait," I told them, but Rufina told the Captain to pick out a present I would like.

He stood up and looked over the presents looking as though he was trying to find the right one. He studied them and then very carefully pulled out a very thin one.

I looked at him with a puzzled look, and he said, "Go ahead, open it!"

I looked at Rufina and she nodded 'yes,' too. I was still puzzled at this thin, little package, but I knew it must be something since he had taken so much time to find it.

I carefully untied the string that held it together and unwrapped the paper around this curious little thing. When the paper was off, I noticed it looked like a letter. I looked up at both of them with tears in my eyes, but I was afraid my eyes would give me away if it wasn't what I was hoping for.

I closed my eyes and slowly opened the back of the envelope to see what was inside. As I pulled out the paper, I immediately noticed Brody's handwriting. I shouted with glee!

I jumped up and hugged the Captain, screaming from joy at the thought of finally receiving something from home.

"Have you already read it?" I asked the Captain.

"No, I haven't" he said, "It is yours to open and have for yourself."

I was thrilled beyond words. "I don't care what it says!" I told him, "This is the best Christmas ever. I do not need one more thing!" and I hugged Rufina and the Captain, again.

"Go ahead!" He told me, "and read your letter."

I had waited so patiently and he and Rufina had conspired to hold it from me. I grunted at them. I knew why, but I hated waiting. This really did make it special, so I folded out the paper and began reading. I was so excited I actually started skipping placing trying to find certain words or phrases that would catch my eye. I had no idea what I was looking for, or if I was actually looking for anything in particular, but I scanned quickly until something caught my eye.

I stopped at something about Ma's disappointment with Uncle Brennan and she was grateful the Captain had offered to adopt me and take care of me and give me security.

I stopped, looked up at the Captain, and then looked back down at the paragraph and re-read it, this time much more slowly. That's what it said, she was grateful for the Captain 'to offer to adopt me and take care of me until she could be with me again.'

I looked up at the Captain again. I didn't know whether to be angry or happy. How would she know about this? I had not said anything in my letter to her about this. Nothing!

I stared at him as tears began to swell in my eyes. Rufina began to cry, also.

"Tell her," she told the Captain, "tell her what is going on! I can't take it anymore!"

"Come here, Allie, and sit by me." he said

I did, and he took my hand, and looking in my eyes.

"After you went to bed, I wrote your Mother a separate letter the same night we wrote yours to her. I then made sure they mailed the two of them together. I told your Mother about how you had grown to be a part of our little home and how very special you were to me and Rufina. I told her about everything I want to be able to do for you, and that I see you as a special blessing brought into my life."

I was flabbergasted and as tears swelled in my eyes, Rufina came up behind me, sat, down, and hugged me from behind. I had nothing to say. I couldn't believe it. This had nothing to do with why I wanted to read my letter from Ma, but now it had totally overtaken any thoughts I had. I was so surprised by the thought of it. I was once again speechless, and so was Rufina.

The Captain sat their quietly. He had released my hand, but we all sat in the exact same place for hours it seemed. Rufina and I leaned back on the sofa, her arms still around me, and my head facing the Captain. This was a huge moment, broken only by the Captain explaining a little more of the story.

"If you read on, you will probably read how I told your Mother this was all conditional on three things. One, her agreeing to it. Two, your agreeing to it, and three, my being able to meet her in person so you would feel comfortable in hearing from her that she was all right with it."

I looked at him and asked, "How could that ever happen? She won't be coming to America for years."

"I know that, but on my next voyage to Ireland, we could meet and she could give her blessing to me. The first step has been taken and agreed to, now it was up to you. Was this something you might consider?"

"I will always love my family and I want to be with them...however, how could I ever turn down your graciousness? I would never, ever have dreamt that a life like this might be possible!" I said, and jumped out of Rufina's arms to hug the Captain!

"This is going to be my favorite Christmas from now on, and you have just made it so! Now," he said, "we can start the paperwork and get everything in order for my voyage back to Ireland in February. You are allowing me to feel as though I have a family!" he said.

Was my name to be Allie McCreary Kiper? I did not know, but I would never lose McCreary as part of my name.

Either way, I asked, "May I get a stamp to press my letters with wax on the back of envelopes just like yours?!"

He laughed, hugged me again, and said, "Without question!"

As we all sat there together, a group of singers were on the street going from house to house singing Christmas songs. It was like a page from a book.

The Captain made sure I felt as spoiled as the most well-to-do child in the world. Every item I tried on during our window shopping day, he bought as a surprise for me and had them sitting out for me when I woke up the next morning – Christmas morning.

I had two new dresses to choose from for our party and new riding clothes. He also bought me a beautiful pair of riding boots. They were a dark, rich leather that came all the way up to my knees. I received two more sleeping gowns, and Rufina bought me a variety of petals and salts for the bath. She knew how much I loved them and went overboard with picking out so many. I could take a bath every day for a month and not be short of fragrances.

The morning was full of memories. We started with my squealing at the sight of all my gifts. I controlled myself long enough to hand out a few items to Rufina and the Captain, but they were more interested in seeing my pleasure with each new thing I picked up or unwrapped. The parlor was a mess. This beautiful room that looked so perfectly festive the few days before was a disaster at the moment.

We left it that way and went in to breakfast where Rufina had a wonderful selection of pancakes. She laid out a delicious assortment of berries to be placed on the pancakes and with the syrup; I ate enough to fill my belly for days. I told them I could not eat another thing for weeks!

We all helped clean up the breakfast feast and talked about the excitement of the week and everything we had to look forward to. When we were done, we went back into the parlor and began laughing at the site of the disastrous mess. We all plopped down in separate spots and didn't move. It was too much to do, and we were too full and pleased with ourselves.

The Captain and Rufina fell asleep right where they plopped. I roused myself enough to pick up my letter. I looked at it and realized I hadn't taken the time to read through all of it completely, and so I did. I rolled on my back on the floor by the fire and began to read.

It was Brody's handwriting, but Ma's words. She was glad I made it safely, but was disappointed with Uncle Brennan. She would be writing him to see what had happened and to scold him for leaving me to fend for myself. She also spoke about Mt. Farraday and his release date. I was thrilled they were going to release him. He would help Ma and Brody so much. Maybe they could get to America that much quicker. She also spoke about Da and his not being able to get out. She said she had been given word he was sick, but she hadn't been to see him, yet. She was hoping to have news the next time she wrote.

Poor Da. Stuck in a horrible place for no real reason. Separated from his family and all alone. Maybe Mr. Farraday could think of something to help him. Ma was lucky to have Brody and Mr. Farraday, I thought. I knew the three of them could make it through this horrible time if they helped one another. Ma also spoke about Patrick and how they heard he was in Australia. It wasn't directly from him, but they were glad he had escaped Ireland and could start a new life in Australia.

She went on to talk about Captain Kiper and how thoughtful he was to write to her and offer to take care of me. She knew she was blessed and felt more so if she knew I would be all right.

She said, "The mills of God grind slowly but they grind finely." She told me to be good and acknowledge and pray for spirituality in my life. I was blessed, she said, and I had a purpose that one day would come to light for all to see.

Brody really didn't say anything on his own in the letter. I was rather disappointed, but I knew their situation might be horrible and I couldn't guess as to how difficult times might be for them. It seemed like ages. Ages since I was there and starving. Ages since people were dying all around us. I knew Ma wanted me to have a better life, but I forever miss them and wish they were here with me.

I fell asleep after having read the letter at least three times. It was mid-afternoon by the time we all woke up. Rufina was the first and she began picking things up in the parlor when the Captain and I woke up and begrudgingly helped her with our mess.

With the disaster cleared, the Captain suggested we all take a walk. Rufina declined his invitation, saying she had an errand to run, so the Captain and I put on our warm things and went out for a walk. He wasn't very talkative, and neither was I.

We walked along the pier and checked out the *Kate*, and then walked up and down some side streets. We could hear other families singing and laughing and playing. On the last street home, Rufina caught up with us, the Captain asked her where she had gone, and she was not too willing to offer an explanation, However, he didn't let it go and we found out she had taken some food to the Baker. He gave her a sly look she chose to ignore.

The Captain and I were holding hands as we turned to his front door.

"This is the way it should be," he said.

"Yes," I grinned, and we headed inside.

As full as we all told ourselves we were earlier, we were none the less hungry when dinner time came around. Rufina made a lovely dinner of roast pig and potatoes, bread dressing, and baked apples. They gave me some wine to drink. Well, it really wasn't wine, I think it was grape juice, but they called it wine to include me in the festivity of the meal. We said a blessing at this meal, and it was the first time I chimed in to say, "Amen." I felt like it, and was appreciative of what I have been given. I was blessed.

I went to sleep that night lying on my stomach and writing a letter to Ma. I was writing on top of one of the books Brody had given me. I paused between sentences and thought hard trying to portray what I felt in my words on the paper. I wanted this letter to be as meaningful to Ma and Brody as their letter had been to me. I wanted Ma to know I was appreciative, and her sacrifice for me was not going to be in vain. I was going to be all right. I would make it.

Our New Year's Party was a wonderful and exciting event! I wore the dark blue dress the Captain bought me. It had a beautiful lace collar at the neck and at the end of the sleeves. My hair had grown beyond my shoulders and I could braid it again without pieces sticking out everywhere. I had a new ribbon and tied it down the back like Betsy had done.

I invited friends from school and music class. I invited Skully and the faithful crew that was still part of the *Kate*. I invited Rufina's roommates from her first few months here, and I invited the Baker, Mr. Angelo Busto, and the Duffields. Even Mrs. Duffield came and was very cordial. Kassidy and Kelly said she was doing much better and a lot of it had to do with me and my story of Kerry. They said their Mother wasn't ready to hear it from me, yet, but she was comforted by what they told her about it. I was glad to hear it. Everyone seemed so happy.

Rufina and I hadn't found anyone for the Captain. I really wanted him to be as happy as I was and have someone he could share his life with. However, my thoughts didn't linger too long on that, for during the party, he seized everyone's attention and made a toast to me. He spoke of his desire to officially adopt me and had not realized what path his life was to take until the fateful voyages of his last two trips. Through all of the hardships and sadness in our lives, he now felt his house was a home.

I knew what he was talking about, and while I couldn't let go of the tree on the knoll, I had made it to America and had a whole life ahead of me. One that was better than I could ever have dreamt about or read about. There were so many people that made this possible. I was blessed.

That night as I went to bed, I picked up Ma's handkerchief and begged myself to please remember her; her smile, her laugh, her everything. Surely I wouldn't forget any of those things. I opened it and placed it against my face, closed my eyes, and thanked her for allowing me to be in this home. This would have to do until I saw her again.

The End